Was it the vibrating bed?

Or was Gage finally reacting to the heat that had been building between them for years?

"Wow," Sugar said, her face going pink, her eyes flickering with startled heat. She seemed to melt into him.

"Yeah. Wow." Emotion rose and rushed through him on a wave of need. And more. Something bigger and more important.

Damn it all, he *was* in love with her.

Now what? He had to think, to figure it out, decide. But Sugar shivered against him and licked her lips, making him lose all reason.

Kiss her.

Are you crazy? Gage didn't go with momentary urges. He pondered options, evaluated outcomes, made the wisest choice.

Kiss her, you ass.

Now.

Acting on impulse for once, he touched Sugar's cheek, lifted his mouth and...

Blaze™

Dear Reader,

How do you keep sex hot over time? That's an issue in this book. My husband and I have a lovely time between the sheets, but I confess I feel wistful about those early blaze days.

The research I did for this book taught me a few things—how the novelty of a vacation can enhance intimacy, how important being relaxed and clearheaded is to sexual response. And as I wrote it, I promised to be more in tune with subtle delights—the sweet smell of my husband's skin, the way he seeks out my hand when we're watching TV together or IMs me jokes from his office just to stay in touch.

Subtle things make sex mean more. And more sex with more meaning is exactly what I want—and what Sugar and Gage got in this book. I hope you enjoy their story. As for me, right now I'm making a late-night date with my man. I can't wait to be in his arms again.

Happy reading,

Dawn Atkins

P.S. Let me know how you enjoy the story—drop me a line at dawn@dawnatkins.com. Watch my Web site for news: www.dawnatkins.com.

WITH HIS TOUCH
Dawn Atkins

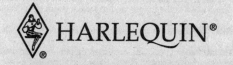

HARLEQUIN®

TORONTO • NEW YORK • LONDON
AMSTERDAM • PARIS • SYDNEY • HAMBURG
STOCKHOLM • ATHENS • TOKYO • MILAN • MADRID
PRAGUE • WARSAW • BUDAPEST • AUCKLAND

ISBN-13: 978-0-373-79298-6
ISBN-10:   0-373-79298-0

WITH HIS TOUCH

This edition published by arrangement with Harlequin Books S.A.

® and TM are trademarks of the publisher. Trademarks indicated with ® are registered in the United States Patent and Trademark Office, the Canadian Trade Marks Office and in other countries.

www.eHarlequin.com

Printed in U.S.A.

ABOUT THE AUTHOR

Dawn Atkins started her writing career in the second grade, crafting stories that included every single spelling word her teacher gave her. Since then, she's expanded her vocabulary and her publishing credits. This book is her sixteenth published book. She won the 2005 Golden Quill for Best Sexy Romance and has been a *Romantic Times BOOKreviews* Reviewers Choice finalist for Best Flipside and Best Blaze. She lives in Arizona with her husband, teenage son and a butterscotch-and-white cat, who lives to interfere with her keyboard. In her spare time she fantasizes about creating a sex resort just like the one in this book. Nude volleyball, anyone? Just kidding... Sort of.

Books by Dawn Atkins

HARLEQUIN BLAZE
93—FRIENDLY PERSUASION
155—VERY TRULY SEXY
176—GOING TO EXTREMES
205—SIMPLY SEX
214—TEASE ME
253—DON'T TEMPT ME...*

HARLEQUIN DUETS
77—ANCHOR THAT MAN!
91—WEDDING FOR ONE
   TATTOO FOR TWO

HARLEQUIN TEMPTATION
871—THE COWBOY FLING
895—LIPSTICK ON HIS COLLAR
945—ROOM...BUT NOT BORED!
990—WILDE FOR YOU

HARLEQUIN FLIPSIDE
11—A PERFECT LIFE?

*Forbidden Fantasies

To David...for taking the risk

ACKNOWLEDGMENTS

I owe unending gratitude to Laurie, Laura and Suzan for showing me that I was limping on a broken leg, introducing me to Ms. Free To Be, and helping me see my way to a new writing life.

Prologue

"HERE'S TO THIRTY-FIVE and our sexual peak!" Sugar Thompson tapped her prickly-pear margarita against her two friends' wide glasses. The burgundy liquid sloshed against the prickly-pear jelly on the sugar-dusted rim before she brought it to her lips for a tangy slurp.

"Hey…" Autumn Beshkin hesitated, glass in midair. "But you said women get several sexual peaks, Sugar. Only men spike at nineteen and decline from there, right?"

"That's true." Sugar had been a couples' therapist before she opened her sex resort with a partner five years ago, so she served as the intimacy expert for the trio of friends who celebrated their birthdays together each year.

As a stripper, Autumn knew a thing or two about sex herself, though from a different angle than Sugar's. Sugar valued Autumn's down-to-earth practicality, a trait they shared. Both believed what they could see, taste, touch or smell over anything emotional or theoretical or certainly romantic.

"The point," said Esmeralda, "is the seven-year lunar shift." A nail tech, Esmeralda McElroy also read palms and studied all things psychic. Sugar thought her theories goofy, but she loved Esmeralda's big heart and generous spirit. She was always helping her clients with loans, a place to stay or a shoulder to cry on. Sugar could tolerate a ton of woo-woo for a few minutes in the warm sun of Esmie's kindness.

It was Sugar's secret weakness.

"We're thirty-five. Our fifth cycle. A biggie and it's palpable. Can't you feel it?" Esmeralda closed her eyes and took a yoga-style breath.

"Cycle, schmycle," Autumn said. "I've already changed my life." She'd gone back to school the previous year to become an accountant, since she had a gift for numbers. She was still dancing, but the shift to school had eased her gritty defensiveness, made her more sunny and hopeful. Sugar was happy for her.

"Here's to becoming a CPA." Sugar lifted her glass again. Under Autumn's bravado, Sugar sensed a core insecurity that even top grades in her first year hadn't eased.

"Here's to all of us," Esmeralda, ever the mother hen, said.

Sugar clicked glasses, then gulped the rest of the icy drink so fast she got brain freeze. Damn. Her partner, Gage, was always after her to slow down. But that's not how she worked. Progress was her mantra, movement her mode.

She was desperate for change at the moment. Spice It Up, their sex resort in San Diego, seemed stagnant and she had a proposal to shake things up that she intended to spring on Gage at the Sex Expo this upcoming weekend. Unlike Sugar, Gage wasn't big on change.

"Tea leaves, Tarot or a Chinese reading?" Esmeralda asked. A psychic encounter was one of Esmie's contributions to their birthday celebration, a tradition they'd kept up even after Sugar had moved to San Diego, leaving the other two in Phoenix.

No matter what, Sugar made time for the gathering.

She counted on her friends as her private pep squad, her sounding board, her heart's voice, which was the role she served for them, too.

"Tea leaves," Sugar said. "Never done that before."

"Doesn't matter to me." Autumn shrugged. "Read my roots for all it will mean." Autumn's cynicism hid a fear of disappointment. Sugar hoped school and whatever wonders befell Autumn this year would resolve that pain.

"Tea leaves it is, then," Esmeralda said, and fetched a baggie of tea from her huge satchel, which clunked with whatever she had in there. Chicken bones? Tibetan bells? A crystal ball?

Sugar smiled, but kept an open mind. When Esmie had read Sugar's palm, she'd accurately interpreted the meandering lines as proof of her restless nature, so she had something going on.

"Chinese tea," Esmie said, waving it under their noses for a sniff. She ordered a pot of hot water and instructed Autumn and Sugar to sprinkle the loose leaves into their cups, then sip slowly to the dregs, swirling the leaves so they made patterns she could read on the sides and bottom of the cups.

Sugar was the first to hand over her cup, eager to see if her plans would show up. Esmeralda swirled the leaves, whispered a request for clarity and wisdom, then studied the leaves.

"What is it? What?"

"Give her a minute," Autumn said.

"Big changes are afoot," Esmeralda said slowly. "Open your eyes and see what you've ignored."

"What I've ignored? What does that mean?"

"Your hunky partner Gage, maybe?" Autumn said.

"No way." There had been heat between them, back in college when they met and again when they started the resort, but they'd stuck to what mattered—their partnership. "Is that all?" she asked, leaning over to see the sprinkle of leaves. She was startled to see what looked like the outline of Gage's lower face, complete with five-o'clock shadow, and she got a little shiver.

"That's all for now," Esmeralda said, wearing a cat-with-cream expression. "The psychic's skill lies as much in knowing what not to reveal as in what she sees." Esmeralda said that every time Sugar pushed for details. And she always pushed.

"Hmm," Autumn said, staring into her cup. "Looks like I'm getting acne…or maybe chicken pox."

Esmeralda motioned for the cup, which she studied. "Changes? Oh, yes. In the three Hs—head and hearth and heart and the heart will lead."

"*Head* is school, I guess," Autumn said. "But I'm not moving, so forget *hearth* and, as to my *heart,* it's just along for the ride." Autumn thought sex was safer than love—an attitude Sugar shared, but for different reasons. Sugar wasn't built for love. Some people weren't.

"Just don't kick your heart to the curb," Esmeralda said, exasperated. "Have faith."

Autumn shrugged. Esmie sighed. Sugar cleared her throat, determined to avoid a debate between Autumn Glass-Half-Empty and Esmeralda Glass-Endlessly-Overflowing. "What about you, Esmeralda?" she asked. "Did you get a reading?"

Esmeralda looked troubled. "More than one, actually. Because of the odd message."

"About your job?" Sugar asked.

"No. That's fine. By the way, my final interview is Monday." Esmeralda had applied to staff the Dream A Little Dream Foundation created by a client of hers, an eccentric heiress who wanted to fund people's dreams. "No. I must begin anew with a man from my past. That's the message."

"Your ex-husband? The financial sinkhole?" Autumn asked.

"It wasn't clear. So I had a second reading."

"I would, too," Autumn said. "Jonathan was a los—"

"Easy." Sugar jabbed Autumn, who was a tad blunt.

"I always wanted another chance with him," Esmeralda mused, "but the cosmos rarely gives you want you want."

"Of course not. That might make you happy." Autumn blocked Sugar's next jab.

"But the second reading said the same. So, I'll just see."

"Sounds like exciting times for all of us, huh?" Sugar said. "Anything else in there?" She thrust the teacup, with its appealing suggestion of Gage's face, under Esmeralda's nose.

Esmeralda only smiled. "Just open your eyes and smell the roses."

"That's all she gets? Mixed-up clichés?" Autumn again.

"And, you, Autumn, must give the benefit of the doubt."

"You read that in there?" Autumn peered into her cup.

"Just keep me on speed-dial, you two," Esmeralda said smugly. "I promise I won't say I told you so. Now drink up so I can do our nails. I created a special design." A manicure by Esmeralda was part three of their birthday tradition.

"Here's to turning thirty-five and turning it around," Sugar said, lifting the dregs of her margarita.

"Here's to turning thirty-five and having it all," Autumn said, clicking her glass.

"Here's to turning thirty-five and doing it *better*," Esmeralda said firmly.

They all laughed, gulped their drinks and grinned at each other. Thirty-five would be big, all right. Sugar could see in Esmie's wistful smile, in Autumn's don't-dare-hope expression and in her own breathless eagerness.

She would definitely keep her friends on speed-dial. She couldn't wait for the adventure to begin.

1

GAGE MAGUIRE watched Sugar twist the dial on the vibrating water bed so it started up a rhythmic rocking that would have given a stone statue hot thoughts.

Lately, around Sugar, even mundane moments did that to him—balancing their budget, clearing a copier jam, accepting a shake of Tic Tacs. Three days with her at the Sextique International Expo checking out erotic products for their resort had been pure hell.

And now they lay body to body on a vibrating bed.

His usually sturdy defenses were failing him—had been ever since his amicable breakup with Adrienne two weeks ago. It was not the breakup per se, but something Adrienne had said.

You're in love with your partner, you big dope. She'd shaken her head at him as though he were blind or stupid. Maybe both.

He'd scoffed then. And later, when he thought about it. How could he be in love with Sugar? Sure, they'd been attracted to each other when they met twelve years ago in college, but they'd wisely ignored it. Sugar always had a boyfriend and Gage wasn't interested in elbowing his way to the front of the line.

And, yeah, there'd been a flare-up when they became

partners six years ago, but they'd sensibly squelched that. Since then, the sparks had been muted, like fireworks through clouds. Nothing he couldn't handle. Until now.

Sugar rolled toward him, a breath away on the shivering sheets. "Would that turn you on?" she teased, her green eyes glowing, big and luminous as a cat's. She reminded him of one—sensual and quick, purring with pleasure, then dashing away at the slightest noise. And she never came when you called. "Maybe not you," she amended, "but most guys."

She harassed him about his self-control, a trait that had served him well for the six years they'd been partners.

"If you're into paint spinners." He fought to keep the tension out of his voice.

"Good point." She turned it down a notch, then fell back beside him on the roiling surface, their arms rubbing gently together. "Better?"

Just great. The new rhythm suggested serious thrusting. "Fine, Sugar."

"I can't tell. Maybe it takes an all-night test."

Good Lord, no. "I think I'm getting the idea."

Maybe the problem was his birthday—tomorrow he'd be thirty-five. A benchmark year and about time for the other shoe to drop in his life. He felt as though he'd been holding his breath for years.

"You think so?" Sugar's voice vibrated with the mattress.

"Yeah." Just to prove he was still in control, Gage pushed up on his elbow and looked down at her.

Just look at her. His heart punched his lungs so hard he couldn't haul in a breath. Her breasts jiggled gently under the clingy top, her black hair brushed his arm, but it was her face that got to him. It was sturdy, yet delicate, with a small nose, soft, mobile mouth and huge green eyes lit with intelligence and a no-bullshit gleam. And fire. Lots of fire.

"More like a MixMaster on low, don't you think?" she said, her easy smile going smart-ass in a heartbeat. Sweet with a bite, that was his Sugar—like a margarita with that scorpion sting of tequila whapping you a good one up the back of the head.

"Maybe." He couldn't take his eyes off her. What was going on with him? *Was* he in love with her?

"A gentle sway would be better." Sugar turned to adjust the dial, but when she rolled back, she misjudged the wave and landed right on top of him, breasts pressed against him, thick hair a curtain between their faces. She smelled of vanilla and skin and the spearmint gum she favored.

"Wow," she said, her face going pink, her eyes flickering with startled heat. She seemed to melt into him.

"Yeah. Wow." Emotion rose and rushed through him on a wave of heat and need. And more. Something bigger and more important.

Dammit all, he *was* in love with her.

Now what? He had to think, figure it out, decide. But Sugar shivered against him and licked her trembling lips, making him lose all reason.

Kiss her.

Are you crazy? Gage didn't go with momentary urges. He pondered options, evaluated outcomes, made the wisest choice.

Kiss her, you ass.

Now.

Acting on impulse, he touched Sugar's cheek, lifted his mouth, and—

"Enjoying the Good Vibrations?" The bonehead

salesman loomed over them, eager and unctuous. "I guar-
antee the Good Vibrations 3000 is the best bed on the
market today."

"We're not sure about the levels," Sugar said, rolling to
look at the guy. She sounded relieved to be interrupted.
"It's hard to tell in such a short time."

"We do offer a thirty-day, money-back trial," the rep
said, practically rubbing his hands together.

While the doofus and Sugar discussed that possibility,
Gage sorted his thoughts. He was in love with Sugar. When
had that happened? A while back? Years ago maybe? Had
he just blocked it?

And what should he do about it? Hope it would pass?
Or take action? Go for it? He had to do something. First,
he had to get rid of Mr. Good Vibrations.

"We'll let you know," Gage snapped at the guy, who
backed up as though Gage had aimed a pistol at his belly.

When the salesman was out of hearing, Sugar shot Gage
a look. "Too pricey, you think?" She scooted off the bed
and pretended to study the price sheet. He knew she was
avoiding the moment. "Our guests prefer to make their own
tsunamis anyway, right?"

He didn't speak, just watched her from the swaying
mattress.

"Shall we check out the sex toys then take a break?" she
asked, her voice breathless and high. She was freaked.

"Think I'll skip the gadgets." He wasn't capable of
movement, even if he wanted to pretend everything was
normal.

"You okay?" she breathed, standing at the edge of the bed.

"Not bad." For someone who'd mentally been run down
by a Mack truck. He was in love with his partner. Probably

had been for years. "You go on. I'll try a couple more speeds on this thing." He made as if to reach for the dial.

"So, birthday dinner in your room?"

"Eight sharp. I already ordered the meal." They always celebrated their week-apart birthdays together and tonight was the night.

"Good." She blew out a breath, obviously intending to do what they always did when things heated up, treat it like sparks on a carpet—a sharp jolt, quickly over.

Not this time. The decision swelled in him, as inevitable as a wave in this water bed. This time he would do something.

Sugar faltered, bit her lip, turned away, then back, confused and unsure. So *not* Sugar. Sugar was sure about everything. She had more opinions than any woman he'd known. They argued constantly, though she liked to call their swordfights *discussions.* Sugar claimed that was how they got to the core truths. He found the process wearying, but worth it.

But just now, Sugar didn't know what she wanted with him and that gave Gage a strange hope. She wiggled her fingers and backed away, shaky in the silk she wore. She belonged in silk. Or maybe leather.

He'd seen her admiring a red leather skirt and jacket in the hotel gift shop. That would have been a much better birthday gift than the PDA he'd bought to replace her failing one. Too late.

Or maybe not. Maybe tonight was the night to act on impulse. Maybe tonight he'd violate his very nature and not think this thing into the ground. He'd buy the outfit and tell her how he felt.

Almost as if she'd read his mind, Sugar spun and fled as if fearful he'd chase her. He'd almost been ready to. He turned off the damn water bed and lay there, swaying softly, trying to settle himself the hell down.

It wasn't too late to forget the attraction. They'd done it before. He didn't have to rock the boat.

But he couldn't go back. The truth had hit him too hard. It all made painful sense. Sugar was the reason none of his girlfriends worked out, why the settled life he craved had proved so elusive. This was the other shoe he'd been waiting for and it dropped inside him like a gravity boot.

It had always been Sugar. Her laughter rang in his head like the purest music. He loved the way her wild ideas knocked his plodding thoughts clean off their tracks. She threw open doors where he'd only seen walls.

She revved him up, made him run on guts and testosterone, made him want to give her anything she wanted, hell, the world. She made him feel alive.

And he was in love with her.

He had to talk to her about it.

Over their birthday dinner? Sure. He'd go gently, the way you coaxed a cat onto your lap. Sugar treated the R word like it smelled bad and the L word like poison.

Let's see what can happen between us. That sounded about right—easy and casual and fun—not threatening at all.

The Sextique International Expo might not be the best venue for a declaration of love, but they were here, dinner was arranged and he was a practical guy.

He'd get flowers and buy her that red leather outfit. Maybe before the night was out, he'd be peeling her out of it…or ripping it off her.

However she wanted it. He just wanted her. In his bed, in his life. Sometimes a bold move was the most sensible, rational, reasonable thing to do.

But all the while, he felt the dangerous tug of a crazy undercurrent. There was nothing sensible, rational or reasonable about falling in love with Sugar.

SUGAR STUMBLED AWAY from the water bed booth toward the long table of sex toys, so dazed she could hardly see, let alone think. What the hell had just happened?

Looking down at Gage on that water bed, she'd felt as if someone had opened an oven in her face. Hugely, impossibly hot.

They'd been through this, Gage and she. They'd pushed past the college crush, then cleared the air for good on the Night of the Mad Margaritas. The resort's grand opening had been in the morning and they'd sucked down one too many celebratory drinks and leaned into an embrace that felt inevitable until their operations manager had snapped the tension with a cell call over a last-minute issue.

They'd laughed in relief, agreed that sleeping together was not worth the risk to their partnership. It had been the mood, the moment, the magic.

They'd *agreed,* dammit.

But just now, he'd looked at her *that way* and she'd *liked* it. A lot.

That was all wrong. Gage was not only her partner, he was her best bud, the person who held her hand through bad times—her mother's cancer scare, her father's roller-coaster relationships, her sister's rocky divorce and her own occasional blues. Gage was a great listener, wise and funny and so different from her that his comments felt like a window of fresh air opened in a stuffy room.

She counted on Gage and he counted on her. She'd thought he did, anyway. She glanced back at him, lying on that damnable bed. Her insides still vibrated—as if someone had banged a tuning fork against her innards. Not from the bed, from Gage and the way he'd looked at her. As if he'd been waiting for her all his life. As if she and no one else would do.

Her knees gave way a little.

Shit. Shit. Shit.

She turned, bit her lip, fought the stupid, impossible surge of joy. Wrong, wrong, wrong. Pointless, really.

To distract herself, she focused on the sex-toy table. The arousing items seemed like so much silly plastic after those blazing hot seconds on that paint-spinner of a water bed with Gage.

Birthday dinner in your room? she'd said. In his *room.* Where there was a *bed.*

Her blood felt so hot that every heartbeat sent a burn to the tips of her fingers and toes and out the top of her head.

Maybe she was simply, well, horny. She'd been between men for months now, though she hadn't really thought about it. Which was odd, since, at thirty-five, she was supposed to be at a sexual peak.

She'd peaked all right—or come close just now. With *Gage.* Her *partner.* Her *friend.* Off-limits since *forever.*

What was she thinking?

Maybe it was Esmeralda's psychic command zipping around in her brain. *You must see what you've ignored.* The advice irritated Sugar. Just because she kept moving, aimed forward, didn't mean she ignored what mattered.

She hadn't missed the important stuff with Gage. What they had was far more important than any affair could offer. And that's all it would be—a fast fling that would burn bright then fizzle to ashes.

Gage was a wonderful man, but Sugar never wanted any man for very long. She didn't seem to have the happy-ever-after gene. Not great news, but it was better to accept who she was than fight it or whine about it.

Still, that moment on the water bed had filled her heart with an ache for something she hadn't thought possible, something that might be there for her if she would reach out and grab it.

Too crazy.

Maybe it was the changes she wanted to make with Spice It Up. Maybe the excitement of growing the resort through franchising had gotten her all stirred up. She planned to talk to Gage tonight. Maybe once she got him excited, too, they'd be okay again.

It wouldn't be easy. Gage was Mr. Stay Put, Stand Pat, Play It Safe. He never drew a card in blackjack when he had sixteen or bought a new suit until his old one had an un-patchable hole. He had the same furniture from his college apartment. Quality brands and classic designs, of course—leftovers from his father's small hotel—but, sheesh, didn't he get tired of seeing the same sofa every damn day?

Of course, this attitude made him a great partner. Their working relationship was a series of negotiated agreements and careful compromises, polished by their debates to a fine gleam.

She and Gage had achieved a delicate balance in their partnership, a perfectly calibrated seesaw of push-pull, rush and calm. Throwing in sex would be like dropping an anvil on one side. Somebody would get flung across the playground. Probably both of them.

Which meant they had to get past the Water Bed Moment—even as it continued to throb through her. She scrubbed at her arms, still covered with goose bumps, and smoothed back her hair, which prickled with awareness, then picked up a box to examine the elaborate vibrator inside. Her task was to find innovative items to add to the inventory of Le Sex Shoppe, the boutique at the resort. Leticia, the manager, was counting on her.

Sugar focused in. Thinking about the resort always steadied her. Maybe she was too intent on her work, letting her personal life fade in importance, but the resort had been all-consuming from the beginning, and reaching this level of success had been a major achievement. Spice It Up, a combination resort and sex-therapy retreat for committed couples, was unique. Therapy-focused, Spice It Up used relationship theory to boost intimacy in long-term relationships, very different from sex-themed resorts and luxury spas.

Their success hadn't gone unnoticed. Competitors were in the wings. After four years, it was time to grow. Grow or die was basic business law. It happened to be her personal mantra, too. Having a new challenge filled Sugar with adrenaline and relief. She liked making progress.

She would talk through her plan with Gage tonight. The Sextique International Expo, with its theme of *Sex Sells... Everything,* made a compelling case for her idea. With porn going mainstream and strippers making *Entice Your Man* videos, sex and all things spicy had never been more legitimate.

She needed to settle herself, focus in on her goal.

Maybe a drink in the bar would help. She had time before dinner. She could distract herself, clear her head, maybe network with conference-goers, get fired up for her pitch to Gage.

In the quietly busy hotel bar, she spotted a guy she'd exchanged a comment with during a marketing presentation. Handsome, he wore a crisp shirt, sleeves folded back, tie loose, and was drinking a martini with olives.

Sex was an appealing possibility and, if not, they could talk business, so she slid onto the stool beside him. "Enjoying the convention?" She tilted her head, accepting his pleased smile.

"I made some contacts," he said, turning to more fully face her, also indicating interest. "You?"

"Me, too. I'm learning lots."

"What can I get you to drink?"

"If that's gin, I'll take one."

"A martini girl. Bombay okay?"

"Excellent." Very classy. "I'm Sugar Thompson, by the way."

"Conner Jameson. ExerSystems. Exercise suites for hotels and motels." He gave her a card, which she exchanged with one of her own. "We spoke, I believe, at that workshop."

"I remember you," she said.

"So… 'Spice It Up,' huh? 'An adventure in enhanced intimacy,'" he read from her card. "I've heard of you."

"Really?" Though she wasn't surprised. Spice It Up had lots of buzz, she'd learned from other attendees. A woman from the Singles Travel Network had mentioned two resorts were adding sex counselors to their amenities—further proof that Sugar and Gage had a brief window to expand before competitors stole their edge.

"I was looking at your brochure at a convention in Nevada and a woman commented that the place was a gold mine."

"Oh, really? Who was she?" A possible contact for franchise possibilities.

"She was with Travel Something… Quest, I believe. TravelQuest. Yeah. Business travel. Her name escapes me. She was very knowledgeable. Tall…blond…"

"And gorgeous? Had to be Rionna Morgan." The woman was the queen of networking.

"You know her?"

"The travel industry's a tight group." Plus, Rionna had a thing for Gage, Sugar was sure. At the Business Association luncheon the month before, she'd complimented his *incisive mind,* batting her eyes so hard Sugar couldn't resist asking her if her contacts were bothering her.

Gage seemed oblivious, but then he'd been dating Adrienne at the time.

"Good point. Makes me wonder how I've missed meeting you until now." He held her gaze. Definitely into it.

She wanted to talk business still. "I hope Rionna's right because we're considering franchising."

"Seems to be the thing do," Conner said. "Big money-maker."

"I know. I had a great preliminary meet with a consultant who's done motel-hotel franchises."

"Which consultant?"

"Foster Matthews of Matthews and Millhouse. You know them?"

"Heard of them. They're solid. We looked into the concept, too, but it wasn't right for us."

"Why was that?"

"Too many competitors, really, and it would have taken too long to build a franchise team. That's crucial."

She nodded. "Foster mentioned that. The next step is for them to come out for a diagnostic workup."

"Have you targeted any franchisees?"

"Not yet. No." She wanted Gage's help for that. They would prepare a package for the regional travel convention coming to San Diego in a month. "Any other advice?" she said.

"Make sure it's a good fit," he said, holding her gaze. She could tell he was finished with the topic and was considering how he and she might fit in an entirely different way. "So how did you get into the sex resort business?" he asked.

"That's a long story." Her martini arrived and she took a sip, loving the warm sting of the gin.

"I've got time." He smiled at her. Getting warmer.

Except she felt no responding warmth. The vibe was as distant as a faraway train, the whistle barely audible.

So annoying. Sex with Conner would be the perfect palate cleanser after that bed jiggle with Gage. Except she was more hot for what he knew about franchises than for what might happen in bed with him.

She sipped more gin, then told him how Spice It Up came to be, how she and Gage had conceived of it six years ago, opened it after a year of prep and planning.

"Very interesting," Conner said, though he seemed to be talking about her mouth, not her resort.

Sugar still wasn't fired up. She glanced toward the bar entrance and noticed Gage walking by, headed for the gift shops. Why, she wondered? He wasn't the type to forget a toiletry item and he never snacked. He looked so purposeful.

Sometimes watching him made her want to stand still and just breathe—slow the hell down for once in her life. Lying on that bed with him, she'd really seen his face. Strong and broad, with nice cheekbones and dark, steady eyes and a firm mouth. She normally liked soft lips, but—

"Penny for your thoughts," Conner said, honing in. No sense dawdling over cocktails when they could be upstairs.

"Nothing important," she said, trying to shake Gage off.

"Then you won't mind if I interrupt them?" Conner leaned forward for a test kiss that could lead to the wild and lovely ride she usually loved.

His lips looked soft, the way she liked them, but she kept thinking about Gage's firmer ones. *Focus.* She was about to get a great kiss.

Which, abruptly, she didn't want.

She felt a strange longing, like a dream where you searched room after room for something you weren't even sure you'd recognize if you found it.

She put her hand on Conner's chest. "I'm sorry. I just realized how tired I am."

His eyes widened. "Did I—"

"Misjudge me? Not at all. I just changed my mind. I'm sorry. I would disappoint you."

"Oh, I doubt that." He smiled ruefully. "Another time?"

"Maybe," she said, then squinted down the bar. "There's a very hot woman over there. Her line is erotic pastries, I think. Talk about a great icebreaker."

He looked where she indicated, then smiled back at her. "You have good taste in women."

She shrugged. "I help where I can." She pushed her martini away, not wanting more alcohol when she already felt funny, and stood. "I'd better take off. Listen, if you run into anyone who might be interested in a franchise, would you mind giving them my card?" She handed him several more.

"I might know of a limited partnership. I'll let you know."

"Great."

"Keep us in mind, too. Custom systems at prefab

prices." He smiled, showing her the man beneath the pitch. She liked the guy. She just didn't want to sleep with him.

He kissed her goodbye—softly and with regret—and she really liked his mouth. "Get some sleep." He cupped her cheek.

"I will." What the hell was the matter with her? She might not be at a sexual peak, but she sure as hell wasn't in a slump. She knew her body, knew her needs. She handled her own O, as a matter of fact, and always had.

Maybe she needed her thyroid checked.

She was uncomfortably aware that the Water Bed Moment was proof positive that her libido was in full working order. Something else was going on here and she wasn't happy about it.

2

THE GIFT BOX CRAMMED UNDER one arm, Gage froze in the bar doorway and watched a guy kiss Sugar right on the mouth.

He was stunned. That Armani-suited bozo was trying to pick her up. And she was letting him. After what had just happened between them even.

That ass couldn't possibly *get* Sugar. He'd hit on her because she was hot and lively and fun. But Gage understood the tender woman beneath the fire and bluff.

Motivated by his new feelings, Gage wanted to march in there and knock that lounge lizard right off his stool. Luckily, before he could pull a Neanderthal, Sugar pushed to her feet, smiled goodbye to the guy and walked away—straight for Gage.

He didn't want her to think he'd stalked her, so he backed up and ducked into an elevator before she saw him.

In his room, he paced, thoughts reeling. What was Sugar up to? Who was that guy? How long before she'd be here for dinner? He looked at his watch. Too long.

He tried to calm down. Everything was ready. He'd worked his plan like the sensible guy he was. He'd bought the leather suit for her and roses in a vase curved like Sugar's figure. Dinner would arrive in an hour, along with Sugar.

But what if she'd made a date with Mr. Armani? What if he was heading to her room this very minute for a quickie?

She hadn't been seeing anyone for a few months, Gage knew, but that wasn't typical. Sugar kept busy to avoid the quiet. Unlike himself, who always took his time. He was too careful, dammit, too slow to act. Look at all the time he'd wasted, without even knowing what he wanted. He'd been doing the breaststroke down the biggest river in Egypt for years and, man, were his arms tired.

It hurt to laugh at himself.

He was done with denial and done with waiting. And at the moment, he had no intention of letting some ass-passing-in-the-night get between him and the woman he…loved. Yeah, that's right. He loved Sugar.

The idea made his head spin. This wasn't how falling in love was supposed to work. You were supposed to gradually realize the depth of your feelings, not get clubbed over the head and dragged down the hall.

But that was what had happened. And he was too much of a pragmatist to deny it. No, the practical thing was to go for it.

Flooded with adrenaline and determined as hell, he barreled down the hall to Sugar's room. He had the fleeting thought that he'd completely lost his mind, but he pounded on her door anyway. He wasn't himself and whoever he'd turned into wasn't backing out now.

In a few seconds, Sugar opened up, her eyes startled. "Gage? What are you doing here?"

"This." He cupped her face between his palms and kissed her, kicking the door shut behind him with one heel. He threw everything into that kiss—all the heat and need— holding her face the entire time.

She made a little whimper, stilled, then softened against him for a few seconds as she'd done on the water bed.

Then she yanked away. "Hold it…. Stop." She sagged, bracing her hands on her thighs, struggling for breath. "Wait."

What about his plan? Be casual and easy and fun? Okay, not too late. Slow down, give her a second, start over calmly. Instead he said the worst possible thing. "Sugar, I'm in love with you."

"I HAVE TO SIT." Sugar felt as though she'd been dumped into a washer and tossed around the drum until her brain rattled in her skull. She backed to the closest bed and sank onto the spread, the satin cool against her stocking-covered thighs. She'd only managed to get her jacket and shoes off when Gage began pounding on her door like the hotel was burning down and her room was next.

She couldn't catch a solid breath and her whole body trembled. Much worse than the Water Bed Moment. She dug her toes into the thick carpet, pressed her soles flat, desperate for solid footing. "What did you say?" She lifted a hand to stop his answer. "Never mind. I heard. Give me a second."

Her sensible partner had just come at her like an avenging angel or an EMT giving her the breath of life.

And what a breath it had been. That kiss had *you're mine* force combined with *how do you want it?* tenderness. He'd held her face between his palms, adoring her, making her feel every millimeter of his mouth—strong lips, coaxing tongue. Now her sex felt like an overwound rubber band about to snap.

And then he'd gone and said it. The L word.

"You love me?" she asked weakly. He couldn't, could

he? The possibility made her feel two things at once: *Oh, hooray* and *Ah, shit*.

Gage dropped onto the bed beside her. Taking her hands in his, he laced their fingers together and rested the clump on his thigh. "That wasn't how I wanted this to go."

"It wasn't?" Maybe they could erase it and start over. Hope rose.

"It's true, though," he said. "I do love you."

Damn.

"I don't know what to say, Gage." Her head was still in the washing machine, banging into the sides so that her ears were ringing and her mind was mush.

"You're saying it." He managed a wry smile. "You're freaked. If it makes you feel any better, so am I. I mean, we worked this all out, right? Way back in college."

"Exactly." They were still on the same page, at least. She'd almost gone for him back then—his quiet solidity had attracted her—but she'd been with Dylan, who was hot, also Riley for a while, and others. The great thing about college was that no one got serious. Except Gage. And he hadn't approved of how actively she dated. She'd concluded he was kind of a tight ass, but forgave him because he'd been a dependable friend. "And when we started the resort, we talked it out, right?" she added.

"Right."

"So this is just chemistry?" she asked weakly. More like the Fourth of July, nuclear fission and an exploding comet all rolled into one.

"Chemistry?" He wasn't buying that, either.

"The important thing is our partnership. And we're friends. Don't forget that."

"Couldn't forget that." He sighed and squeezed their

fingers together. "Maybe if we're good at being partners and friends, we could be good at…more."

"It was that water bed!" she blurted. "I mean, shaking and bumping and rocking like that."

He shook his head.

"I guess not."

"I think it's always been there. For me." He leveled his gaze at her. "I just blocked it."

This isn't fair, she wanted to whine. They'd figured this all *out.* They knew what *mattered.* How could a giant quivering mattress full of water make them forget?

She had to get them back on track. "We're so different, Gage." That's what she told herself whenever she had hot thoughts about him. She liked variety, action, late nights. He was Mr. Same Old, Mr. Rut, Mr. Early To Bed, Early To Rise. Probably predictable in bed, too—all missionary, all the time.

"We can work that out…." The tiny hesitation in his voice told her she'd made some headway, so she kept going.

"I don't do permanent, remember?" Gage was the kind of guy who got married for good. In fact, she was surprised he wasn't already ringed up.

His eyes held hers. *With me you could.*

She knew better. She'd let a couple of guys get serious on her. They'd wanted to spend every minute with her until she felt smothered. The breakups were dreadful. She'd felt as though she'd led them on. She'd been in love with love—the guys, too, no doubt—and she'd vowed to never put anyone through that again. She was just better off sticking with short-term sex.

Plenty of women were built like her, though many refused to accept it, got married and made themselves—and their husbands—miserable when it fell apart.

Sugar wouldn't do that. She couldn't. And certainly not with a man she cared as much about as Gage. "We don't see relationships the same. Look at how we reacted to our parents' divorces." Gage thought his parents quit too soon, while she accepted her folks' breakup without complaint. Relationships were dynamic systems that could fly apart. Especially for people like Sugar and her parents. It happened. No sense torturing yourself, your spouse or your family over it.

"That's different," Gage said. "Completely."

"I'm not built like you, Gage." People like Gage knew how to make love work. And when their relationships faltered, Spice It Up got them back on track. She loved being part of that effort. Somehow, that made up for her own lack. Not lack, exactly, but she did get an empty feeling from time to time.

Which she didn't appreciate being reminded of.

Gage was looking at her with so much hope, she panicked. "I need change, Gage. New furniture, for God's sake." That was lame, but she was flipping out, almost getting sucked into Gage's fantasy.

"We're talking about couches now?"

"It's just a symbol. I need variety. You want sameness. You've had those shoes since Clinton's second term."

"Hey, I had them resoled." He studied them briefly, then looked at her. "What's wrong with sticking with quality?"

"Nothing. It's just not me. I'm cheap, disposable fashion. You're solid, classic traditions."

"This is you and me, Sugar, not *Better Homes & Gardens*. Pretend I didn't blurt what I blurted. Try this— Hey, Sugar, how about we see what develops? Better?" He gave that self-mocking smile she loved so much.

"Not much, no." The truth was out. And the fact that he'd behaved so out of character told her how big his feelings were. Shutting him down felt criminal, but what choice did she have? Her stomach joined her head in the churning washer.

"Let it sink in," Gage said.

But there was no point and too much at stake. She had to sort this out. *What would Gage do?* That was her mantra when she got emotionally overwrought. Gage was so rational, so sensible. When he wasn't around to argue her through something, she imagined what he'd say. Now she was using him against himself. But it couldn't be helped.

"Let's think this through," she said. "Why is this happening now? You just broke up with Adrienne, right? So you're lonely. You and I spend a lot of time together. We're close friends. Plus, it's a big birthday for both of us. Thirty-five is time to turn the corner. I know I've been thinking about shaking things up. But not..." She hesitated. "Not like that."

"Shaking things up?" He frowned. "Like how?"

"By doing something different with the resort. I planned to talk to you about it at dinner, but—"

"No, no. Go on. Tell me now." He folded his arms.

"Maybe later. When we get back home."

"Let's have it," he said wearily. "What are you cooking up, Sugar?"

They needed a change of subject, that was certain. "Promise you'll hear me out before you start arguing?"

"Go on."

He hadn't promised, but she went ahead anyway. "Okay... You know how we've been overbooked during busy months?"

"Yeah?"

"That's revenue just disappearing. There's growing interest in sex resorts. That's obvious from this conference. Think of all the travel reviews we've had lately. The buzz is that we've got a gold mine on our hands. If we don't get ahead of the curve, we'll lose out."

"What are you proposing?" He spoke slowly, considering the idea. Thank goodness. His analytical side had kicked in.

She felt safe to babble on. "At first, I thought we could buy a second location, but that's capital-intensive and we'd be spread thin staff-wise. Then I read a big trade journal piece on hospitality franchises. The consultants in the article were based in San Diego, so I called them."

"Franchising?" He lifted his eyes to hers. "You want to franchise Spice It Up?"

"Franchising is the way to go. I was talking to a guy earlier about it. Plus, it's a cash cow, Gage, and—"

"And you met with consultants? Without talking to me first?"

She preferred Gage's business bristle to the hurt from before. "It was just a preliminary discussion. No money changed hands. I wanted to tell you about it, share my other research and get your ideas about possible franchisees we could target. It's all there." She nodded at her briefcase on the table by the door, ready for her to carry to Gage's room.

Back before she got dumped in a washer set on heavy-duty.

"A franchise is a package. Spice It Up is too unique to be packaged." He shook his head. *That's that.* A good sign. This was how all their debates started.

She barreled ahead. "I thought that, too, at first. Then I did some reading. There's a book—*Franchising For*

Dummies, can you believe that?—which has checklists and tips and screening tools. You have to check it out." She nodded at her case again.

"What about us, Sugar?" His eyes bored into her.

Us sounded *sooo* good just then. Like a long hot bath with nothing in her mind but the pleasure of it. She sank into that feeling and into Gage's eyes. She'd never noticed the swirls of caramel in their melted chocolate depths.

Stop it. Enough with the hot baths and candy eyes.

"The only *us* that counts is us as partners, Gage," she said. "We got carried away. We have history and attraction. You're lonely. I'm lonely, too, I guess. And that water bed…wow. Who could blame us?" She was trying to joke, but her throat hurt and she couldn't make herself smile.

"You won't even consider it?" He dug at her with his dark eyes. "You don't feel—"

"We can't." She wasn't sure how she felt, but she wouldn't lead him on, so she shook her head. "Even if I did feel— Well, anyway, no. Just no."

"Oh." Gage released her hands, which fell back to her lap. She stared down at them. Without Gage holding them, they felt numb and empty. Hands were for holding.

Oh, stop. She was so *not* sentimental.

"Now what?" Gage asked softly, sadly.

She took a deep breath. "Now we do what we do best…." She faltered. "We're partners. So we'll debate the franchise idea until we agree and—"

"I can't do that," he said slowly. "I can't go back."

"What are you saying?"

"Or maybe I just don't want to. Now that I figured it out."

"What does that mean?" Her heart leaped to her throat. She was startled to feel Gage back away. Always when they disagreed about an issue, Gage engaged, fenced with all his might until they were exhausted and the best idea won out.

Not this time. She felt chilled to the bone.

"Maybe I need a change," Gage said.

"What kind of change?" She felt scared and thickheaded.

"I mean, maybe it's time for me to go."

It was as if someone had plunged a hot knife into her chest. "You can't leave Spice It Up." This was not the kind of shake-up she wanted at all. "Is it the franchise? Because you don't know enough yet. Look at what I've got before you dismiss the idea."

She rushed to her briefcase, opened it and grabbed the franchise research folder, Gage's silence behind her like a wall or a threat. She held out the folder, but he simply looked at her.

"I don't see how I can stay, Sugar. You don't really need me anymore."

"Of course I do. Especially with the franchise, I—"

"Things between us are different now."

"They don't have to be." But they were. She felt it, too. "What would you do instead?" she asked faintly, sinking to a seat beside him.

"I haven't thought about it. You could buy me out, I guess." He shrugged.

"I don't have that much cash. How would that work?" She was flailing for a delay, anything, until she could come up with a fix. The resort was everything to her. And Gage was so much a part of the resort in her mind, she couldn't imagine going on without him.

"I can be flexible about terms. I'm not in a rush."

"But I'd need a new partner and everything." A lump filled her throat, making it hard to speak. "With the franchising…"

"You could take over my work or Oliver could step up to the job. And, as far as the franchise goes…I don't think that's wise."

"Look, we're both upset, Gage. Let's not say things we'll both regret."

But he looked dead serious, not flipped out, not over-wrought. She was the one on the edge of hysteria. Gage seemed…resigned. He stood, as if to leave her room.

She stood, too. "Read over this stuff." She pushed the folder at him and this time he took it.

"I don't see the point," he said.

"I'll come over for dinner in an hour and we can talk it through." Debates had always worked with them, so why not now?

When he was gone, she rested her back against the door. He just needed a little time to come to his senses, right?

Why couldn't he leave? Sugar believed in moving on when the time was right, so why couldn't Gage? Even Mr. Stay Put had his limits, right?

But this was totally for the wrong reasons. It was practically emotional blackmail. *Be with me or I'll break up our partnership?* She should be furious.

But she wasn't. She was scared. The idea of Gage leaving made her mind stutter and spit like a candle in a draft.

She didn't want him to go.

3

AN HOUR LATER, Sugar stood outside Gage's room, holding his birthday gift, determined to be positive. No way would Gage leave over something as crazy as a sudden surge of lust. It was as though they'd gotten drunk at a high-school reunion and confessed an old crush.

Gage had had time to read what she'd given him, so they'd debate the franchise through to the other side and be fine. One day soon, they'd laugh about that silly Water Bed Moment and the Amazing Washing-Machine Kiss.

She tapped on the door. For a second, she wished he would yank it open and kiss her mindless again. That kiss had been wild and free and safe and sure all at once. She'd been almost afraid to relive it in her mind. It was like too much ice cream too fast. It gave her brain freeze.

The door opened. Gage stood there. He looked…normal.

Disappointment stabbed her. What was wrong with her? Normal was good. Normal was her only hope.

"Come in," he said and backed up.

Inside, she smelled dinner. Something sweet, orange, garlic with an under note of…what?

Roses. On the rolling dinner table in a vase surrounded by white tea-light candles, their gold tongues turning the transparent vase into a dancing prism of colors.

"You got roses?" She bent to the flowers. The cool petals brushed her cheek, the fresh musk filled her nose.

"So you would stop and smell them," he said, smiling sadly.

"Saying it with flowers, huh?" Esmeralda had urged that, too. To avoid his eyes, Sugar ran her finger down the curve of the vase, which suggested a sleek woman's body.

"The shape reminded me of you," Gage said.

She started to joke about her waist being thicker and her hips broader, but she didn't feel like laughing and he didn't seem to, either.

She saw two packages on one of the beds—one small and hand-wrapped, the other large in fancy gold paper with a huge bow bearing the hotel's gift shop sticker. He'd bought that since they arrived. Probably where he'd been headed when she'd seen him from the bar. A gift to go with his blurt of love.

Her heart pinched. If only she were a different person, the kind of person who could say yes to Gage and mean forever. "Gage, about what happened—"

"Let's forget it for tonight," he said. "We both have things to think about and decisions to make."

"Did you read my stuff?" She nodded at the far bed, where her folder lay, hoping against hope that would solve everything.

He shook his head. "Let's just celebrate our birthdays, okay?" He sounded weary.

"Sure. That's smart." The tradition of celebrating birthdays together had started the year they met in a psych research class at Arizona State. She had asked Gage to be her study partner—he took great notes—and she'd invited him to her small birthday party, where, with some probing, she learned his birthday was within days of hers. It was so like him to keep that private. All his emotions roiled under the surface.

Except for tonight, evidently.

She held out her present. It was a Global Positioning Unit, which held satellite maps of practically the entire planet. Gage was into orienting himself in the world and she'd seen him studying GPS models on a Web site.

When he accepted the box, their fingers brushed and Sugar's knees gave way. Again. That was weird. They touched each other all the time at work, brushing bodies, bumping arms, playfully hip checking each other. Gage often led her with a hand to her back and she would link arms with him as they walked together.

But just now, the brush of his fingers made her breathless.

Which told her she'd been ignoring her reaction. Just as Gage had blocked his feelings about her, she'd numbed out whenever they touched.

That no longer seemed an option.

And, damn, he smelled good. Of cologne and soap and just him. And he looked taller…broader…more *there*.

It was as though she'd been happily wandering around in the dark and someone had flipped on the light, forcing her to notice new and lovely details about the man—his warm, smart eyes, those delicious laugh lines around his firm mouth, the way his thick hair curled a little against the back of his neck, the way he carried himself with quiet assurance and easy strength.

She needed the lights off—*now*—if things were ever to be normal again.

She put her gift beside the ones for her on the bed.

The *bed*. In his *room*. Where they were *alone*.

She suddenly lost all strength in her legs and practically fell onto the chair behind the linen-covered table. The water glasses sloshed and the warmers rattled on the two dinner plates. Gage caught the wine bottle, which jiggled in its low holder, and sat across from her.

"So, what's for dinner?" She smiled cheerfully, determined to enjoy the meal, put everything else on hold.

Gage uncovered the plates to reveal gorgeous entrées—golden-brown duck displayed over a small-grained pasta patty, with an exotic-looking salad. "Low-carb duck à l'orange. It's sweetened with Splenda. I worked out the meal with the chef. That's a soy polenta, which is lower in carbs. Plus, hearts-of-palm salad—"

"Hearts of palm?"

"There's that jar in the fridge, so I figured it was on the diet."

She used it to spiff up her tuna salads at work. "You don't miss much, do you, Gage?"

"Not about you, no." He said it so matter-of-factly, as though it was as basic as breathing and her heart filled up tight as a balloon about to burst. She felt *cared for*.

It's just a crush. They had crushes on each other. All they had to do was let it fade—like having a sex dream about someone you knew. As the day wore on, the memory extinguished.

He lifted the lid from a smaller plate, which held a tiny cheesecake, crusted with nuts and topped with sliced strawberries. "Five carbs per piece. The crust is cashews. Strawberries are low carb."

"The lowest of any fruit," she added, her throat tight. "You went to so much trouble, Gage. I'm so sorry that this meal didn't go like—"

"Don't worry. I arranged the meal yesterday, so you wouldn't feel guilty about indulging."

Not even knowing he loved her, he'd fussed like this? That was supposed to make her feel better?

"I brought the wine with me. The guy said it has a clean taste and nice finish."

She turned the bottle to read the label and saw that it was the low-carb merlot she'd read about. "You are such a dear friend."

"Don't rub it in." Another joke that fell flat. "So dig in," he said, gesturing for her to start.

She bit into a morsel of duck, feeling his eyes on her. "Mmm," she said. "Exquisite. Try it."

He began to eat, too. She paused to watch, enjoying how his fingers moved on his utensils, the muscular workings of his jaw and throat as he chewed and swallowed, his tongue, which had felt so perfect in her mouth. That kiss had made her feel a way she didn't remember feeling in a long time, maybe ever.

But it wasn't love. It was lust and longing and surprise and denial and…God, she wanted him *so bad*. Heat flooded her face and her body, reached down her arms and legs, flew up through the roots of every hair so that the strands that brushed her cheek felt like flames licking her skin.

"Sugar? You okay?"

"Uh, fine," she said, embarrassed. "Just savoring…everything." She held her wineglass with both hands to keep from grabbing Gage by the collar of his oxford shirt and savoring him. For hours.

The sex couldn't possibly be that good. Or maybe only at first. Lots of couples came to Spice It Up because their sex life had gone flat as day-old soda.

And even if the sex stayed hot, what about the day-to-day dullness? Gage would read the paper every morning over breakfast and want his eggs a certain way—he'd probably fix them, at least, since he was a great cook. They would set off for the resort together, listening to public radio news in the car, making observations about the traffic, the weather, the work ahead.

After work, repeat conversation. Back at home, ritual chitchat, *The NewsHour* on PBS, the *Daily Show* on Comedy Central, early to bed, a quickie and the next day the same routine. On the weekends, movies and concerts, the monotony broken by the occasional vacation. Gage wanted to go on an Alaskan cruise. What could be duller than being trapped on a boat with nothing to do but eat and lounge and play bingo?

She would try to make him happy, to be happy herself, but she'd be miserable. She'd end up buying herself a café racer just for the rush of taking the curves fast.

"Was it good?" Gage asked.

"Uh, what?" For a second, she thought he meant her fantasy, but he meant the food. "Scrumptious. The duck. The polenta. The salad." In the time it took to nibble a few bites of the meal, she'd had them on the brink of divorce. Good grief. "I'm just so full. Why don't you open your gift?" She was too upset to eat.

He wiped his mouth, tossed his napkin on the table, then turned to the bed to grab her gift to him. He cut the ribbon with his pocketknife—Gage was ever prepared—tore open the paper and smiled at the box he saw. "You got me a GPS unit. Great."

"The guy at the store said it's the best nonprofessional model. And you can download more maps if you want."

"I've wanted one for a while." His eyes connected with hers, full of affection and appreciation. "Thank you."

"I saw you checking them out." It seemed that she'd been watching him pretty closely, too.

"Your turn," he said and handed her the remaining packages. "Open the little one first."

"You shouldn't have gotten me two gifts."

He only shrugged.

In the small box was a Palm Pilot. "How did you know? Mine is—"

"Failing. Yeah. I noticed."

Of course. "Thank you."

"Now the other." His eyes lit with anticipation.

She tore open the paper. In the candlelight, the red leather suit she'd almost bought gleamed up at her. It had been very expensive. "This is too much, Gage."

"It seemed right at the time."

When he'd planned to declare his love. Her heart ached at the thought. She held the jacket under her chin, breathing in the leather smell. "It's gorgeous."

"Is the size is right?"

She checked the label. "Perfect."

"Maybe you should try it. That way you can exchange it before we leave if you need to." He swallowed. He wanted to see her in it.

She wanted him to. "Okay. I'll try it on."

The suit fit like a second skin, she saw in the bathroom mirror, with a front zipper for the jacket and a side one for the skirt, and she even looked slimmer in it. She stepped, barefoot, into the heels she'd kicked off earlier and walked out to him.

Gage's jaw dropped at the sight of her. "Men will follow you like dogs. Howling."

"Hardly." She blushed, walking closer, stopping when she was a breath away.

"Are you kidding? They'll rip each other apart to get to you first. But then, I knew that when I bought it."

"It feels good on." She ran her hands down the sides of the skirt. Gage's eyes followed like a breath on her skin.

"Let me see." He fingered the open collar, brushing her collarbone with his knuckle. "Glove leather. Very soft." She could tell he was contemplating ripping the suit right off her.

She swayed in the magnetic pull of his desire. Two zipper yanks and she'd be nude except for panties. She'd skipped a bra, which she did whenever her clothes were opaque enough.

"It's gorgeous, Gage, but you spent too much on me."

"Worth every penny to see you in it."

Or out of it?

She forced herself to step back, breaking the force field. "So, did you bring birthday candles?"

He patted his pocket. "What do you think?"

"You're always prepared." Did he have condoms? She had some in her purse....

He held out the box. "I say we do seven," he said. "Thirty-five twice is seventy. A candle per decade between us."

"Sounds good."

She made her way shakily back to the table, the suit creaking as she moved.

Together they found room for the candles among the plump strawberry slices on the yellow-cream surface of the cheesecake and Gage lit them all with one match. What great fingers he had.

All the better to stroke you with.

Stop. But it was tough, with the candles casting mysterious shadows on Gage's face in the room's low, golden light. Her entire body was alive to Gage's every breath, the twitch of each muscle, the gleam of candlelight in his dark hair, those caramel-swirled chocolate eyes.

It's just lust, Sugar.

So, go with lust. Lust is good.

Could they just sleep together one time? Get it over with?

What about the L word? Maybe he'd mistaken lust for love. Maybe *lust* was the L word he meant.

"Make your wish," Gage whispered.

I wish we could sleep together.

Too risky, even for a wish. She shook her head to clear it.

"What's the matter?"

"Just figuring the best wish." She shut her eyes. *I wish we would come to our senses.*

They leaned over the cake, faces close, the candle flames making Gage's pupils seem on fire. Whatever he was wishing was something hot and sweaty.

They blew out all the candles in a sweep of warm breath. And the swirl of smoke and burnt smell made her think of sad endings and lost chances.

"What did you wish?" Gage asked, his face close over the tiny cake.

"If I tell you, it won't come true."

"Maybe we don't want your wish to come true," he said softly. "Maybe we want mine."

Maybe they did. She realized Gage had always been there for her. Comforting her during the bad times, celebrating the triumphs, always with his wry smile. They'd been through a lot together, the early years of financial pinch, the fat of recent success. They'd shared everything. They were close.

And all this time, she'd blocked her attraction. But that ability was gone for good. Now, wearing the suit he'd given her, looking into his dark, hungry eyes, desire flooded through her so strong and inevitable she was powerless to resist it.

Screw thinking, screw being sensible, going numb, waiting until it faded. She wanted this man *now*. She grabbed Gage's face in both hands and kissed him with all her might.

He tasted familiar, but new, of himself and the meal and the wine. He leaned into the kiss and held her face, too. The table jiggled and she realized they'd both leaned into the cheesecake, getting some on their clothes, but she didn't care.

Gage stopped the kiss, but held her face still. "What are we doing?" He seemed to be struggling for breath.

"What we both need," she said. Before she went for him again, she threw in, "Friendship with benefits." What*ever*.

The steel plate covers clunked to the floor. Silverware rattled, a wineglass toppled, but neither of them seemed to care. All she knew was that she had Gage's tongue and he had hers and they were turning their faces from side to side, bumping noses, gasping to breathe while gobbling each other up as though they were the Splenda-sweetened cake neither had tasted.

Wanting body-to-body contact, she pushed to her feet, taking Gage with her, moved away from the table and walked Gage backward, still kissing, until they both landed on the bed, her on top.

Gage slid his hands under her arms to cup her breasts through the spongy leather, then tugged at the jacket zipper. "Why is this okay again?" he murmured.

"Because we're friends and we want each other and what's the point of saying no when it's driving us crazy?"

Her jacket flapped open, exposing her breasts. "Good enough for me," Gage said, taking one breast deep into his mouth, greedy for it, his breath hot on her skin, the suction thrilling her. He ran his tongue across her nipple, making her squirm against him. Her skirt rode high on her thighs. "Ohhhh." Lord. When had this ever felt so good?

Except there were so many damn clothes. She went for Gage's belt, but he shifted to the other nipple and she was lost to the sensation—the pull, the heat, the pressure, the tease.

Her mind flitted, like static electricity, flaring and zipping everywhere. *What are you doing, Sugar?... Don't think.... Stop thinking.... What's the deal with this belt? Can I tear it open with my teeth? You're thinking again....*

She gave up on the belt and touched him through his pants. She wanted the hard length of him inside her. Now. Now. Now.

She hadn't been this frantic since, well, forever. She wanted him more than she'd wanted anyone. Ever.

He shoved her skirt higher, reached between her legs and stroked her through her panties.

"Oh. Yes. Yes."

He slid two fingers beneath the elastic to find where she was wet for him, and she lost complete control, crying out, moaning, managing garbled syllables.

"I've wanted you so long," Gage breathed. "I never let myself know how much."

"I know," she said. There was so much here. Too much. Her body responded as though someone had blown open a door that had been barricaded shut. She rocked against his fingers. He held her gaze. She felt pinned to him, locked to the feeling only he could give her. She was afraid she might never, ever get enough.

She felt the twining sensation of her body warming up for release.

I could come with him. The fact startled her. She handled her own climaxes, pushing herself over the edge after her partner came or sometimes just before. A minor glitch in her system, but many women didn't come during intercourse. Or at least not all the time. It was fine. She was in charge of her own pleasure and maybe that was best. No disappointment that way.

Except now she seemed ready to fly through space at Gage's touch. Which thrilled her and scared her.

And distracted her.

"Are you okay?" Gage stilled, sensing her hesitation. He looked at her, not allowing her to escape.

"I'm just…I'm on the pill. Are you healthy?" The birth control discussion would buy her time.

"I'm good," he said.

"Oh, I'm sure you are," she said, going for his belt, fighting to get back in the groove.

He gently eased his fingers away from her spot and stopped her hand. "What just happened, Sugar?"

"Nothing," she said, embarrassed that he'd noticed. "I guess I expect Oliver to interrupt us with a call."

He smiled at the joke, but he was watching her. "Do we need to be interrupted?"

"Of course not. Friends with benefits is definitely the way to go. We—"

Amazingly enough, the phone did ring. They stared at it, then at each other and burst out laughing.

She fell to the side beside Gage, who picked up the phone. "Yes?…Oh, hello, Chef Winslow." He grinned at her, then focused on the caller. "The meal was wonderful. We enjoyed it very much… Yes. Very moist… Definitely… Yes, a terrific choice for the menu. Absolutely. No problem…thanks again."

He hung up and looked down at her lying beside him.

"The chef?" she asked.

"Yep. He's working up a low-carb menu. I didn't have the heart to tell him we hadn't tried the cheesecake. Wait." He slid his finger across a spot on her suit, then licked it. "Excellent."

He ran his gaze down her body, making her feel naked, even though her jacket had fallen closed and she still wore her skirt, then he seemed to gather himself, get control. "Probably good we got interrupted, huh? We're not thinking clearly."

"Forget thinking," she said. "Let's finish what we started." She moved to kiss him, but the expression on his face stopped her cold. He wanted more than just sex.

Sex was all Sugar could offer him.

Which meant he would go. Cold fear clawed at her. "I don't want you to leave Spice It Up," she said softly.

"How can I stay?" He took her hand, linked their fingers.

Things change. People change. Even Gage could change. She understood that clearly. "But I'll need your help."

"The franchise is a bad idea, Sugar."

Thinking fast, she came up with a solution. "We need time. You said it yourself. We have to let things sink in before we make any decisions."

"How much time?" Gage said, his eyes searching hers.

"A month. Until the travel convention. Give me a month

to convince you franchising is the way to go." A month to convince him to stay.

"Franchising won't work, Sugar."

"You have a month to prove it to me."

"Are you serious?"

"You can't just walk away, Gage. Not yet."

They were great partners, dammit. Great partners hips didn't grow on trees. She refused to think beyond that, not while Gage still looked at her, his eyes clear and hot, and held her hand so tightly she never wanted him to let go.

That's what had happened. She'd been trying to hold on to him, and that need had turned sexual. It was just human nature. As simple and conquerable as that.

SUGAR WANTED MORE TIME.

So did Gage. He'd been foolish, pushing for too much too fast. Had he thought he was in some romantic movie with violins and pink sunsets? Lord. This was Sugar, who treated men like library books—check 'em out and turn 'em in before they're due.

On the other hand, they'd had twelve years. If they were meant to be together, wouldn't it have happened by now? Maybe he was grasping at straws.

No. Something wonderful had brimmed in Sugar's green eyes when he'd touched her—surprised hope. Arousal, too, which he'd loved. Then she seemed to scare herself. What exactly frightened her? How she felt? Or what she'd seen in his face?

"One month, huh?" One month to decide. One month to get her to fall in love with him.

A month of making love? God, how he wanted that.

But Sugar hid behind sex—rushed into it, used it,

ironically enough, to keep people away. Except she hadn't kept him away. He'd seen that, too, in her face. Connection, closeness. Was that what scared her?

Maybe she hid her fear behind detachment. What did she say about her parents' divorce? *Nothing stays the same. Love and let go.* He didn't buy that. It had to be fear that made Sugar crave motion.

If he could only show her another way, make her see that if she would just hold still for a second, happiness could settle around her.

Since everything between them was negotiated, it was his turn to propose terms. *Think, man. Get it together.*

But he could still taste her sweet breasts on his tongue, feel her lush wetness under that slip of underwear, where she was soft and needy and eager.

Say something rational.

She was waiting, her cheeks pink, her breasts peeking from the unzipped jacket. What about that *friends with benefits* option?

Nope. Not even close to what he wanted with Sugar. He zipped the jacket all the way to the top, shutting away temptation, before he could get a word out. "Okay. One month. But you have to do something for me."

"What?" She tilted her head, lips pursed, ready to haggle.

"Let me show you the magic of Spice It Up."

"I know the magic. I helped create it." They both shared the conviction that couples' therapy required deep examination of intimacy in a relaxed environment, which was what they strove to create at Spice It Up. Gage came to that knowledge through research—he'd done extensive studies of the literature. Sugar had formed her opinions after three years as a couples' therapist. A weekend retreat was often just the start of transformation, so she'd wanted an environment to comfortably pursue more success, more intimacy.

"You've forgotten a lot. We both have. I want us to sample the guest experience."

"You want us to stay together? In a suite?"

"Not stay. Just get a feel for it. We can register, go through the orientation with Erika, plan a schedule, choose workshops, even participate, all to gather impressions of how it is to stay at Spice It Up."

"And what about…this?" She motioned between them, her eyes hot. She was excited, but also nervous.

"Sex would be too easy."

"Too easy, huh?" She sighed, but he felt her relief. What had just happened between them had upset her.

"We're doing this as partners."

"But the whole point of Spice It Up is to improve a couple's sex life. Intimacy through sex. Healing through sex. Exercises for sex. Sex, sex, sex."

"We can work around that, can't we? We're more than our urges." *Yeah, right.* There was just a bit of glove leather between him and her naked body and if she said *sex* one more time with those lips, he couldn't be held accountable for his actions. He shifted his body to hide the proof of his distress.

"You would say that." She sighed. "Mr. Self-Control."

She had no idea. Just two zippers and he'd have heaven. Forget soothing her doubts, forget the plan, just get *in.* Why the hell not sleep with her and be done with it?

Because he was more than a chest-pounding primate. He wanted sex with Sugar to count. He wanted all of her—heart and soul, body and mind. He'd waited this long. What was one more month?

She shifted beside him, making the leather jacket swell over her breasts, and her skirt ride higher. Her panties had felt thin. Lace? Black, maybe?

One more month would be hell on wheels.

He would manage it somehow. He would surprise her with the resort and with himself while he was at it, show her she was safe with him. She could fall in love and be happy.

"It would give me ideas for the franchise package, I guess." She flipped her hair over her shoulder, crossed her legs and wiggled one foot—a sure sign she was intrigued. Her skirt shot even higher, so he focused on her feet.

She had puffy toes and a high arch he would love to massage until she moaned. Muscular calves, too, that would feel so good locked around his ass and…

"So, no sex?" she asked, as if she'd read his mind.

"No sex." He pushed to his feet, slightly hunched.

"You okay?"

"Charley horse," he said, knowing she'd caught him. This was merely the first of countless moments of sexual agony he would endure in the coming weeks. Worth every twinge if it got Sugar in his life.

4

BACK HOME in San Diego, Sugar pushed ahead of Gage into the Spice It Up lobby, headed for the check-in desk, ready to launch their plan. Gage caught up and took her hand. "Hold on. Look at what we built." He gestured at the lobby spread out before them, pulling her closer. When he released her fingers, the warmth lingered.

Damn. Since the Expo Incident, there was extra warmth to every breath or touch or smile they shared. Ridiculous, really, and it complicated everything.

Sugar's gaze floated from the cream marble tile to the polished mahogany walls, from the overstuffed velvet love seats and sofas to the lush Oriental rug in the cozy conversation pit, everything in the resort's colors of violet, teal and gold. On cool evenings, the massive fireplace crackled and popped with licking flames. She sighed with pleasure.

Gage had a point. Every subtle element was deliberate—meant to create an atmosphere of warmth, sensuality, intimacy and connection. She had to be certain the franchises included the crucial items.

A gigantic flower arrangement stood on a huge table in the center of the lobby. Violet bird-of-paradise, apple-green orchids, purple irises and marigolds stood out against a background of white roses, baby's breath and freesia.

A few feet away was the gleaming grand piano where music students from the nearby college played for the guests each evening.

For now, piped-in romantic music filled the air, along with the alluring scent of the flowers, lemon oil and vanilla-lavender candles in clusters large and small. Behind the elegant, dark-wood reception counter, staff was busy with guests. Completing her visual sweep, Sugar found Gage waiting for her. "You're right. We did good, huh?"

Gage smiled in what seemed to be triumph. What was that about? Oh, yeah. She'd forgotten they were in the middle of a debate.

To show him she hadn't given an inch, she popped the steno pad from the pocket of her laptop carrier and readied a pen. "Mahogany and marble aren't essential," she said, writing her thoughts, "but the franchises must include a fireplace, the piano and real flowers, don't you agree?"

Gage blew out a breath. "I suppose so. Yeah."

She'd made her point—she was working toward the franchises—and fought a grin. "Shall we check in?"

"Sure you don't want to wait until after the staff meeting?" Every Monday at eleven, the staff gathered to touch base on the upcoming week's events.

"More fun to get a natural reaction from the front desk."

To avoid alarming employees, they'd agreed to tell everyone they were working on a new marketing campaign, which was true enough, since they would use what they noticed in all their promotional materials. Once they'd decided about the franchising, they'd bring staff on board. Less anxiety that way in an industry fraught with turmoil.

"This could start rumors about us being a couple," Gage said, picking up his briefcase.

"We'll be absolutely clear, that's all," Sugar said.

"Oh, you bet," he said. "That'll do the trick." But he seemed entirely too peppy and pleased with himself. Why? His plan fit perfectly with her own. She'd hardly given in at all, but he acted as though he'd bested her.

"Allowing rumors won't help either of us, Gage," she warned. What did he think was going to happen? They'd check into a room, rip each other's clothes off and fall madly in love? That only worked in the movies. Or for some of their guests, of course, which was the point, after all.

Gage gave her the moony look from their birthday wish, full of hope and yearning. It was as if a romantic pod person had taken over his body. His incredibly buff body.

She had to admit that since the Expo Incident, Gage seemed different to her. Taller, broader and more muscular. That erection had been…impressive. If only she'd ripped his clothes off to get the whole effect. That had been her last chance. They'd agreed—no sex. Still, she remembered Gage sucking on her nipple, stroking her beneath her panties and she felt all shivery and woozy.

She was off-kilter. Plus the flight home had worn her out and she'd slept poorly last night. Whatever. She had to forget the Expo Incident and focus on what a terrific team they made. Gage was smart and savvy and sensible. A great partner.

Well, except for that damn smug smile he wore at the moment. Which was worse—the smug smile or the moony daze? They both irritated the hell out of her. "Quit grinning like you won something, Gage," she muttered.

"What? I'm just happy to be here with you, partner." He patted her back. Could a pat be smug?

"So how was the convention?" Brittany asked eagerly, catching sight of them as they approached.

"Bring back anything good?" Luigi said, holding a hand over the phone. "Something new in condoms maybe?" Snap. Snap. The guy's jaws worked over the inevitable piece of Juicy Fruit. That was one signature element they could leave out—gum-popping receptionists.

"I got a few samples you can have. I'll bring them into the meeting," Sugar said. "Some joke items—condom lollipops, key chain penises, tropical-flavored lubricants. Nothing revolutionary."

"Oh, give the lollipop to Oliver," Brittany said. "He has a great blush." Brittany had a crush on their operations manager, Oliver Noble, who was a no-nonsense guy—single, but ten years older than Brittany, and easy to embarrass. To counteract that problem, Oliver blustered at her, which seemed to accelerate the fire, not retard it.

"Jeez. You're so predictable, Brit," Luigi said. Snap, snap.

"So, what's up?" Brittany asked. "Why are you two on that side of the desk?"

"We're checking in," Gage said.

Luigi's jaw froze midchew and he joined Brittany in staring at them.

"It's for new marketing materials," Sugar added. "Gage and I are test guests so we can sample the experience. We need a room and an orientation."

"You're checking in? The two of you? As a couple?" Brittany's eyes went wider. "Wow. That's great! Really great."

Luigi resumed chewing, but very, very slowly.

"Strictly for research, right, Gage?" Sugar jabbed him with an elbow.

"Ouch." Gage nodded.

"Sure. I get it." Brittany winked.

Luigi double-popped his gum.

"Really," Sugar said wearily. She noticed that Clarice, the Pleasure Concierge and the resort's biggest gossip, had stopped working and was watching intently. If her ears had been antennae, they'd have been twitching.

"Wait," Luigi said suspiciously. "Is this, like, going to show up in my performance review?"

"Not at all."

But he wadded his gum into a pink message slip and tossed it into the trash, stood very tall and smiled a fake smile as he clicked into the system. "So, how long will you be staying with us, Mr. and, uh, Mrs. Maguire?"

"Don't you have reservations to confirm?" Brittany said, bumping Luigi out of the way to take over the task. She was always eager for extra responsibility.

Luigi shrugged and moved to the second terminal.

"It's Mr. Maguire and Ms. Thompson," Sugar said firmly to Brittany. "And it will be for one day."

"Two, don't you think?" Gage added mildly. "We'll need the overnight in case we work late."

There was a thud, then a swishing sound, as the rack of brochures Clarice had been pretending to neaten tipped over, spraying pamphlets across the glossy marble floor.

"We won't be sleeping there, so no need for maid service," Sugar said to be absolutely clear. She shot a frown at Gage.

"But, otherwise, we'd like the full guest treatment," Gage said. "As you can see, my partner is reluctant about our stay. Wouldn't you say so, sweetheart?"

Brittany just blinked at them.

"She doesn't see how a vacation can fix our, uh, problem." Gage seemed to be taking on a guest persona.

"I imagine you've heard that before from guests checking in, Brittany?"

Brittany seemed frozen.

"He wants you to say what you say when couples seem torn about being here," Sugar said. "When one thinks it's a waste of time or a pricey experiment. I'm the reluctant mate, Brittany, get it?"

Brittany blinked.

"If it saves our marriage, it's worth every penny, correct?" Gage said, prodding the stunned clerk.

"Uh, oh, yeah," Brittany said, finally catching on. "Absolutely right. Our happiest customers arrive in doubt and leave in bliss." She grinned. "Hey, put that in the brochure!"

"Why not?" Gage said to Sugar. Then he winked at her.

Sugar's knees turned to water. Over a *wink*, dammit. Gage winked all the time, but since the Expo Incident, the gesture was a lightning bolt straight to her sex.

Dazed, Sugar copied down Brittany's words.

Brittany beamed. "Okay, you two, welcome to an adventure in enhanced intimacy." *An adventure in enhanced intimacy* was their tagline. Sugar noted that franchisees should use it when welcoming guests.

"Oh! Wait! Here's another one," Brittany said. "We change relationships from so-so to oh-wow. Write that down!"

Sugar sighed and scribbled. "Got it. Now how about checking us in before the staff meeting?"

"Happy to! Would you prefer our luxury suites or one of our themed casitas? The casitas cost a tad more, but they're so wonderfully…um…what's the right word? Atmospheric! That's it," Brittany said, then tilted her head at Sugar's pad.

"I'll remember."

"Can you show us what they're like?" Gage asked.

"Oh. Yes. I'm so glad you asked!"

Luigi, listening in, rolled his eyes.

Brittany whipped out the two laminated display cards. The first, a single panel, showed a sample suite from the tower, where the opulent rooms had their patented multi-layer, pillow-topped bedding, an in-room hot tub, multiple-headed shower and a two-person sauna.

The second was a three-panel foldout of the fantasy bungalows scattered throughout the property—an aspect of the resort that Sugar didn't expect to include in the franchise package because of the cost factor. While theme-room resorts weren't unique, Spice It Up's niche was the commitment to sex and relationship therapy in strengthening couples' success.

"A tower room will be fine for our purposes," Sugar said.

"But the casitas are special." Gage studied the card as if he'd never seen the rooms before.

"They're very popular," Brittany said.

"Which is why we don't want to tie one up," Sugar said.

"These are open." Brittany skipped over the occupied rooms, hesitating over Harem Room, the Wild West Cabin, the Roman Holiday and the Fairy Tale Castlette, then she used her wax pencil to check mark the Victorian Romance Retreat, the Atlantis Cave and, Sugar's personal favorite, the Jungle Bungalow.

A Hollywood set designer in love with a famous actress had created the property as a novelty honeymoon resort. The affair fizzled, the actress and her money disappeared and Sugar had happened onto the place at the exact right moment to snap it up.

"Which one would you like, *dear?*" Gage asked her, still in character.

"I think you should choose, *darling*," Sugar said, her voice dripping with fake syrup.

Brittany looked from one to the other, speculating on the dynamic between them, no doubt. Clarice, meanwhile, had given up any pretense of work and was watching, chin on palm.

"We'll take the Jungle Bungalow," Gage said abruptly, folding the brochure and handing it to Brittany.

"Perfect," Brittany said and got busy at her keyboard.

Sugar stared at Gage, startled. "That's my favorite. How did you…?"

"Know? That's easy. I know you."

She gazed at him, while Brittany babbled about their choice, not noticing the vibe, thank God. Lord knew what Clarice had detected and at least Luigi was away from the desk.

"It's my favorite, too," Gage added.

"Oh."

Finished, Brittany turned to them with the glossy folder all guests got upon check-in. "Allow me to show you our amenities." She lifted out the main brochure and pointed her wax pencil at each item as she described it.

"For evening entertainment, we have two bars. Spicers, with live music or a DJ for dancing, and Intimates, designed for private drinks for two." She paused to look at them, trying to figure out which they'd prefer, Sugar guessed.

"Our restaurant, Edibles, is exquisite. Emile Fine, our chef, trained in Europe and specializes in room-service dinners for two. We also have a deli that offers romantic take-out picnics."

"Sounds fun, don't you think, darling?" Gage grinned at her.

"Lovely, *dear*." She rolled her eyes at him.

"We have two gift shops. The first offers our signature body lotions and toiletries and our exclusive chocolates, designed by European chocolatier Sebastian Rocque. The second, Le Sex Shoppe, contains a unique mix of erotic books, toys and games to enhance your intimate experiences."

The sex shop would definitely be part of the franchise. It had been her idea, but Gage had found the wholesale vendors and hired Leticia, the manager, who had exquisite haggling instincts and great taste.

"Of course, we have a heated pool, indoor and outdoor hot tubs, a spa and exercise space, as you'd expect. But what is unique about Spice It Up is our immersive therapy environment, including workshops and fantasy role-play rooms you can reserve.

"Our Intimacy Director, Erika Hauf, will help you tailor your experience to your interests and needs, which is also what distinguishes us from other couples resorts."

"I imagine that uniqueness is why your customers love the place," Gage said. "Where else in the world could they have a comparable experience?"

"Gee, makes you wonder why there isn't more than one, doesn't it?" Sugar said, making her own point.

They locked gazes.

The phone rang.

Brittany grabbed the receiver. "Spice It Up, how can we thrill you?" Then she dropped her bright tone, obviously talking to someone she knew well. "Yeah, they are." She covered the mouthpiece. "Maribeth," she whispered. Maribeth Bonner was their marketing manager. "They're doing a fake check in," she said into the phone. "They're being test guests…. Yeah… It's a marketing thing….

What…? I don't know exactly." She glanced at them and mouthed, "Wanna talk to her?"

Seemed like the resort grapevine was alive and well. Clarice had probably called Maribeth, who was now bristling that they hadn't filled her in first. Maribeth liked to be in the know about all promotions.

"Tell her we'll explain at the staff meeting," Sugar said. "And say we'll need her help." That should make her feel better.

They would need Maribeth on the franchise team. Possibly her assistant, Daisy Glover, too. The more Sugar thought about the franchise, the more excited she became. She just had to get Gage on board.

Brittany repeated Sugar's words to Maribeth, then clicked off. "She thinks you're mad about the November lag."

"Of course not. We've always had a holiday slump." They'd have to mention that in the franchise agreement. Franchisees needed to clearly understand revenue ebb and flow. Though that might vary, depending on the target city, and aggressive marketing might solve the problem. Sugar wrote a note to herself.

"So, okay, where was I?" Brittany said. "I've shown you the amenities…. Oh, yeah, the Ecstasy Orientation with Erika." She clicked some keys. "She can fit you in at noon."

"After the staff meeting," Gage said. "Sounds good."

"Now Jolie will introduce you to the pleasures of your room." Brittany lifted her gaze to someone behind them and Sugar and Gage turned to find Jolie, who was also a massage therapist, as was her twin sister Jade. Many employees performed double duties at Spice It Up. Waiters served as Intimacy Associates, playing bit parts in guest-couple fantasies, for example. Sex occurred only between the couples, though, since enhanced intimacy was the goal of a stay at Spice It Up.

Cross training. She wrote that down, knowing she'd have to add more time to the training portion of her franchise plan.

Gage would help her balance it all out and provide crucial information for the Operations Manual—the bible for franchisees. Gage's hospitality industry experience had been crucial to their success—he'd worked at his father's hotel. She counted on that expertise now. In fact, she didn't know how she'd handle him leaving. Oliver knew a lot, but he was no Gage.

"Gage and Sugar will be staying in the Jungle Bungalow," Brittany explained to Jolie, widening her eyes to invite Jolie's speculation.

"It's research for new marketing materials," Sugar said quickly. "We'll tell you all about it at the staff meeting."

Jolie smiled and tilted her head, speculating away.

Sugar felt herself blush. For the first time, it dawned on her that staff probably already wondered whether they slept together, since they were so close. Their innocence had made her oblivious. They weren't so innocent anymore.

Jolie held the door for them, her gold-and-teal wraparound skirt—part of the staff uniform—flapping in the flurry of outside air. Sugar passed in front of Gage into the sunny May morning, loving the hint of the ocean on the light breeze. She loved spring—summer, too—in San Diego. So did guests, since this was their busiest time.

Right now, everything was so vivid. Since the Expo Incident, her senses seemed heightened. Colors seemed brighter, smells stronger, the air on her skin more intense. So odd. It was as though she had a fever or her water had been dosed with a mild and lovely hallucinogen.

They started down the path, neat bricks beneath their feet, vine-covered archway overhead.

"Just explain everything to us the way you would any guest, Jolie," Gage said.

Jolie smiled, one brow lifted. "Okay. Sure. Let's see…"

"Like what's this?" Gage motioned at the gazebo in the grassy area to their right, where four couples in the resort's teal silk robes sat cross-legged, eyes closed, stroking their partner's face, taking instructions from the therapist.

"That's a class called Bonding Touch. The couples are describing the sensations and emotions they get by touching each other. The instructor is Mary Ellen Isley and she's wonderful."

"I imagine it's difficult to find sex therapists," Gage said, again trying to point out a flaw in Sugar's plan.

Jolie shrugged. "All I know is we have two great ones. Mary Ellen and of course, our director, Erika Hauf. Our couples love Mary Ellen's tantric workshop. And nobody knows the G spot better than Mary E. You should try her multiple orgasm class."

"We'll have to check that out." Gage grinned.

"I think we get the idea," Sugar muttered. No way was she observing a sex workshop with Gage.

"Write down 'uniquely talented staff,'" Gage said. "For the new materials."

She huffed out a breath.

Jolie motioned to the left of the walkway and pointed out the workshop rooms, spa and therapy center. Most of the rooms had their wooden blinds open to the spring sun. Sugar could see the Romantic Meals for Two cooking class going on in what had been a snack bar when they bought the place. Franchisees without a spare kitchen wouldn't be able to hold cooking classes.

Jolie led them to the top of a hill, then started down.

Gage paused and caught Sugar's arm. "Take a look."

Jolie waited a few yards downhill. The staff was trained to allow intimacy between the couples wherever possible.

Together they surveyed the resort grounds—tennis and volleyball courts to one side and, to the other, the low, rolling hills and varied plant life that marked off each casita's landscape. There were pine trees and a stone wall around the Fairy Tale Castlette, a Japanese garden near the paper-walled Asia Room, and cactus and a split-rail fence near the Wild West Cabin. "It is an amazing place," she said.

"You spotted it, remember?"

"Yeah." She'd gotten lost on the freeway, pulled into the resort to ask directions and found the owner bleary-eyed, nursing a Scotch at noon.

"You talked the guy into selling it to us."

"I just listened to him." He'd taken her on a tour, poured out his heart—and another Scotch—telling her that the love of his life had left him and that his dream, this resort, was about to plunge him into bankruptcy. All he wanted was out.

"I was just lucky." When she told him what she and Gage wanted to create, he offered her an incredible deal. She waited until he was sober to sign any papers, but she and Gage were overjoyed at the price they settled on.

"It was more than luck. You know people, Sugar. That's something else special about Spice It Up. You."

"You don't need to flatter me, Gage."

"You don't realize how rare you are." He turned to look at her full-on, as though she was the answer to all his questions. That was impossible, she knew. And it made her feel sad for him.

"We've built a great place," he said, taking her hand and squeezing it.

"We have." She liked standing there with him, surveying what they'd made together. "That's why I want to share it."

"We have room to grow, Sugar. Maybe all we need is more aggressive marketing to fill the schedule gaps."

"Maybe."

"Just keep an open mind, okay?"

"You, too," she said.

"I will," he said, but she watched that stubborn muscle jerk in his cheek. They were both pretty obstinate. What if they couldn't work it out? She got a bad taste at the back of her throat and her stomach churned.

They moved on, joined Jolie and soon rounded the low-rise to the Jungle Bungalow, where the landscaping was lush with vines and giant houseplants, the air dense and earthy. Colorful flowers accented the space and the outdoor sound system emitted tropical birdcalls, frog croaks and the buzz of insects.

Sugar watched Jolie unlock the door, feeling herself sink under the spell of her favorite casita, where Gage and she would be alone. For hours. Surrounded by primal beauty. With a bed.

5

"TAKE A MOMENT to absorb the atmosphere," Jolie said, holding the door for Sugar and Gage to enter. She flipped the sound switch so that the outdoor jungle sounds now emerged from hidden speakers in the room, enhanced by the quiet gurgle of the miniature waterfall that streamed over faux boulders in the center. God, Sugar loved this room.

Plants filled the place. Rubber trees and banana plants and mother-in-law's tongue stood in the corners. Schleflera and asparagus fern seemed to grow from the false stone walls. Vines of philodendron and ivy ran just under the ceiling all around.

Each casita was equipped with a scent that matched its ambiance and the Jungle Bungalow smelled of jasmine. Yum.

"We've preselected sounds themed to your casita, but you can choose different music," Jolie said, changing the sound to salsa, then resuming the jungle track. "You can also adjust the lights." She dimmed them to a romantic gold. "If you prefer, there are candles." She opened a drawer full of white pillars.

Sugar's eyes gravitated to the bed tucked into a cave of fake sandstone, which Gage seemed to be studying, too. It was big and round and soft, covered by a satin spread decorated with banana leaves, toucans and bird-of-paradise.

This was a bed to hang off the end of, throw each other across, burrow under, tie each other to—anything but sleep.

Gage's gaze met her own. *Great bed.*

"This is your Pleasure Center." Jolie meant the materials along the far wall, but Sugar could only think of her body's own spot, which had gone abruptly tight.

"Here you'll find books on sexual intimacy, romance novels, erotica and intimacy board games, including one invented by our own Dr. Hauf," Jolie continued, motioning at the shelves. "The carousel holds instructional DVDs and sexy films."

Pleasure Centers would be moneymakers, Sugar had concluded, so while they were here, she would catalog the items to be included in the franchise package.

Jolie showed them the hot tub and sauna. "Help yourself to the resort's signature body oils, lotions and bubble bath." She waved at the shelf that held them. "You are also entitled to a daily in-room massage. Together or separately…as you wish." She paused, waiting for them to tell her which they preferred.

"We'll figure that out," Gage said too quickly.

"Jade and I had a cancellation this afternoon if you're interested."

"Pencil us in," Sugar said, pleased that Gage was blushing. If the idea of lying naked beside her getting rubbed with oil made him uneasy, good. Besides, Sugar hadn't had a massage in forever and Jolie and Jade were the best.

"So, any questions?" Jolie asked.

"Not from me," Sugar said. "You, Gage?"

He shook his head.

"If you were guests, I would ask if you needed me to come back for you when it was time for your orientation, but I'll assume you can find your way?" That was another instruction—encourage guests to participate fully in all activities.

"We'll get there, thanks, Jolie." Gage reached for his wallet.

"Please." She shook her head, refusing a tip. "It was my pleasure. I'll leave you with our complimentary welcome gift." Jolie tapped the handle of the basket, which rested on the faux boulder that served as an entry table.

Pulling the door almost closed, she said, "Enjoy," with a mischievous smile, as though she knew exactly what temptations they faced.

And then they were alone in an exotic jungle, with bird-calls, tumbling water, jasmine in the air, romantic gold light and that big, beautiful bed.

Sugar avoided Gage's eyes and went to check out the basket for franchise potential. There were sample condoms, flavored massage oils, lotion, a novelty thong and men's bikini underwear, along with a box of the resort's lip-shaped truffles. All easy to package.

She picked up what she thought was lotion, but it turned out to be flavored lubricant. "Heats with friction," she read from the side of it. "Ever use any of this?" She tilted the tube at him.

"Uh, no." Gage cleared his throat, watching while she squeezed a dollop of gleaming red liquid onto her fingertip. She sniffed it, then touched her tongue to it. "Cinnamon." She ran it between thumb and forefinger, then blew across the moist surface. Heat flared where her breath met the oil.

"Oooh. You have to try this." She grabbed his palm, squirted a blob, then rubbed their palms together. When she blew across the surface, a delicious heat rose.

"Wow. Warm," Gage said, his breathing uneven.

"With the right friction, we'd produce quite a blaze." She put her hot hand against his cheek. Her heart thudded in her ears so loud she was afraid he could hear it, too.

"I think we'd do just fine on our own," he said huskily.

"I'm surprised this is your favorite casita," she said, needing to change the subject. "I would have thought you'd be more into the Atlantis Room, since you like water. Or maybe the Victorian. Not for the doilies and pillows, of course, but for the seriousness and the dignity."

"And the repression?" he asked wryly. "I may have timeless furniture and classic shoes, but that's not all there is to me, Sugar."

"I know." She was certainly beginning to. She was pretty sure he wouldn't be a missionary-only guy after all. Damn. "I do love this casita."

"We couldn't get you to leave during the walk-through."

"It's the waterfall, the colors, all the plants. It's so earthy. So primitive." So me-Tarzan-you-Jane. But she wouldn't say that, even though the heat in Gage's eyes made it easy to picture him pounding his chest for her.

"Maybe it reminds me of the trip to Hawaii my mother won from the restaurant where she worked. It was a contest for who could sell the most froufrou drinks in all their outlets."

"Nice prize."

"Yeah. She worked hard for it, too, and she really needed the getaway. It was right after the divorce and she was a mess. My sister was crying all the time, picking fights in kindergarten and she'd started wetting the bed. The three of us had such a good time—we forgot all the yelling and sadness and just went nuts.

"I remember we went to this huge jungle park and there

were humongous plants all around us and my sister and I ran down that winding trail, screaming with joy. We stopped at this lookout spot where there was this big, roaring waterfall and I just pictured myself down there, the water pouring over me, feeling scared and wild and alive all at once."

"I can see you like that." He kept his gaze on her face. The waterfall bubbled behind them, the bed easy inches away. The jasmine in the air made her dizzy—or maybe it was the way Gage was looking at her—and her heartbeats sounded like frenzied jungle drums in her ears.

Don't get carried away. We have a deal.

She closed her fists and dug her nails into her palms, except she felt the sticky cinnamon gel. "Gotta get this stuff off." She moved across the room and crouched beside the water feature to rinse her hands in the bubbling water.

Gage joined her, squatting so close she wanted to lean against him, feel his arms around her.

Which was ridiculous.

She noticed that one of the bubblers along the stream bed was clogged. Two of them. No, three. "These need to be fixed," she said. "There's some algae pitting, it looks like, too." She scraped at a black streak with a nail.

Gage surveyed the feature. "The whole thing needs to be replastered." The softness of his tone told her he knew she'd just been changing the subject. "I'll tell Nestor." Nestor Obregon managed repairs and landscaping throughout the resort.

"Great." She pushed to her feet, shaking the water from her fingers, then drying them on her skirt. She went back to the basket and replaced the tube of cinnamon gel. "We'll want these baskets in the franchise," she said. "The vendors will love us and we'll make money. Think of the chocolate order alone."

Her fingers were shaking when she peeled back the plastic from the truffle sampler. "Remember how you argued with me about commissioning these?" She breathed in the spice and chocolate.

Gage had balked at the expense of the dark-chocolate-covered truffles in three flavors—gingersnap, passion fruit and nutmeg-orange. Guests adored them. The spicy flavor lingered like the memory of their stays.

"Yes, but do you remember the time-share idea?" Gage said.

She grimaced. She'd been jazzed to partner with a time-share condo group, but Gage had correctly assessed the idea was a loser. "Everybody makes mistakes. We balance each other. That's my point. Here…see if this is as fresh as it should be."

He leaned forward, then seemed to think better of nibbling the chocolate from her fingers and took it from her and popped it in his mouth. "Mmm. Good." He licked ginger cream from his lip and she released a shuddering sigh.

He held a truffle out to her. "Just one won't hurt." As if it were the chocolate that tempted her, not his lips and tongue and how they would feel on her body.

She returned the chocolate firmly to the box. "One is never enough." She let the double meaning hang between them, like the humid mist from that long-ago Hawaiian waterfall.

"True," Gage said.

"So, together or separate for the massages?"

"I'm thinking that's not such a good idea," he said shakily.

"You want us to experience the resort, don't you?" She didn't know why she was teasing him. The idea of the massage seemed dangerous to her, too. The air between them was as heated as if they'd drenched themselves in that red-hot gel. "Jolie and Jade are the best. And after that, we can unwind in the hot tub, throw a sexy DVD on or maybe play an intimacy game?"

"You're trying to torture me, aren't you?" Gage said.

"Would it be torture?"

"You know it would." His voice was a low growl that vibrated through her.

"We all have to make sacrifices. If we want to truly understand the magic of Spice It Up, that is."

"If you can take it, Sugar, so can I."

"Oh, I can take it," she said. But standing there in the man-made jungle, with Gage looking so wicked, that bed just a tumble away, she wasn't so sure. "We'd better get to the staff meeting," she said, hoping it was time. Gage agreed without looking at his watch, so she assumed he felt as uneasy as she did.

In a few minutes they stood outside the glass wall of the conference room where the Monday meetings were held. The room was packed, every chair filled and people stood against the walls.

"What's with the promptness?" she said. The employees usually trickled in, but they were all there today, many munching cookies shaped like the Mexican flag, since it was nearly Cinco de Mayo and Brittany, the unofficial Sunshine Lady, made sure there were themed refreshments for each meeting. She tracked birthdays, weddings and childbirths and one Friday a month organized a party for employees celebrating the anniversary of their hire dates.

"Whatever it is, Maribeth's got them enthralled," he said. Maribeth stood at the head of the table, talking to the group.

"Must be about our marketing plan," she said. No one could possibly know about the franchise idea, since she'd only had two phone conversations with the consultant, Foster Matthews, and met with him in his office, not at the resort.

"Maybe they're waiting for us to announce our engagement," Gage said, pushing open the door, leaving her standing there slack-jawed for a second.

All heads turned their way as they entered.

Maribeth stopped speaking and smiled. "I was just explaining that you two are test guests for our new sales materials. I've urged everyone to do their usual fine work."

"Perfect," Sugar said. Maribeth seemed to have jumped in front of the parade, which pleased Sugar, since they should have tipped her off earlier anyway.

"And no one's getting hung out on their performance reviews, correct?" Oliver asked pointedly, shooting a look at Luigi.

"Of course not," Sugar said. "We're looking for things we want to highlight about the resort."

"No shake-ups, no mass firing, right?" Oliver added, this time looking at Brittany.

"We have full confidence in all of you," Gage said. "We're always looking to improve, of course, so if you have suggestions, please let us know. We always—"

"How about more direct mail?" Daisy interrupted. "The list of people in court-ordered marriage counseling is public record and we could send them brochures."

"We already advertise in the court newsletter," Maribeth said tightly.

Uh-oh. Tension there, Sugar saw. Maribeth had lately been acting impatient with Daisy, who was eager as a puppy. Sugar needed to talk to them both, assure them of her support. She did not want them to try to outdo or deflate each other.

"I know," Daisy said, "but I just thought—"

"It's worth considering, Daisy," Gage said. "We'll look into it."

"All good ideas are welcome," Sugar said, watching as Maribeth rolled her eyes. Now if Maribeth were on the franchise team, Daisy could take on more marketing duties, which would give them both a chance to shine.

"How are bookings?" Sugar asked Maribeth.

"We're still low for November and December."

"I scored the Reviving Relationships Retreat for February," Daisy said. "Two hundred people. They lost their L.A. venue and the planning committee is jazzed about coming to San Diego."

"Good work, you two," Sugar said. "What would we do without such a great team?"

"Like I said, the winter months aren't looking so good," Maribeth said.

"We know the holidays are tough. Keep working it," Gage said. "Moving on. How tight are we booked for Happily-Ever-After Week next week?"

"We should be full," Maribeth said.

"Excellent. And what about inventory, meals and special events?"

They swung into the usual agenda, running through the coming week's dinner specials with Emile Fine, the chef, discussing the supply order with the maid supervisor, along with maintenance issues with Nestor. Gage asked him to send out someone to fix the Jungle Bungalow's water feature.

When the discussion had wound down, Sugar said, "Anything else?"

"One thing," Clarice said. "I think we had a spy."

"A spy?" Sugar perked up.

"Last week. Louise Waters was what she called herself. Tall, black hair in a bun, fierce face. She was taking lots of notes, talking to herself. At first I thought, phone earpiece, but then I saw the minirecorder. And while I was signing her up for a sunset sail, I happened to get a peek at her notepad. She'd scribbled room dimensions and what looked like booking estimates. The tablet was from TravelQuest. I don't know if that means anything."

"I remember her," Jolie said. "She had a solo massage—major neck tension—and I saw her husband hit on Mario at Spicers." Mario, their regular DJ, was gay.

"Sounds like a fake couple to me," Clarice said. "Spies, for sure."

"She could be a travel critic," Gage said.

Travel writers registered incognito to evaluate properties and hoteliers were known to use spies to check out competitors. Spice It Up had never had a spy before that they knew of. The appearance was proof the resort was ripe for imitation. She felt the adrenaline rush of knowing her instincts were dead-on.

Why TravelQuest? Seemed strange that a company specializing in suites for business travelers would consider a sex resort. On the other hand, hadn't Rionna told Conner Jameson that Spice It Up was a gold mine? The woman had a great nose for making money.

"Should we find out more?" Clarice asked. "I know the concierge at the flagship TravelQuest in L.A. I could see if there's any gossip about us. Or, wait, Daisy, what about that PR guy you dated? Wasn't TravelQuest his account?"

Daisy went pink. "We're not…um…seeing each other anymore." Her last words were mumbled at the table. Poor thing.

"There's no need to pursue this," Sugar said. "We have a great concept. Spies and copycats are inevitable. Just keep up the great work—give them more to envy."

Smiles filled the faces around the room.

"That's all I have. Gage, anything?"

"Nothing except to say how much Sugar and I value you. You each make the resort special in your own way. Loretta, folding towels into wedding bands on the beds for turndown…Emile, with your 'Takes Two' couples desserts…Clarice, getting Mario each couples' special song for karaoke night. Even the walkway stones spelling out guests' initials in a heart, Nestor."

He made eye contact with each person as he spoke. He was such a warm and solid guy. She knew that his message was dual—to give staff a pep talk and to tell her that their success was due to a combination of people and place that could not be copied.

He was wrong, though. Between them, they knew all its secrets. Sharing them through a franchise would be a gift to the world. Well, to Phoenix, San Francisco and Orange County, their likely first franchise locales.

"These touches make a trip to Spice It Up utterly memorable," he continued. "Never forget how important you are to making the guest experience a highlight of their lives."

"Very true," Sugar said, leading the applause. When it had died down, she said, "If that's it, then, let's go thrill 'em!"

"I still need contributions for Friday's luncheon,"

Brittany piped up. "We all celebrate, so we all contribute. Five people are having hire anniversaries! Don't forget!" She shot a look around the room. Brittany loved the resort like it was home and the staff like they were family, even if she sometimes got heavy-handed about it.

Sugar, accompanied by Gage, followed the staff out of the conference room, smiling as she watched them set off to their work. Gage was right about the quality of their employees. Brittany tracked things like a hawk. Clarice's nosiness made her perfect at discerning the right off-site amusements for their guests. And, tension notwithstanding, Maribeth and Daisy worked hard to keep bookings up. The operations staff was skilled and thorough, the sex therapists consummate professionals and the kitchen and waitstaff miracles of efficiency.

For a second, Sugar's chest felt tight, like maybe she was wrong to disrupt the resort's operation with this franchise project. But change was opportunity. Some employees might want to work at a new franchise, perhaps, to be near family or to explore a new city. Though Spice It Up offered competitive wages now, more revenue meant bigger salaries for everyone. Most important of all was the need to keep the business strong. Stagnation would hurt employees, too.

In the empty hall, Sugar turned to Gage and whispered, "I think they bought our story on the marketing materials."

"Seems like it."

"I hope you didn't overdo it with the pep talk. That could make staff think something's going on."

"Sooo…you are to be *test guests,* is it?" Erika Hauf's Scandinavian accent held laughter, telling Sugar that Erika hadn't bought their story.

"Yes," Sugar said. "We're sampling the guest experience."

"And I am to be meeting you in my office now?" Erika said.

"For an orientation, yes," Gage said.

"I will see what I see." She breezed away as silently as she'd arrived.

Sugar motioned Gage into an alcove.

"Everyone bought the story but Erika," Gage said.

"Maybe we should tell her the truth. We'll need her to help hire and train the therapists if we decide to do the franchise."

"We're only exploring, Sugar."

"We'll tell her that. We have to run the idea past Oliver, too. I see him as the franchise team leader. He'd be great at that, don't you think?"

"What makes you think he'd even be interested?"

"He's smart and ambitious and you said yourself he might want to step into your shoes." But that possibility made her head hurt.

She heard the hum of water running in the kitchen on the other side of the alcove, so she put her finger to her lips. "We can talk about it in Erika's office," she whispered.

As they passed the kitchen doorway, Sugar saw that Brittany sat at the table. She smiled at them, waving with half of the Mexican-flag cookie she was eating. She likely hadn't heard anything, but it was a reminder to be careful where they talked about the plan.

Now they would be meeting with Erika, who clearly knew something was up. What if she'd picked up on the attraction between them? That made Sugar cringe.

Except…Erika had a light touch as a therapist. She might be able to gently help Gage see that he'd turned lust into love. Maybe that would painlessly end the problem.

Yeah, right. Wishful thinking if she ever heard it.

Gage's blurted words hung between them, ringing in the air like a brass bell that couldn't be unrung. There was no way someone wouldn't end up getting hurt.

6

EVEN IF ERIKA had figured out what was going on between him and Sugar, Gage was happier in her office than alone with Sugar in that damn casita, where he'd felt his self-control trickling away like the waterfall behind them.

After the orientation, they were due back for a Jade and Jolie massage in their room, then the hot tub and maybe a video? Just great.

He was stronger than his urges, dammit. Strong enough to lie naked next to Sugar, while she got rubbed in warm oil? Just to torture him, she would throw in some moans, no doubt. Of all the women to fall in love with, why did it have to be Sugar?

He had always figured the woman he fell in love with would be a soul mate, a twin under the skin, and they would be compatible and easy with each other, effortlessly blending their lives.

Sugar was a tease and a pain, who thought arguments were fun. She never slowed down. She never made it easy. She required effort and full-on attention. She wore him out.

And made him feel alive.

And he was in love with her.

Erika had stepped out of her office, promising to return in a moment. He dropped into one of the overstuffed chairs, padded so it hugged the body. His arm brushed Sugar's as it rested on the curved top of the chair. Intimacy was Erika's theme in furniture and art, as well as therapy. The room was filled with tasteful artwork showing couples kissing, hugging, making love. Oils, line drawings, charcoals and sculptures.

His favorite was a reproduction of Rodin's *The Kiss* that rested on the corner of Erika's desk. He loved the roundness of the couple's shoulders and leg muscles, their solid strength and a warmth that defied the cool metal from which the statue had been cast. The way the man's hand rested on the woman's hip suggested pent-up passion and the way the woman seemed to fold into the man's body reminded him of how Sugar had melted against him.

He caught Sugar's gaze. She'd been studying the sculpture, too. *Yeah. Us. Like that.* The shared thought made hope swell. Hope and, well, another thing.

"What do you think about the spy?" Sugar asked him, obviously wanting to change the subject. "Do you think she was from TravelQuest? What's Rionna up to?"

"We're hardly TravelQuest's business model."

"I know for a fact she thinks we have a gold mine."

"Rionna's an astute businesswoman."

"Who wants to have your love child."

"That's not true." He shifted in his seat. Rionna's flirtatiousness was just her style, he knew.

"Come on. She's hot for you. Admit it."

"She flirts with everyone—men, women, doesn't matter. That's how she networks."

"'Oh, *Gage*, you have such an incisive *mind.*'" Sugar was mimicking Rionna.

"She's smart, like I said." He grinned. "You're not

jealous, are you?" He could hope, couldn't he? He was relieved that they were at least engaged in their usual back-and-forth. His wild blurt of love and the snap decision to go for Sugar had been out of character. They'd settled back into their usual mode, at least. He felt a little more like himself.

"Of course not. Rionna's hot. Why not date her?"

He ignored the suggestion. "I probably should give her a call, though. She once mentioned they'd considered franchising some business hotels in Europe, but it didn't work out."

"If you need an excuse to call her, sure," Sugar said, giving him a strange look. "Ask her about the spy while you're at it." She fiddled nervously with the edge of the chair, the action telling him she wasn't entirely happy with the idea of him actually seeing Rionna. Maybe she *was* jealous. A good sign.

"She didn't send a spy. And when did Rionna tell you we had a gold mine, anyway?"

"She said it to a guy I met at the Expo. Conner Jameson. ExerSystems." She dropped her gaze and he realized abruptly who she was talking about.

"He that guy who kissed you in the bar?"

"You saw that?"

"I happened to be walking by, yes." Jealousy stung again.

"We were talking business. We exchanged cards."

"And made out? And you criticize Rionna for a little compliment and too much eye blinking."

"He knew a lot about franchises." She shrugged.

"He wanted in your pants."

"Like Rionna wants in yours?"

"She admires my business acumen."

"And your buff body."

"You think I'm buff?" He flushed with unreasonable pride.

"The point is that if Rionna is after our business, it's proof that it's time to build."

"The woman Clarice was talking about was likely a travel critic who happened to have a TravelQuest scratch pad."

"You take things too much at face value, Gage. That's your whole problem."

"Your whole problem is making too much of next to nothing. What seems true likely is true."

"Not if you pay attention to the subtleties. The devil's in the details and you tend to—"

"Sorry to keep you waiting."

Gage and Sugar jolted at Erika's sudden appearance. How did she manage to pop in so silently? Maybe it was just the zone he and Sugar got into when they argued that cut them off from everything else. "But I see you've managed to keep each other interested." She gave them a knowing look over her half-glasses, before she sat in the straight-backed chair angled toward them, a clipboard thick with folders in one hand.

"So," she said crisply, removing her glasses and leaning forward, "in our meeting you were guilty children. Explain for me what is happening here." She waved the glasses in the space between them.

Gage looked at Sugar, who looked back, her expression as sheepish as he felt. No way was he telling Erika the whole story. "We're exploring the guest experience, as we said in the meeting, but there is more. We have a bit of a quandary."

"A quandary?" Erika asked.

"This has to be confidential," Sugar said.

"Absolutely. You are my clients, no?"

"I guess." Sugar frowned. "In a way. Maybe."

"In a nutshell, Sugar wants to franchise Spice It Up and I don't."

"He says if we can't work it out, he'll leave."

"So your partnership is at risk," Erika said, cutting to the chase. "Not so different from couples who come to us to save their marriages, yes?"

"Not so different," Gage said softly.

Sugar wiggled in her seat, uncomfortable about the comparison, he guessed. "We've given each other a month to work it out."

"So then—" Erika tapped her pen against her lip "—I begin as I do with guests. I ask of their hopes for their stay. So, we start there? Tell me your aspirations for this month."

"Well, we want to change each other's minds," Sugar said. "I want to convince Gage to stay and work with me on the franchise. And he wants me to give up the idea and just…" She glanced at him, then swallowed. *Fall in love with him.* That's what he wanted and Sugar obviously knew it. "Go back to the way things were," Sugar finished in a rush.

"Is this true, Gage? Is this what you want?"

"I think we want each other to be happy," he said, "whether we remain partners or not. I know I want that for Sugar." He turned to her.

"Me, too. For you, Gage." Her eyes shone at him with so much earnestness, he wanted to declare his love all over again.

Erika smiled. "Excellent. Many couples do not have this wish. Please remember that as we proceed. A positive indicator."

They nodded at Erika and each other.

"Good. A bit of history will help. Tell me about the beginning. The how and when of your coming together."

He thought of that crashing kiss over the cheesecake, of kissing her bare breasts on the bed, of touching her, but that wasn't what Erika meant. "We knew each other from college," he said, "but it's been six years since we started working on Spice It Up."

"A long time," Erika mused, looking from one to the other. "Long enough to take each other for granted."

"Exactly," Gage said. That was the problem. Sugar didn't appreciate either him or the resort anymore.

"And long enough to negotiate new terms," Erika said.

"Precisely," Sugar said, giving him a triumphant look. "That's exactly what we need."

"So, how did you decide to form this partnership?" Erika asked.

"I was working for a research firm and Sugar went into private practice as a therapist, but we stayed in touch."

"I was doing couples' counseling, which I enjoyed," Sugar said. "Except I got restless. Like I always do." She gave him that look again. "I had been to a couples' retreat and I mentioned to Gage how nice it would be to have a way to enhance the experience with more time, more activities, more pampering for the couples."

"My father has a thirty-room hotel and I'd always worked with him, followed the industry, all that. So Sugar's concept intrigued me." And, thinking about it now, he'd leaped at the chance to work with her. If she'd wanted to open a car repair place, he'd have done that, too.

Sure he valued applying the psychological techniques and theories that he knew made a difference when relationships got rocky, but he'd wanted to work with Sugar far more than he'd wanted to open a sex resort. In his mind and heart, Spice It Up and Sugar were inextricably linked.

"So we worked out a plan," Sugar said. "Gage got us investors and we opened up, made a go of it."

"You make it sound easy. We had trouble getting loans, remember? Figuring out how and where to advertise was tough and our overhead was way high at first." They'd struggled and endured, growing closer through the crises.

"But by the second year, we were doing okay," Sugar said. "And now we're in danger of going flat. Grow or die. That's how it is in business."

"In relationships, this, too, is true," Erika inserted.

"We are far from flat," Gage argued. "Bookings are up for the season and we're up ten percent in overall revenue. We're doing well."

"For now, sure. But we have to think long-range. And we're turning away guests during our busy times."

"You're confusing motion with progress, Sugar. Action for the sake of action leads to waste."

"Inertia is anathema. You can't grow from a dead stop. Momentum is essential."

"I disagree. You have to stop and make a clear decision."

"Time out." Erika put her hands in a T. "This argument is spinning wheels. We shift gears for an exercise."

"An exercise?" they both said at once, looking at Erika.

"As I do with all my clients. To remind them what it was that brought them together. Please turn your chairs facing."

Gage shifted his chair to face Sugar as Erika indicated.

"Closer, knees fit." Erika showed them with her fingers how she wanted their legs to interlock and Gage scooted closer, making it happen. Sugar met his gaze with tense eyes.

"Put, each of you, hands on the other's thighs and look into eyes, please," Erika instructed.

"How does this help?" Sugar asked, nervously licking her lips, a move that gave Gage a hot jolt.

"Just do it," he muttered, not any happier than she was.

Tentatively Sugar rested her palms on his thighs.

Good God that felt good. He put his hands on her legs, muscular under the silk dress. Her tight muscles jumped under his fingers.

"Now, hold for three minutes," Erika said. "I will time. As you look at the other, think what attracted you."

"What attracted us?" Sugar asked weakly.

"As partners, yes," Erika said. "After three minutes, you will share."

"Out loud?" Gage said. "Say it out loud?"

"How else?"

"I'm not sure that's such a good idea," Sugar said.

"Resistance shows importance," Erika said. "Try."

They both took deep breaths, blew them out and steadied their gazes on each other's face.

"Ready, begin," Erika said, as if she'd fired a starting gun.

On a very slow race, Gage noted. Each second ticked painfully by. Worse, looking into Sugar's eyes, he immediately remembered the wonder and arousal on her face back in that hotel bed. Her thigh quivered under his palm, just like it had when he'd touched her…there. He remembered the rush of heat, the desperate need to be inside her. He'd loved that he'd put that wild look on her face.

Sugar shivered, then her eyes danced away, flitted here and there.

Don't look down, he silently begged her, fearful that his bulge was visible.

He fought to ignore it, struggling to remember the things that had made him want to work with Sugar, not sleep with her. The reasons overlapped, really. He loved her energy, her style, her intensity, her ideas. It was who she was that got to him at—as a partner and as a woman.

When Erika finally called time, they both exhaled in a blast, as if they'd been holding their breaths for all three minutes. Both jerked their chairs back.

"Stay as you are, please," Erika said. "How was that experience for you?"

Reluctantly they scooted back in place.

"Exhausting," Sugar said. "Staring like that is…hard."

Gage hoped she hadn't noticed exactly how *hard* it had gotten. "It's not natural to look that closely at someone," he added.

"Unless you are lovers," Erika said softly. "And then you spend hours, seeing everything in the eyes, in the mouth, in the twitch of muscle, the hitch of breath, no?"

Yes. Sugar's gaze locked with his and they stared and breathed and remembered.

Erika let the silence hang for an agony of time.

"So, we share?" she said finally. "Please tell Gage what attracted you to him, Sugar."

"Okay…" She took a deep breath and blew it out. "What I liked was how smart you were; the way you pinpointed issues. How you put your finger *right on it.*" She caught herself, then grinned at the words she'd chosen and the obvious double meaning. Her eyes twinkled wickedly and he could only think of the warm pulse of her beneath his finger.

Stop it. Now.

"Gage? And you? What attracted you to Sugar?" Erika again.

He had to clear his throat to get out the words. "I liked

your, uh, sensitivity." Two could play this game. "How responsive you were to the ideas *I touched on.*"

"We were good together," Sugar breathed, definitely meaning what he thought she meant.

"Yes, we were," he said. "Very good."

"I liked how we went back and forth, moved with the ideas, intensified them, made them do what we wanted." She sighed shakily.

The silence held and Erika didn't break it. Sugar seemed to catch herself, realizing, he was sure, how strange that exchange had sounded. When she resumed talking, it was in a normal voice. "I liked the way we balanced each other. I had the wild ideas and you had the practical applications."

"But you think practical is boring," Gage said.

"That's not true." But it was, he knew. She thought he was dull and predictable. "What I meant was—"

"Just because I'm practical, doesn't mean I don't have an imagination, Sugar."

"Or fantasies," Erika said calmly. "Correct?"

They swiveled their heads to her, hands still on each other's thighs. "Fantasies?" they both said at once.

"About your partnership, yes?" But Gage had already slipped into sexy mental images of Sugar. She took a shaky breath as if she'd stumbled onto some lusty pictures of her own.

"So, Gage, share your fantasy with Sugar, please."

"Share my—"

"How do you see your partnership?" Erika clarified.

"Oh. Well." He shifted in his seat, fought for coherent partnership thoughts. "I don't see a lot of changes, except that we value what we have more."

"How would that be, Gage? Describe it."

"Mostly, we would do what we already do. Meet with staff every week, walk the grounds, greet the guests at the restaurant and in the bar, go over the books, touch base with marketing, keep in contact with our managers, make sure things run smoothly. The only difference would be that we would enjoy each moment to the fullest, celebrate every success. We thrill hundreds of couples every year. What's more satisfying than that?"

Being with Sugar every day, every night, all night. That would be better. That would be all he wanted in the world. The hope of that was what infused his every moment at Spice It Up. If he didn't reach her, there was no way he could stay.

And he wasn't reaching her. That was obvious. With every word he'd spoken, she'd shrunk away from him. The light in her eyes was gone, her lips were thin, her jaw locked, cheek muscle flickering. She looked like a cat forced into a carrier to be dragged to the vet. He'd described his ideal world and she wanted to run screaming from the room. How would he ever get through to her?

"You desire the intimacy of the familiar," Erika said.

Gage nodded. That was one way to put it.

"And you, Sugar? You do not?"

"No," Sugar said firmly. "I do not."

Gage's heart sank with a thud he could almost hear.

WHAT COULD BE MORE DULL? Sugar wondered, shaking herself back to reality. Gage's ideal partnership was so ordinary, so routine and, at the same time, so sunshine-and-rainbows that she felt sick to her stomach. The only thing missing were cartoon bluebirds tweeting on his shoulder.

However, for one weird blip of time, she'd been into it.

Probably because of Gage's husky voice, which could hypnotize her. Also, since his love blurt, she was so much more in tune with him. Staring into his eyes was like staring at the sun. You could burn out your corneas—and every truth you knew.

His fantasy was dangerous. She'd seen what happened when you got too caught up in wanting things to be a certain way. Her mother had been a mess over her divorce. Her sister, too, clung to the past to the point of misery, as a child, and in her own messy marriage years later. Sugar had seen it happen to friends, too. They'd lost themselves, gotten stuck with wanting the old days—even when the old days had been full of fights and tears.

Better to hold it together, don't go so deep you couldn't come back to the surface. It wasn't as though she'd had huge personal traumas or anything. Hell, no. She'd been too careful. Maybe she just didn't feel things as intensely as other people did. She was just wired that way.

"How about you, Sugar?" Erika asked her. "What is your partnership fantasy?"

She was glad to get back on track. "Okay. I see us working on a killer franchise, hunched over the laptop, elbowing each other off the keyboard because we're so anxious to get our ideas down. I see us completely enthralled, debating, revising, creating, adding and deleting, letting the tomato soup burn to black on the stove because we forget to eat. I see us energized, fully alive."

"So you prefer the thrill of the new?" Erika said.

"Exactly." Erika knew her stuff.

Erika nodded sagely. "Many seasoned couples face this quandary."

"But we're not—" Sugar said.

"A couple? No. But there are similarities, no? At the beginning of a relationship, the flood of norepinephrine and dopamine in the brain mark the infatuation phase—which you had as partners, as well. You were high, happy, floating on air, filled with excitement and focused completely on your partnership. Many people, like Sugar, crave the rush of these hormones signifying infatuation."

That made perfect sense to her and Gage seemed to get it, too, nodding as he listened.

"Then, as time passes, the brain pumps other chemicals—those that urge attachment and bonding—serotonin, the calming hormone, for example," Erika continued. "This leads to permanence—marriage, or, in your case, a long-term partnership. You, Gage, prefer the constancy of attachment, correct?"

"You could put it that way, I guess."

"Isn't it true, Erika, that people can confuse infatuation with attachment?" Sugar asked. "Misread the hormonal impulses?"

"That is sometimes the case, yes."

"Or cling to infatuation because they underestimate their ability to form strong attachments," Gage said.

"This also is true," Erika said. "Human relationships are complex and we struggle with differential meanings."

Dammit. This wasn't helping a bit. Erika was being carefully neutral. Like any good therapist, of course.

"So how do we solve this problem of competing needs?" Erika continued.

"How?" Sugar asked. They both leaned forward, eager for the answer.

"By giving you each what you want. Gage, you must thrill Sugar. And you, Sugar, must give Gage constancy."

"How would that work?" Gage asked. "How am I supposed to, uh, thrill her?"

"Why do couples fall in love on vacation? Novelty. Novelty tricks the brain, stimulates it, offers elation and arousal. Here at our resort, we are very purposeful about this. We ask our couples to do new things together—sexually, of course—but also by trying different foods, doing new activities, exploring new places."

"That's for couples, Erika," Sugar inserted. "And we're not—"

"A couple? Yes, you've made that quite clear." Erika pursed her lips and her eyes twinkled. "Still, as her partner, you can do something new for Sugar, Gage. Considering this franchise concept is an example."

"Perfect," Sugar said. So far, so good.

"And, Sugar, you can also better value what you have in the resort. And in Gage, your partner."

"Which is what we agreed to do," she said. "So you're telling us we're on the right track."

"It would seem so. On the surface. Though you may want to look beneath—at deeper issues."

"Great, then," she said, relieved to wrap this up. "Before we go, though, we need to ask you if you'd be willing to serve on our franchise team, Erika. If we go that route." She nodded at Gage to acknowledge the objection he was no doubt ready to raise. "We'd need you to help us find and train the therapists for the franchises."

"I would be traveling?" she asked.

"A little. In the west, mostly, since that's our logical expansion market."

"Provided I can meet my obligations here, then, yes, that would interest me."

"We'll work around your schedule, don't worry. We'll be talking to Oliver, too. We want him to head the franchise team. But please don't say anything to anyone in the meantime."

"We don't want to upset the staff unnecessarily," Gage added. "Not until we've decided yes or no."

She remembered the other help she needed from Erika. "Also, we need testimonials from our reunion couples next week. The franchising consultant recommended a video and we can use it for marketing purposes, too." Which was the only way she'd gotten Gage to agree to the idea.

"Since you meet with all the couples and know their history, we thought you could pick out the ones we should interview."

"It would be my pleasure," Erika said.

"We're looking for colorful stories and couples who are articulate and deeply in love," Sugar said. "Three couples, I'm thinking, to be sure we get enough good footage."

"I'll be happy to help."

"Terrific. So is that it?" Sugar scooted forward, ready to stand.

"Hang on," Gage said. "We're test guests, remember, and we haven't finished our orientation. After you ask about the guests' hopes, then what happens, Erika?"

Sugar sat back in her chair, fighting her impatience.

"Next is the *Intimacy Inventory.*" Erika pulled two folders from her clipboard and handed them to Sugar and Gage. A mechanical pencil had been clipped to the three-page quiz—multiple choice and short answer—on top of each folder.

Sugar skimmed the questions. *Do you enjoy being touched? Do you easily experience orgasm? Do you like a lot of nonsexual physical contact from your partner? Do you feel you are attractive?* The bottom half asked her to answer the same questions about her partner.

The last thing Sugar wanted to do was think harder about sex with Gage. She was already struggling. "This isn't really pertinent to us," she said.

"If we were guests it would be," Gage said, busy bubbling in his answers, not even looking up.

She read through more questions, her pencil poised. *How inhibited are you? How comfortable are you with sharing your intimate needs with your partner?* She wasn't in the mood to get into this. She knew herself well enough.

She read down to the questions about her partner. *What part of your partner's body, beyond genitals, does he/she find most arousing?*

She looked over at Gage, who was writing a short answer at the moment. Hmm. Chest? Nipples? Thighs? Biceps? She had no idea. She'd barely touched him. She had no idea what physical contact turned him on the most. Personally she loved having her neck and ears stroked and licked and…

Gage raised his eyes to hers. "What's up?"

Afraid her thoughts were written on her face, she frowned. "I don't really see the point of doing the entire test. We should really get to work back at the bungalow." Where the twins were due in a bit—a whole new challenge she wasn't sure she was ready to meet.

"We can spare five minutes," Gage said, holding her gaze, insisting she stick it out. She could almost hear him repeat Erika's phrase. *Resistance shows importance.* "You use this inventory to suggest workshops and exercises for each couple, right, Erika?"

"That is correct." Erika slipped two papers from her clipboard and handed them each one. It was the workshop list.

"So let's give Erika something to analyze, huh?" Gage said. "Just for fun? For something new?" Then he winked at her.

If she'd been standing, her knees would have wobbled. It was like some reflex. The man lowered a lid and she trembled. What hormone caused *that?*

Gawd. Sugar bubbled in the first two answers, then stopped. No way would she let Erika compare her answers to Gage's. The last thing she wanted to learn was that she and Gage were sexual soul mates. She also didn't want to poke around about her orgasm issue, either. She just hoped Gage hadn't caught on to why she'd faded away while he was touching her.

"Done." Gage put down his pencil. He finished everything he started, all right. What a terrific trait in a lover….

He looked over at her paper. "Are you finished?"

She folded her form in half. "Enough for now. Let's not waste Erika's time tabulating the results."

"The results show compatibilities, conflicts, the gaps the couple must bridge," Erika said.

"Maybe that would help us," Gage said. "As partners, of course." He shot Erika a knowing look, sharing the joke.

"I think we're fine." Sugar took his form and shoved it into his folder, then put her form away, too. "What happens next, Erika, for the guests, I mean?"

"I usually recommend workshops, as I said, and sometimes therapy sessions or other activities—time in the fantasy rooms perhaps?" She looked at Gage.

"Interesting." Gage nodded. It was as if the two of them were cooking something up. "Knowing us as you do, Erika, what advice would you give us…as partners?"

"I hesitate to speculate."

"Exactly." Sugar rose, wanting to get out of here.

"Hang on." Gage caught her hand and tugged her back down. He was always doing that, catching her on the move and stopping her. She had her usual mixed reaction— annoyed at being stopped and pleased he wanted to share something with her. "By all means, speculate."

"All right." Erika studied them, a finger to her lip, then leaned forward. "You must risk what you know about each other—and yourselves. Surprise each other. See each other with new eyes. Build trust to reach the next plateau… assuming you want the climb."

Gage looked at Sugar.

Sugar looked away.

"You have within you all you need to solve this… quandary, as you call it," Erika said. "So do not worry."

"And what workshops would you suggest…if we were a couple?" Gage said. "Since we're test guests."

"All right. I would suggest Intimacy For Couples. Bonding Touch, too. Then something fun, say Cooking For Two. Since you know each other so well, you might enjoy the Newly Renewed Game." She paused. "Mary E.'s tantric sex class can be illuminating. And, if you're feeling ener- getic, Exploring Multiple Orgasm is a great skill builder."

Sugar's face felt so hot she was sure she glowed. "Very nice, Erika. And more than thorough." No way could she endure one of those sessions with Gage.

"Yes, thanks," Gage said. He seemed a little flum- moxed, too.

They all stood. "I am happy to meet again with you to assess your progress."

"You've done plenty," Sugar said. *Enough already.*

Erika hugged Gage first, warm curiosity in her gaze

when she looked at him. Had she guessed his feelings? She had made that remark about fantasies. What was that about?

When Erika got to her, Sugar broke away quickly, but Erika held her gaze until she felt as though the woman was seeing straight to her soul. *You must risk what you know....* Sugar was perfectly happy with what she knew about herself and Gage.

Erika took them each by an arm and drew them close. "I'm so happy you came to me. You're my favorite couple—" She raised her hand before Sugar could object "—I mean, partners."

"And we're happy you're with us," Sugar said. "I'll check with you on the couples to be interviewed."

Erika nodded. She tapped the folder Sugar held. "Inside are the materials we give each couple. Tip sheets and intimacy techniques. You may find them useful."

Useful for what? What the heck was Erika suggesting? Sugar doubted it had to do with the franchise package.

Outside Erika's office, Gage turned to Sugar, a mischievous light in his eyes. "How about we check out the fantasy rooms?"

Her stomach did a flip-flop. "Why would we do that?"

"Research for the franchise, of course. And to explore the resort. What else?"

"Nothing. I didn't...I just...we don't..."

"You're not afraid of a little fantasy, are you, Sugar?" The wicked glint in his eyes told her she should be.

"Of course not," she said firmly, breaking out in a nervous sweat. What else could she say?

7

YOU MUST THRILL SUGAR. Erika's words resonated in Gage's head as though someone had banged a gong between his ears. Leading her to the three role-play suites, he vowed to do just that.

It was a tall order, since excitement was a way of life for Sugar, but he'd figure it out. Sugar thought she had him nailed. Predictable, classic, dull. He had to show her she was wrong.

Their session with Erika had made a truth about Sugar even clearer to him. Intimacy scared her to death. The mere word on Erika's inventory had stopped her cold. He'd concluded that sex would be too easy with her, but it would also be the fastest way to reach her.

He just had to stay in control of himself. He could do it. What was a little short-term agony if it earned him forever with Sugar?

It was tougher now that he'd tasted her mouth, heard her moans, felt the curve of her breast, the wet silk of her sex. Which meant he was in for a new level of abuse. He felt like Tantalus, the Greek king doomed for eternity to be inches from the fruit and water he craved but could never consume.

Outside the first fantasy suite, which had the Available card in the door slot, they put their folders on the outside table. Sugar stopped to read the framed chart on the wall: The Top Ten Fantasies.

He read them, too. *Sex with more than one person...sex with a stranger...sex with someone of the same sex... watching someone have sex...sex with domination or submission...* Playing with sexual power would be one of Sugar's fantasies, he'd bet, since she liked to stay in control.

"So, which are your favorites, Gage?" she asked, turning to him. She was acting bold to cover the alarm she'd felt when he'd suggested the suites. He'd thrown her. A good start.

"So hard to choose." He shrugged.

"How about girl-on-girl? Men usually like that."

"I'm more into me-on-you, Sugar." The truth was always best, he'd found. "Whatever fantasy I might have, you would star in it."

"That's an incredibly sexy thing to say." Her words came out shaky and she grabbed the table, as if to steady herself.

"It's true. Does that make it sexier?"

She blinked. No, it made it scarier, he realized, so he changed the subject. "This is one of yours." He tapped *semipublic sex.*

Her eyes went wide. "How did you know?"

"Because the elevator lag was your idea." They'd rigged one of the cars for a ten-minute pause before the alarm would sound. A placard warned riders, Caution: This Car Stalls Between Floors, with a picture of an embracing couple.

"You're good."

"I like to think so," he said.

She sighed. "You seem so...different."

"You've never really seen me."

"Maybe not." She faltered. "Maybe I blocked it, too." She bit her lip, pondering the idea.

Pleased, Gage turned the availability card to Occupied and led her into the empty room, which was arranged in small sets suggesting common fantasies—a classroom for a teacher/student role-play, an office desk for boss/secretary, a three-way mirror and chrome pole for a stripper/customer, and more. The backdrops and props had come from a photographer closing out her business.

As they walked, Sugar took notes and made comments about each set—staying busy, he thought, to avoid thinking about the erotic possibilities that surrounded them.

"Apple for the teacher?" He lifted the wooden fruit from the teacher's desk. "Since I've been such a bad, bad student."

"Are you bribing me, young Master Maguire?" she said with an English accent, instantly getting into the role.

"If that's what I must do to get what I want, Mistress Thompson." Their gazes caught and held.

Sugar swallowed, then jerked her eyes away. "I don't think a franchise would need three fantasy rooms, if space is an issue. Costumes with a single room and collapsible walls would work. Especially when the resort grounds can be used for stranger in a bar, sex in an elevator and sex outdoors." Here, guests could reserve one of three private grottos if their fantasies required a fresh-air setting.

She led him out of the room. The second room was occupied, so she skipped that, then breezed past the third, which had the Occupied card in place, though its door was open.

He called her back. "This we can't skip." It was the Control Room, so named because it was used for fantasies related to restraint and power.

Lupe, one of the maids, emerged with her cleaning cart. She took out the card, ready to turn it to Available, but Gage held out his hand to stop her.

She gave him a smile, then pushed her cart down the hall and away.

"It's lunchtime or we'd never get in," Gage said.

"This room's popular, true." Sugar gave him a brief, nervous smile and walked in front of him into the room.

He followed. The room's colors were black, dark blue and red, the fabrics plush, the drapes thick velvet. There were sets as in the other rooms, but fewer. The biggest was a faux stone wall with two sets of shackles. A nearby table held whips and cuffs and other dangerous items that had been softened into plastic or covered in velvet.

Costumes hung from coatracks near each set—black-leather outfits, velvet hoods, masks and capes, sexy hooker outfits, cop uniforms and motorcycle helmets. Jack boots and stilettos in several sizes rested in small cubbies beside each rack.

It was all subdued and tasteful, but every item suggested one person's will being imposed on another who enjoyed being restrained and taken.

Sugar strode to the mock jail cell, where bamboo poles served as the bars and a plush cot rested against the inside wall. She grabbed the cop cap off the rack and put it on Gage's head, then held a transparent red top against her chest. The sight made him dizzy.

"Did I do something wrong, Officer Maguire?" she teased.

He had to clear his throat to speak. "That depends."

"It's not illegal to want a little company, is it?" She batted her eyes at him.

"If you take money for it, it is."

"But I wouldn't charge you, Officer. You look too good in your uniform." She moved close, behaving in character, but when she ran her finger down his chest, he grabbed her hand and pulled her tight against him.

"You're playing with fire, lady," he growled.

She looked into his eyes, not quite sure he was acting. Neither was he. She turned and tried to put the see-through thing on a hook, but missed and had to try again.

He replaced the cap, smiling to himself. So far, so good.

Sugar went into the "cell," and rattled the bamboo bars. "Not too believable, but I guess it works."

"The action's in your head," he said, gripping the bars above her hands. He pictured taking her on that narrow cot, her hands cuffed to the bars behind her head, her legs wrapped around him, locked on tight....

"The biggest sex organ is the brain," she breathed, then slid out of the cell, uncomfortable, it seemed, standing there with only the bars between them, their fingers touching.

She went to the wall with the manacles. "These seem too high," she said, lifting up the higher pair of shackles. "Would you test them?" She clearly needed to take charge and while he hated feeling powerless, he would endure it for Sugar.

He stood against the wall, lifted his arms and let her close the velvet-lined cuffs around each wrist.

She backed away, surveying him. "Feel okay?" She bounced the key in her palm, then closed her fingers around it. *Got you.*

"If you're into it, I guess." He pulled on the chains, making them clank ominously.

"Are you, Gage? Into it?"

Hell, no. "If you are, I'll play," he said, low and even.

Sugar shivered, but tried to hide it by turning away. She played with the items on the table, then chose one—a riding crop, he saw when she turned back.

She slapped it against her palm, moving close. "Perhaps the prisoner needs a little discipline?" She poked the short length of leather at his chest.

"Is that what you want?" he said. "To punish me for wanting you?"

"Is it working?"

"You mean, am I suffering? Yeah."

"Aching?" Her gaze dropped to his crotch.

"Check it out for yourself." He rocked his pelvis forward. Where did that come from?

She seemed surprised, too, but she accepted the challenge and ran the crop down the middle of his chest, over his belt and across his erection. "Impressive. That must hurt."

"It's a sweet pain."

She stroked him with the short whip, watching his face the entire time.

"Do you like this fantasy, Gage?" she asked softly.

Not really. He wanted out of these chains. He wanted to grab her close, erase the distance between them. The only tools he had for achieving that goal were words, so he used them. "Not as much as that elevator you like. Why don't you talk me through that one? Tell me how it works."

"How it works?" Her breathing was as shaky as her voice.

"How does it happen? How does it feel? Describe it to me."

She blinked at him.

"You're not afraid of a little fantasy, are you?"

She leveled her gaze. *Absolutely not.* Nothing scared Sugar. Except love and commitment.

"So, how does it start? You and your lover are going up the elevator…"

"Yes," she said. "We're going to our room and we're so hot we can't keep our hands off each other's body."

"Oh, yeah?"

"Yeah." She stepped closer and dropped the riding crop, which rattled, then rolled a few inches away.

"Keep going," he murmured. "Then what?"

"Then we're touching each other…everywhere." Now she pressed herself against him, stretching her arms up along his. He heard the click of the cuff key hitting the floor, then she squeezed his forearms and closed her eyes. "The elevator ride takes forever."

"Yeah…forever."

"We can't stand how slow it is. We need to get naked. We need to screw. We're desperate. If we don't we'll explode or die."

"Yeah. Dying's a definite possibility."

"We can't stop. We rub against each other." Lost to the moment, she slid against him, her eyes closed, living the fantasy.

He groaned.

"We're moving faster," she said. "We aren't aware of anything but how much we want each other. We don't care if someone gets on the elevator. We can't care. The only thing we can do is rub and slide and stroke each other. I'm against the glass wall, the mirror, and you shove my skirt up out of the way."

She'd used *you,* putting him into the fantasy and he was so glad. He was there, all right. All the way.

She pivoted her hips against him, faster. "You open your zipper…"

"Then what?" he ground out, his cock aching behind his zipper, which he wanted her to open right now. God, get these shackles off so he could touch her, free himself, get *in*.

"Then you're inside me," she breathed.

"Yeah." He wanted that. Now.

"You're moving in and out, pounding into me, hard and fast."

This was way, way out of control, but he didn't care. He wanted to be in that elevator with her, truly inside her, not chafing against his own clothes and chained to the wall. He wanted to touch her where she was soft and needy and primed to go off, to shatter at his touch.

"And we're afraid to get caught," she continued breathlessly, "and desperate to finish and we can't...stop." She rocked quicker and quicker.

At the worst moment possible, his cell phone sounded.

Sugar jerked away from him. "What...? Oh...the phone. Wow." She tried to laugh, pushed her hair back with one hand and flopped against the wall beside him, panting.

"Do you mind? It's there." He nodded down at his waist where his phone rested in its holder. He wiggled his chained hands.

With a dazed smile, she grabbed his phone and held it to his ear.

"Hello," he croaked into it.

"It's Jolie, Gage. We're here for the massage. Where are you two?"

"Oh. Yeah. Sorry, Jolie. We got, um, tied up." He looked at Sugar, who burst out laughing.

"Shall we reschedule?" Jolie asked him.

"No. No, thanks." No way could he stand a massage

with Sugar in the same room. "Sorry for the mix-up. We'll pay you for the time. Bye."

Sugar closed his phone and clipped it in place. "We could have gotten a half hour at least," she said. "But that would have made it even harder." She patted his zipper, teasing now.

"Unchain me, please."

She bent to pick up the key, dangling it in front of him. "This what you want?"

"Sugar," he warned.

"Promise to help me with the franchise package?" She wiggled the key back and forth, teasing him.

He hooked her body with one leg and yanked her close. "Unlock the cuffs."

"Say pretty please," she said, but her body melted against him.

"Pretty please," he murmured into her hair, willing, suddenly, to stay chained like this for hours.

But she was annoyingly cooperative and released one of his wrists. "That was…hot," she breathed, looking at him with new admiration.

"Don't sound so surprised. You underestimate me, Sugar. Maybe yourself, too."

She stilled, pondering the idea.

Gently, he took the manacle key from her fingers and freed his other hand, rubbing his wrist. He'd wanted her so badly he'd been ready to make love chained to the wall. Thank God for the phone call—a repeating pattern in their relationship.

Rescued by a phone call at the worst moment.

Or the best—certainly for his plan. He'd surprised her, at least, made her more aware of him. It was a start, though he'd been close to losing control. That wouldn't help anything.

He bent to pick up the riding crop. "So, we go back to

the room and look over your research?" He absently tapped the crop on his palm.

Sugar shivered at the sight. "Stop that." She grabbed it away from him and slapped it back to the table. At least they were both struggling.

Gage stayed calm and clearheaded right up until they stepped into their private jungle, when he felt like Tarzan, ready to pound his chest, grab Sugar and swing her across the room on a vine to that big, beautiful bed. Maybe he should have brought along a pair of those velvet-lined manacles after all.

"This room gets to me," Sugar said, turning shiny eyes to him. "It makes me feel…strange."

"Like jumping into a waterfall?" Or a bed.

"Something like that." She stepped closer.

The high torture was of his own making, he realized, since he'd chosen this hellishly erotic room. "So, we get to work," he said, carrying the folders Erika had given them to the glass-topped boulder that served as a table. "Forget the massages and the hot tub. Just work."

"Work would be good," she said, blowing out a breath. She busied herself getting her laptop out, plugged in and turned on. "I'll key in the notes I've taken and show you the research I have. Plus, the consultants gave me a checklist you can help me finish."

Gage was relieved. If they could get into their work rhythm, they would be fine. Normal. Like every other day.

"I also want to sketch out the room essentials," she said, going to the bookshelves. She spun the DVD carousel slowly, creating a whirl of soft-focus flesh— hands, mouths, bodies, breasts, bottoms. "We'll definitely include Pleasure Centers." She handed him the inventory sheet. "Check off the must-haves for me, while I read them off, okay?"

He sat in one of the rattan chairs and marked the boxes beside the titles Sugar read off, the hot words rolling off her tongue like a laundry list of lust. So much for normal. Watching her lips shape those arousing words was anything but.

"Which do you prefer?" she asked, holding out two movies showing soft-focused couples embracing.

"That's it for me." He pushed the list away.

"Getting to you?" She looked at the DVD covers. "Yeah. I see what you mean. We have plenty anyway." She put the movies back and gave the rack a spin. "The carousel is great, Gage," she mused, watching the DVD spines fly by. "Inexpensive and practical." She joined him at the table, sitting beside him.

"It was your idea to combine the self-help stuff with erotic films and novels."

"That was obvious. You need the facts and the fun. That's the formula for good sex."

"What about *great* sex? Isn't that what we want? For our guests, I mean." It was what he wanted with Sugar. He remembered something Erika always said and opened the folder to find the quote at the top of the sheet that listed the workshops. "'Good sex is a matter of technique. We can teach you *good* sex,'" he read. "'*Great* sex you must create as a couple. Great sex comes from who you are together.'"

And he and Sugar together would be great. When the time was right. He had to be patient no matter how much he wanted to put an end to the tension of wanting her so much that every glance, every brief touch on the arm had him trembling like a kid.

"*Great* and *good* are subjective," she said, brushing away the idea like so much lint on her sleeve. "Many factors control sexual pleasure—hormonal levels, energy, age, health, imagination, self-concept, expectations, all that." She shrugged.

She was minimizing the wonder of it because it scared her, he'd bet. How could he reassure her?

She opened her folder. "We'll want to include the tip sheets," she said, flipping through the pages Erika had included. "Listen to this—'It is normal for sexual desire to wax and wane during a relationship.'" She looked at him. "See, I couldn't stand being on either end of that—either losing interest or having someone lose interest in me."

He couldn't imagine not wanting Sugar, but he said, "If you love each other, you find a way."

"Not if it isn't in you, Gage." She held his gaze, wanting him to accept that she didn't do *permanent*. "Then no matter what you do, there is no way."

He felt a jolt of doubt. He'd counted on their feelings being mutual, on Sugar simply being afraid to trust his love or her own feelings for him. But what if she was right? What if she didn't love him? What if it was just lust, after all?

Sugar had gone back to reading the list. "'It is normal for men to have an orgasm with every sex act,'" she read, "'and for women to sometimes not.'" She flared pink, then talked quickly. "Kind of sad that people need fact sheets about what's normal. Everyone's afraid they're not doing it right, that everyone else is better at it or more fulfilled by it."

Was she embarrassed because she hadn't climaxed in his room at the Sex Expo? They'd been crazed, so it was no wonder. Sugar was so confident in her sexuality, he couldn't believe that was a problem. "If you care about each other, you do whatever it takes."

She raised her gaze to his and he tried to hold her, tell her he would be there for her, but she hid behind a grin. "Whatever it takes? Like manacles and riding crops?"

"Or elevators with a lag switch."

"Or twin massage therapists," she said, her eyes sparkling with heat. "You have a thing for twins?"

"Only if they're both you."

"Two of me? I can't imagine."

"Oh, I can," he said.

"Oh." Her body sort of caved, then she waved her hand before her face like she was burning up. "You know, it's so hot in here. I think a shower might be just what I need." She jumped up so fast she knocked her folder to the floor, then rushed to the bathroom, slamming the door behind her like she was afraid he'd chase her.

A distinct possibility.

He bent to pick up what she'd knocked down. Her Intimacy Inventory had slid out of the folder and to the floor. He saw that she'd only penciled in two answers. Yes, she liked to be touched in nonphysical ways—he'd known that, but in his answer to the questions about her, he'd added "as long as she doesn't feel trapped or restrained." And, yes, she enjoyed sex. That was no surprise. But the other questions, how she felt about sex, about talking about it, all the details, she'd left blank.

He listened to her in the bathroom. He pictured her leaning back, hands up to catch the water, the waist-high spouts splashing her torso, the one overhead dropping water like a rainstorm.

Then soap. Ah…soap. Bare hands or a washcloth? Bare, he hoped. He pictured her small palms rubbing her breasts, her belly, her ass, her spot. She had no tan lines, he remembered from those moments at the Expo hotel, which meant she sunbathed topless, maybe nude, rolling over like a cat, letting rays warm all her curves and dips and soft places.

What if he just slipped into that shower and took her in his arms? No talking. Just action. She wouldn't object, he'd bet. And they could enjoy each other in their own private waterfall. Why was that a bad idea again?

Because it would be too easy.

What was wrong with easy?

It wouldn't last. That was the problem. Sugar would tuck the experience away and consider it done. And he never wanted to be done with her. He wasn't settling for good sex, remember? He wanted great sex, which would only come when they were truly together, determined to build a life together.

So, he prowled the room, trying to think of anything except what was going on in that shower, focusing on the greater good, his goal.

He was almost calm when Sugar emerged, pink and glowing, in a cloud of sweet-smelling steam, her hair tied high on her head, loose strands curled against her damp neck. She was naked under the resort's green silk robe, which gaped to reveal a tantalizing glimpse of her breasts. Through the silk, her nipples seemed swollen. The thin fabric covered her body, soft and moist and warm, and he craved it like life itself.

She looked like a goddess.

"Better?" he asked, feeling worse.

"Much." She smiled. "Our robes are so comfortable." She held out one arm and rubbed it with the other. "I'm glad you suggested sampling the experience. I'd forgotten all the extra touches. Lavender-vanilla is the perfect scent for the shower gel and lotion. It's so intense you can almost get drunk on it."

"You picked the stuff, if I recall."

"Got a great price, too. But you found the detachable shower head." She sighed dreamily. "So many lovely settings. *Verrry* practical." She leveled her gaze at him.

Good Lord. Had she *used* the thing? Like *that?* He flashed on the picture of her aiming the pulsing jets between her legs, her head thrown back. Watching her pleasure herself…what a fantasy.

"Glad you, uh, enjoyed it," he managed to say.

"Very relaxing," she said. "You should try it."

"I don't think it would help a bit." Even if he could, uh, relieve himself, one look at her and he'd be reinforced steel all over again.

8

DAMMIT. Sugar wanted to growl in exasperation. The relief of the magical shower evaporated the instant she caught sight of Gage—his lust as naked as she was under this robe.

One look from Gage and she was a needy knot all over again.

The problem was denial. They'd told themselves "no" and that made "yes" irresistible.

Gage struggled, too. His eyes were dark with frustration and his jaw rippled with tension.

"So, back to work?" She turned toward the glass-covered faux stone table. They had to quit torturing themselves. They were like kids who deliberately rubbed their shoes on the carpet and touched metal just to see the spark and feel the sting. Enough.

Work would save them. It had to.

"We'll include the workshops," she said, sitting down at the computer and putting her fingers on the keyboard. "Read me the list."

He did and she typed in the most popular classes on bonding, intimacy and sexual technique. "Not sure we can include the Newly Renewed Game. Mary E. loves being the game show host, but not every therapist will be interested. If we get trained instructors, the multiple orgasm and tantric sex classes are popular."

"Remember that couple who thought the tantric class was a special-interest class in geometry?" Gage said.

"Yeah. They confused it with something—tangrams, I think. The husband was an engineer. When Mary E. explained it, his eyes went as round as saucers."

They both laughed.

"In the end, they took the class twice," Sugar said.

"Yeah, that's the magic of this place. You can't help but get into it. How can you duplicate that?" His voice was wistful, not argumentative.

"If we can define it, we can duplicate it. Every franchise started out unique. Starbucks and Massage Envy and Krispy Kreme—heck, Jiffy Lube. All the motel franchises started out one-of-a-kind, too."

"The chef has to be special," he said. "Remember when we couldn't find anyone we liked?"

"Oh, yeah. And that guy who showed up for the interview in a Speedo and a chef hat. He thought that's what we meant by 'cooking sexy.'"

"Don't forget the guy who carved sticks of butter into genitalia. He was fast with that blade."

"You stood there with your hand over your zipper like you thought you were next." She laughed. "He was cute. Too bad his menus were so blah."

"Then you found Emile. It was a leap of faith to take him on, after all the trouble he'd had."

"He was halfway through his AA steps and I could just feel he would make it. I knew he'd never give up on himself again."

"You're good with people, Sugar."

She shrugged away the compliment. "And you got him his dream kitchen, which kept him happy enough to say yes when we couldn't pay him what he was truly worth. At first, anyway."

He paused and looked at her. "We worked hard getting here, you know."

"Burned a lot of tomato soup," she said wistfully. "And we can do it again, Gage. That's the point. The franchise is new, but it's a way to value what we have, like Erika said. And I need you to keep me on track and in balance."

She took one of his hands between both of hers, then examined it. "You have great hands." She liked when he held hers, the way it made her feel necessary. But he could also trap her, hold her back, keep her in place when she wanted to move—*had* to move.

She'd always hated that feeling, even as a child. She remembered wrestling with a bigger neighborhood kid and the agony of having her will stymied, of not being able to escape his hold. He'd been just goofing around, but she'd been wild with fury and retaliated so roughly the kid avoided her after that.

"I like yours, too," he said, turning her hand over to examine the underside. "Strong, but soft."

"Esmeralda says I have *searcher* written right into my palm." She pointed to the line, jagged, with little X marks in a meandering curve across her hand. "See how it suggests movement."

"Looks like a fence to me." He traced the crease, tickling her. "It could mean you want stability and boundaries." He lifted his gaze to her face. "You can see whatever you want to see, Sugar."

"Well, I see phone lines along the highway or a railroad track. Who knows what's around the bend? Could be better. Could be the best."

"You were that way when I met you—restless in class, always watching the clock."

"Why didn't you just ask me out, anyway, back then?"

"Because I knew I wasn't your type."

"And what was my type?"

He released her hand. "I wasn't around the corner, in the next class, or the next bar stool down. I was right there in front of you."

She disliked the edge in his voice. It reminded her of how he'd been about Dylan and her other boyfriends. "You disapproved of me," she said. "You didn't like the fact that I slept with different guys. You used to give me those looks."

"That was envy, Sugar. I envied those guys."

"*All* those guys. That's what you mean, Gage." She was glad of a reason to be upset. Anything to end this odd longing that filled her chest again, made her yearn to hold hands with him again, fingers laced tight.

His voice went low. "I didn't want to be just another guy you slept with."

You wouldn't have been. She'd known it then and had a sudden wish she'd pushed things, slept with him instead of avoided him, afraid for some reason of where it might lead.

Like she was afraid now.

Stop it. The attraction had sprung up because Gage was off-limits, because their partnership was at risk. This feeling was artificial, a trick they'd played on each other.

"Water under the bridge, anyway," she said. "Where were we? Oh, I know." She pulled out the Matthews and Millhouse checklist and handed it to him. "Help me fill in the blanks on this, would you?"

He looked it over, frowning. "This is too generic. A one-size-fits-all list won't work with Spice It Up."

"It's only preliminary. After they do the diagnostic visit, then we'll get down to specifics."

"These consultants—Matthews and Millhouse—what do you know about them?"

"They're well respected and they have an impressive client list."

"When Rionna calls me back, I'll see if she's heard of them. Seems to me the consultants TravelQuest worked with had some kind of racket going—they got paid by the franchisees or something."

"You're so suspicious."

"I'm just careful."

"Fill in the blanks, okay?"

She was relieved when he dug in and before long he'd finished and they began adding items to the sample franchise agreement. Gage leaned close as she worked, reminding her of the partnership fantasy she'd described in Erika's office, except she was naked under a robe, feeling tight between her legs and she was having a hard time breathing. She shifted her chair to make room between them, but the chair leg caught in the flagstone and she tipped backward.

Gage caught her. "Whoa there."

"I was off balance."

"Me, too," he said, "but my chair's fine." His gaze slid to where her robe gaped, then back up, his dark eyes swirling with so much heat it hurt to look at him.

He pushed to his feet, went to the bathroom and returned with her clothes, which he dropped on the table in front of her. "Do me a favor and put these back on while I take a shower. A cold one."

"Sure." She watched him stride away. He had a point. It was crazy sitting here nearly naked, surrounded by books and videos about sex in a room built for it. Her nerves were as taut as piano wire.

Maybe they'd done enough work for today. They'd finished the checklist, drafted the franchising agreement, which the consultants would help them refine before a lawyer would draft the official agreement, and she had lots of notes for the operating manual.

She turned off the computer and straightened their papers. As she did so, she noticed Gage's Intimacy Inventory. Should she read it? He'd been fine with giving it to Erika to analyze, right? Why not?

Gage's favorite place to be touched turned out to be his neck and ears. Her favorite, too. Favorite part on a woman's body and why? *Her face because it holds everything—eyes, mouth, soul.* Could he possibly be that romantic?

His favorite activity? *Being alone with the woman I love.*

Wow. To make matters worse, the man was a few feet away, soaping up his naked body. *If you care about each other, you do whatever it takes.* He was such a patient man and so thorough and he finished everything he started....

Her gaze dropped to the partner questions at the bottom of the survey. How well did Gage know her?

He'd correctly written *ears and neck* for her favorite nonsexual body part. Great guess. For the question on who prefers to initiate sexual contact, he'd marked that she did. His answer to *why?* was *prefers control.*

Exactly right.

Then, the killer question: *What is your partner's greatest sexual need?* And his answer, in his neat block letters: *To feel safe enough to let go.*

Gage knew her. He got her. She felt abrupt relief, like when a stalled car finally started up, saving the day. She released a breath she'd held too long.

She thought about how he'd looked at her when she'd chained him to the wall in the fantasy room. Even as she took charge of him, he'd had power over her. Because he knew her. That made her shiver.

He'd figured out her elevator fantasy, too.

Her favorite one was being surprised by a stranger who knew her better than she knew herself.

A stranger who was also a friend?

On the other hand, how well did she know Gage? Not well at all. She'd blocked the details about him, walking around with her eyes half closed against the attraction.

Maybe she should do something about that. What if *she* made love to *him?* That wouldn't be breaking the rules exactly. It would even the balance between them and hopefully ease the tension. Why not?

Or maybe she just needed an excuse. Whatever it was, she found herself heading for the bathroom, her heart in her throat.

Before she could enter, Gage emerged in a mist of cool air fully dressed. His hair was curly and wet, his cheeks ruddy, his eyes clear and he looked calm. "You're still naked," he said, hesitating at the expression on her face.

"I am." She walked closer.

"What are you doing?"

She decided not to explain, just to go for it. "This," she said and took his face in her hands and kissed him, just as he'd kissed her before the Expo Incident.

He broke it off and held her away by her upper arms. "I just spent ten minutes in ice water to stop wanting that."

"I know. And I just read your inventory. I need to know you as well as you know me."

He opened his mouth to object, but she kissed his neck, then moved up to run her tongue along the edge of his ear. "This is your favorite spot?"

"Uh-huh," he groaned.

"Mine, too." She nibbled his earlobe. "Great guess."

He clutched her body close. "We agreed not to do this."

She leaned back and looked into his eyes. "This time, *I'm* doing *you*, Gage."

"I don't get your logic," he murmured.

"This will be good for us. I know it will."

She felt him give in to her words, the way *Open, Sesame* made the stone rumble away from the cave mouth. He pulled her to him and kissed her deeply, drinking her in. He cupped her bottom through her robe, rubbing and sliding the silk against her body. Then he flipped open the robe to look at her breasts and lower, his gaze so intent it was like actual contact. The sash tickled her calves.

She lifted the hem of Gage's shirt and he helped her take it off. This time the belt was easy and Gage was soon naked in front of her.

She took in his broad shoulders, strong biceps and smoothly muscled chest, followed the hot trail of dark hair that led to his jutting penis. The sight made her feel faint and turned her sex into a hot knot of need.

She looked up and his expression nearly did her in. It was full of yearning and passion and want. What had been his fondest wish? *Time alone with the woman I love.*

She imagined endless hours making love, luxurious hours in bed, in the hot tub. Hell, against a wall.

Gage pulled her against him, their bodies connecting in

all the right places. He slid his hand inside her robe to stroke her back, then her bottom, all the while maneuvering her to the bed.

She fell onto the bedspread and Gage rose over her, looking down at her as though he owned her.

She wanted that—to be possessed, to be overwhelmed. She wanted to just let go, let it all go, sink into the moment.

But she was supposed to be learning about Gage—what he liked, what he wanted sexually. This was about balance and fairness and…hell, she couldn't quite remember….

So she pushed up and rolled over to straddle his hips. Her robe fell from her shoulders and whispered onto Gage's thighs. He grabbed her bare bottom with both big hands.

She loved that.

How could she stay in charge when the mere touch of his fingers made her melt? She had to control him somehow. What she needed were the shackles from the Control Room. Wait a minute…

She tugged her robe sash from its loops and wrapped it around one of Gage's hands.

"What are you doing?"

"Focusing on you," she said, tying his bound wrist to the piece of brass that held the reading lamp above the bed. "Finding out what turns you on."

"Anything you do turns me on."

"Mmm." She lowered her mouth and kissed him, but his free hand found her bottom and it felt so good she wiggled against his palm.

Stay in charge, she told herself. "Stop distracting me." She pulled away to make a slip knot for his other wrist, but Gage took one of her breasts into his mouth.

"Quit that," she moaned, rubbing herself against him for

a few delicious seconds before she made herself move away. She slipped the loop around his free hand and tied it around the pipe. Now his arms were pulled up, making the muscles swell nicely, and she could do whatever she wanted to do, including walk away.

But she wasn't about to do that. The desire in his face transfixed her so much, she might as well be shackled to a stone wall herself.

"You're beautiful," he murmured.

"Flattery will not get you untied," she said, but the words came out shakily.

He caught her with his legs, pulled her against him, making her soften and go tight all at once.

"Do I have to tie your legs, too?" She tried to sound tough.

He held on a second longer, then let go with a sigh and extended his legs. He looked up at his tied hands. "So, now what?" His voice managed to be wryly humorous and husky with desire at the same time.

"Now I discover exactly what you like."

"You already know what I like."

She thought of the welcome basket with its sexy items and remembered the hot cinnamon gel. "Stay right there," she said, jumping off the bed.

"I'm not going anywhere," Gage said, frustration warring with humor in his tone. She loved the way he could laugh at himself.

She fetched the tube and set it beside Gage's body, before straddling him again.

Gage eyed the container. "Looks like I'm in trouble now."

"I certainly hope so." She looked him over. "Where to start? Hmm. I know you like this." She licked his neck, making her tongue firm against his skin, then she nibbled his earlobe. "But how about this?" She slid her tongue into his ear.

"Yeah. That works." Goose bumps formed on his arm so that she felt them against her cheek. She turned to lick the raised flesh.

"That, too. That's good. I told you if you're doing it, I like it." His voice was low and delicious. She rose on her knees and ran her tongue around his wrist, outlining her sash.

He tried to catch her breast with his mouth, but she moved away, liking how he lurched after her, pulling at the restraints. She licked down his arm, enjoying the way the tendons and muscles were tensed in their captivity.

He huffed out a frustrated breath.

"You don't like being tied up?" she asked.

"Not exactly." He tried to smile. Even though he didn't want to relinquish his power, he'd done so for her. She couldn't have done that. She was touched by his generosity.

"I promise to make it worth your while," she said, licking and kissing the side of his chest, teasing each rib, moving up to his underarm.

He jerked and a laugh burst out.

"You're ticklish?"

"Sometimes."

She looked at him. "That's something I didn't know." She moved away from the ticklish spot, using her tongue in a way that made him writhe and groan and move his hips so that his erection stroked her bottom.

She wanted him inside her body. And soon. She was positively liquid between her legs. She wanted to sink into the moment, forget herself, forget everything but the taste and touch and feel of Gage. But if she did that, she'd get swept away into her own pleasure and that wasn't her goal.

Get FREE BOOKS and FREE GIFTS when you play the...

LAS VEGAS
GAME

Just scratch off the gold box with a coin. Then check below to see the gifts you get!

YES! I have scratched off the gold box. Please send me my **2 FREE BOOKS** and **2 FREE GIFTS for which I qualify.** I understand that I am under no obligation to purchase any books as explained on the back of this card.

351 HDL EF5K   151 HDL EF6K

FIRST NAME	LAST NAME

ADDRESS

APT.#	CITY

STATE/PROV.	ZIP/POSTAL CODE

(H-B-12/06)

7 7 7	Worth TWO FREE BOOKS plus TWO BONUS Mystery Gifts!
🍒 🍒 🍒	Worth TWO FREE BOOKS!
🔔 🔔 ♣	TRY AGAIN!

www.eHarlequin.com

Offer limited to one per household and not valid to current Harlequin® Blaze® subscribers. All orders subject to approval.

Reluctantly she moved her body away, shifted herself to slide down his belly, nipping as she went. "Do you like little bites?" She demonstrated, sucking in taut flesh, then biting down. "Or bigger ones?" She bit a little harder.

He gasped. "That's…good. It's all good."

She would make it even better. She grabbed the cinnamon stuff and squirted a thin line down the middle of Gage's chest, using her tongue and blowing as she kissed and tongued her way down, making what she hoped was a line of flames down his body.

"Tell me what you want, Gage," she said.

"I want you. I want inside you."

"Not this time." Though that was her dearest desire at the moment. She'd bet there was something he'd love just as much. She put a dab of the gel on the head of his penis and blew a whisper of air there.

Gage moaned her name and his penis surged upward, wordlessly telling her she was correct.

She wrapped her hand around Gage's cock, very turned on herself. "Tell me what you want." She needed to hear the words.

"Your touch," he groaned out. "Keep touching me."

"What else?" she said. She applied the goo to his shaft and slid her hand up and down, rubbing it all over. "Say it."

"I want your mouth around my cock," he said, his voice deep and husky. "I want you to work me with your tongue and I want you to suck me dry."

"Oh, yes," she said, felled by the rough words in his raw voice. She had her self-controlled partner tied to a bed talking dirty to her. She'd never heard anything so arousing.

She covered him with her mouth, pulling him in, sucking hard, almost wishing the cinnamon was gone so she'd only taste him, his flesh, his fluid. She puffed out a breath, imagining how the sudden heat would feel.

He bucked into her mouth. "That's so good. So hot. So…good."

She took him in deep, her lips tight.

"Your mouth feels…sweet."

She sucked harder, keeping her hand low on the shaft where her mouth couldn't reach, holding tight, working him that way, too. Gage moved deeper into her throat.

Sugar enjoyed the hot human urgency of giving head to a man. Usually, she focused on her partner's pleasure, but this time, with Gage, was different. She felt connected to him, part of his experience.

When he said her name it was like a caress. Her throat opened so the act was effortless, as if his pleasure and her pleasure were one and the same. Her sex tightened, throbbed, swelled with desire.

Every gasp from Gage thrilled her, every twinge was a gift. She wanted this to be the best ever. For Gage. And for her, too, she realized.

Gage tensed, then stilled. "Sugar, I'm there," he gasped, warning her so she could release him if she didn't want the taste, but she wanted every drop. She pulled on him, sucking him strongly. His hips rocked in, he reached deep and filled her throat with his warm essence.

She smiled and swallowed, triumphant.

"Sugar," Gage said, barely able to form words, it seemed. "Untie me. I want to hold you."

And she wanted that, too. She'd made love to Gage, which was her plan, learned what turned him on, but she wanted him more than ever. What she'd done had only made things worse.

No way was this over. Not even close.

9

SUGAR RELEASED one of Gage's hands, then fell against him, tucking herself against his chest, kissing his neck.

He could only grin and hug her, happy to see how swept away she was. Maybe it wasn't so bad that they were having sex. Sugar seemed different.

He might as well think it was the right thing to do. He had no defense against her tongue, her lips and her clever hands. He'd been lost to her.

He cupped her head so he could kiss her mouth, feeling so much tenderness he didn't know how to contain it.

The waterfall trickled near them, the air smelled of that cinnamon junk she'd rubbed on him and of her hair and skin and of him. The moment was primitive and carnal and so damn good.

"I want something else," he said to her.

"What?" she asked, shifting so she could see his face. She looked dazed and aroused and faint.

He untied his other hand and rolled onto her, braced by his elbow to keep his weight off her. "I want inside you." He would make love to her until she felt safe. He would melt her defenses, make her his.

"Ooookaaaay," she breathed, giving in, surrendering to him. Her body was warm and pliable and eager. He tucked his hands under her back, took her breast into his mouth and tongued the swollen tip until she moaned and arched, wanting more.

A song began to play in his head, tinkling softly. Just like in the movies, he was hearing music.

He moved to her other breast.

The music got louder and he realized it wasn't in his head. It was Sugar's cell phone. It seemed to reach him from another time zone, another continent, another planet.

Sugar tensed beneath him.

"Let it ring," he said, kissing her neck. Then his phone went off, its simple trill a rhythmic pulse in the middle of Sugar's tune.

"Something must be up," Sugar said, pushing to a sit.

"I guess." He was reluctant to move. It was as though his bedside alarm had gone off in the middle of a great dream he wanted to cling to.

They stumbled to their respective phones—his in his abandoned pants pocket, hers on the table beside the laptop. Naked and sheepish, they checked their displays.

"Marketing," Sugar read from hers.

"Front desk," he reported.

They said hello at the same time.

"Gage, we need you in the lobby." Brittany. "There was a screw-up on the Happily-Ever-After bookings. A bunch of people are here for the *Coppola* reunion, not the *couples* reunion. There are kids and pissed-off parents all over the place. Clarice is on the phone getting them another reserve, but we need you and Sugar to smooth things out."

"Shuttle them to wherever Clarice sets them up. You have my okay."

"We need you and Sugar up here. You can't just dial it in, Gage." What was that supposed to mean?

"Everyone makes mistakes, Daisy," Sugar was saying. She shot him a questioning look. "No one's blaming you. Just be more careful in the future."

He promised Brittany he'd be right up and he and Sugar disconnected at the same time.

"Daisy spaced out sending the correction fax."

"Brittany wants us there. She's very upset. Something about how as owners we need to be on top of everything? What's going on?"

"Your pep talk probably made her nervous. Maybe she thinks we are looking to evaluate staff. I don't know."

They dressed fast, not talking. Over the swish of her dress, the buzz of his zipper, he could practically hear Sugar's thoughts. *Back up. Get away. Erase this.* The distance between them stretched with each ticking second.

"We got saved." She waved her phone in the air.

"We got interrupted," he said, wanting to bring her back to him. He reached for her, but she stayed where she was.

"I shouldn't have done that. I thought it would make it easier. That was stupid."

"Maybe not. Maybe it's right." But he should have held off. Sugar was tucking this away, pretending it was nothing already.

"I got carried away." She was shaking like a leaf.

"Maybe we shouldn't fight it," he said—one last shot.

She hesitated, opened her mouth to speak—

Both phones went off at once. Sugar looked relieved.

They each took a "hurry up" call, then set off for the lobby, Gage's heart heavy in his chest. Sugar might not come around. He had to allow that possibility, as miserable as it was.

In the courtyard, they gathered up two kids ogling the bonding class in the gazebo. In the main building, Gage heard a crash coming from the Power Room.

Inside, he found a man dressed like a cop and his partner in a bikini trying to talk a kid in a velvet cape and a motorcycle helmet down from the stripper pole.

Gage promised him Brittany's leftover Cinco de Mayo cookies and the kid slithered to the floor and let Gage lead him into the lobby, where he found Sugar and Clarice calming three thirty-somethings—two women and a man.

Gage noticed a red-faced woman dragging a young girl out of the gift shop. "Those are toys for grown-ups, Ariel," she hissed.

"But how do you *play* with them?"

"Ask me when you're older."

"How much older?" the girl said.

"Fifteen years. Maybe twenty."

Gage smiled at the woman, who groaned in frustration.

When he reached the front desk, Brittany introduced him to Benjamin Coppola, the bemused patriarch of the clan. The people Sugar and Clarice were soothing were his adult children.

Gage was still apologizing to Mr. Coppola when Sugar joined them. "We're getting your reservation squared away," she said.

Mr. Coppola nodded. "This seems like a great place to me. I don't know what happened to my kids' sense of humor. We didn't raise 'em to be prudes, did we, Gloria?" He put his arm around his wife.

"Certainly not."

"Now that they're parents, everything's a bad influence on their kids," he continued. "I just don't get it."

"Perhaps you and Mrs. Coppola can stay with us another time," Sugar said. "We'd like to offer you a fifty-percent discount." She wrote that down on a resort note card, signed it and gave it to Mr. Coppola.

"We do have our thirty-fifth anniversary coming up. June 17," he said, tucking the card in his pocket.

"Thirty-fourth, dear, and it's on the nineteenth," his wife corrected. "You always want to rush things."

"Nothing says we can't celebrate early." He hugged her close.

Gage smiled at the couple's obvious affection for each other. He caught Sugar's eye. *See how it's done?*

She gave a little shrug. *It works for some people.* She didn't think she was one of them. But he knew she was. If she'd just let him prove it to her.

Soon, most of the Coppolas were filing outside for the resort van and Gage turned to Sugar to say something to fix the problem, calm her down.

Then his cell phone rang.

"Take the call," she said. "I'll go settle those two." She motioned at Maribeth and Daisy who seemed to be arguing, then headed their way.

His display said TravelQuest. Rionna returning his call, no doubt. He flipped open his phone and said hello.

"Gage!" she gushed, more chipper than usual. "I was so *happy* to get your *call.* It's such a *coincidence,* since I wanted to call *you,* too."

Wow. Maybe Sugar was right and she did have a thing for him. He glanced over at where his partner was soothing the marketing team.

"I called to ask about TravelQuest's experience with franchising. Didn't you consider it with that European hotel chain?" As he talked, he moved to the phone alcove for privacy.

"Yes, but it didn't work out."

"Can you tell me why?"

"Sure, but first hear me out. I have a proposition for you."

"A proposition?" Damn, Sugar was right.

"Our VP of new properties just retired. We need new blood and a fresh vision, so I thought of you, of course."

"I'm flattered." His first thought was *I told you so* to Sugar about Rionna's attraction to him.

"It's not about flattery, Gage. You have great instincts, you're experienced, you know the industry, and I like your take on development."

"I'm not looking for a job, Rionna. I—"

"Hear me out. You wouldn't be a partner. Not at first, anyway, but our compensation package is strong. You'll be pleased."

"Thanks, Rionna, but, like I said—"

"You're not looking, yeah. Got it. Sometimes the job comes looking for you. You had some great ideas when we talked."

At the luncheon, he'd shared some thoughts on targeting and demographics. TravelQuest had always fascinated him. "Still, I'm committed here." He paused.

"We all need to shake things up from time to time."

"I suppose." That was Sugar's philosophy. That's what the franchise idea was all about. And if he and Sugar couldn't be together, he would certainly need a new direction for his career.

Being around Sugar, business as usual, after all this, would be impossible. He'd be going through the motions, his heart a twist of pain. She'd soon enough snag another lover and that would kill him. Since that night at the Expo, he could no longer hide from his feelings about her.

"You'd have free rein with the department," Rionna continued. "We've got a decent budget and you'd have management support. My team is progressive and flexible. You'll like everyone. You'd probably need to relocate eventually, but not right away."

"Like I said, I'm flattered—"

"You know we would work well together."

They would. Rionna was savvy and practical and, unlike Sugar, would actually listen to him. What would it be like not to have to argue every single point to death?

Sugar would see the move as pure treason. She did not want him to leave at all, let alone go to work for Rionna, despite urging him to date the woman. She would be furious.

"Sugar counts on me." But he hesitated a beat too long and he knew Rionna had caught it.

"Loyalty is good. I respect that. We value loyalty at TravelQuest, too." She paused, then spoke in a lower voice. "You shouldn't feel guilty when it's time to move on, Gage. You'd love it here."

"It would be interesting work," he heard himself say.

"Too much of life is habit. We go on automatic pilot. Think about what you really want for yourself."

"Like I said, I—"

"At least think about it."

"Okay. I will," he said finally, his mouth dry, his heart pounding. What was he doing?

"I need to know by month's end. If you say no, I'll have to get a headhunter on it."

"I don't want to hold you up, so if you need an answer now, it's—"

"If there's a chance to lure you, I can wait two weeks. Tell you what—I'll send you the job description and you shoot me a current résumé, how's that?"

"Sounds good." If being with Sugar was impossible—and it was looking that way—a challenging new job would be exactly what he needed.

Everything had changed, just as he'd said that first night. Even their partner debates felt different to him, more frustrating and pointless. He'd put up with them to be with Sugar, like some lovesick fool. He couldn't turn a blind eye to himself anymore.

So, he'd send the damn résumé. Where was the harm? "So, about your franchising experience…"

Rionna answered his questions and as they finished up, he watched Sugar head his way, smiling. The sight made his heart bang a hole in his rib cage. He had it bad. And to no good end, it seemed.

"Stay in touch, Gage," Rionna said.

The little girl from the gift shop shrieked and ran by waving a pink lozenge-shaped balloon…with a tip. A tip? Lord. She'd blown up a condom.

"That is not a balloon, Ariel," the mother yelled, hot on her trail. "Take that nasty thing out of your mouth."

"What's going on?" Rionna asked.

"Just a booking snafu," Gage said.

"If you've got kids in your adults-only lobby, I'd say so." She laughed. "We'll talk next week then?"

"I don't think that I'll—"

She hung up before he could reinforce the fact that it was only a résumé, not a yes. All the same, the possibility made him feel less trapped, like he had an escape hatch, a future beyond the coming disaster.

"Who were you talking to?" Sugar asked, tilting her head at him. "Your face is the color of the condom Clarice is making into a balloon animal." She nodded to where the concierge was bending the item into a doughnut for the mortified mother and her delighted daughter. They needed to get out to the van ASAP.

"Rionna returned my call about the franchise," he said, knowing he sounded even guiltier.

"I see." Sugar's eyes lit with awareness. "And she wants to discuss it over dinner?"

"It was a business call, Sugar."

"You don't have to BS me, Gage. You can date anyone you want. Rionna is hot. She's smart, too. Go for it. You don't need my approval."

"You know I don't want Rionna," he said, glancing around to be sure they couldn't be overheard. "You know what I want."

The mischief drained from her face, replaced by tension. "I'm hoping we can get past that. We're more than our urges, right?"

He would have been pissed at how easily she'd dismissed them, except she was obviously shaken up, pale and anxious and uncertain. "I keep saying that."

"I know what will help," she said, brightening.

"Yeah?" He flashed on heading back to that jungle bed and screwing each other's brains out.

"Let's book the diagnostic visit with Matthews and Millhouse."

"We're supposed to be doing research, not dragging in consultants, Sugar." This would not help at all.

"But the more we know, the sooner we can make a decision."

"Rionna said TravelQuest nixed the franchise because the consultants had a sweetheart deal with the franchisees. You have to be careful whom you work with."

"True, but as I said, Matthews and Millhouse are well respected."

"You're going to do this, aren't you? Push into the franchise no matter what?"

"If we don't meet the profile, I'll forget it. You said you'd give this a chance. That was our deal."

"What about being test guests? That was our deal, too. We should sit in on some workshops, enjoy one of Emile's couples dinners, check out the bar, do some dancing." Even as he said it, he felt how pointless and painful that would be.

Her eyes flitted across his face. "We can't risk that. Look what happened after a couple of hours together."

True. "What did that mean to you, Sugar?"

She sucked in a breath. "What did it mean?" Her gaze fluttered and danced. "It was wonderful, of course. Intense and fun…" She gave a weak smile. "I don't know…."

"But it was just sex, right?"

"What's wrong with that?" she asked, her voice crisp. "Why isn't sex enough for you? You can't make me into someone I'm not, Gage. I'm perfectly happy with who I am."

"I get it. I hear you. I had to ask." If that was all that was between them, then he had some thinking to do and a decision to make.

You did the right thing. That was all that kept Sugar from crumbling right there in the phone alcove. She'd made Gage give up. What else could she do? Even if she wanted more, the end was inevitable. She knew herself too well.

She would only disappoint him. Why drag out the agony? Why put either of them through unnecessary heartbreak?

So what if her chest was so tight she couldn't catch a breath and her legs felt like wooden stilts under her?

She told Gage she was going back to the room for the laptop, then clumped numbly away on her stilt-legs, confused and aching. She wanted a place to hide for a while.

What if Gage left?

If being together was impossible, Gage might decide he couldn't stay her partner. The idea made her dizzy with pain. It was his choice. She couldn't force him to stay.

She hurried across the resort grounds, smiling and greeting the guests who strolled by, waving at Mary E., who was holding a body awareness class on the lawn. Soon Sugar was climbing the hill above the Jungle Bungalow, and found herself practically running down the path to the door.

Inside, she could still smell cinnamon on top of the jasmine. The waterfall bubbled its greeting, the golden light warmed her, and her sash hung from the lamp over the bed. She threw herself on the mussed spread, arms out, breathing in Gage's cologne—which had soaked into the fabric—letting it all come back, vivid as a movie on a screen behind her eyes.

Oh, Gage.

She could see his muscular arms stretched up, his smile wry as she wrapped the sash around his wrists. She remembered how he'd tasted, how he'd felt in her mouth, how good she'd felt lying against his chest, his arm around her, lost in the moment and hungering to have him inside her.

Of course it was more than sex. She'd felt a new yearning, like mad dominoes tumbling through her, head to toe, each one registering need, awareness and pain.

Now she knew what she'd been missing. Dammit. She'd always been perfectly happy with herself.

Oh, Gage.

She wished she'd never let him into her room on Expo Night.

She heard a key in the slot. Was it Gage? Come to demand another chance? Ridiculous, of course, because Sugar made up her own mind and always had.

The door opened. She jumped to her feet, heart in her throat and—

Three men in painters' overalls and caps lumbered in carrying tool boxes and sawhorses. They'd come to repair the water feature. While they set up, she packed up the papers and shut down the computer.

By the time she left, the casita's atmosphere was different. The bubbling waterfall was silent. The romantic dimness had been overpowered by sunlight flooding in from the propped-open door. The workers had brought in the smell of paint, plaster, wood and metal so she could hardly detect the jasmine. They shouted to each other over the heavy metal they were blasting from the sound system.

The romance of the room was utterly gone. Just as well.

It was time to move on.

If she wanted to save their partnership, Sugar had to get her and Gage back in normal mode. That was her new plan.

In the office, Sugar got busy. She put in a call to Foster Matthews, worked on details for the Happily-Ever-After Week reception, refined the questions she would ask the three couples whose testimonials they would videotape and put in some work on the franchise operating manual.

As she worked, she kept an eye out for Gage, who

usually popped into her office several times a day. He was noticeably absent—avoiding her, no doubt.

Maybe that was best. They had to adjust to the change. The "test guest" idea was over. She couldn't handle any more couple stuff with Gage. A candlelit dinner in Spicers would be cruel, a cooking-for-two class brutal and a sex workshop, even as observers, plain murder.

What would fix things? If Gage got a girlfriend, of course. Rionna Morgan? She seemed an obvious choice. Sugar had even encouraged him to ask her out, though the idea made her blood boil black. It was crazy. Rionna was smart, attractive and interesting. They would make a great couple.

But Sugar wanted to claw the woman's eyes out.

What a mess she was.

The only good thing that happened was that Foster Matthews called back with an opening next Friday for a diagnostic visit. Maybe Gage would be so intrigued by the meeting he'd forget all thoughts of leaving. She could hope, couldn't she?

Buoyed by the news, she popped out of her office to tell Gage and was startled to find Brittany standing at the door, looking nervous.

"Hi," she said, jerking her hand in a stiff wave. "I just wondered…I mean, I wanted to verify that you'll be at the hire-anniversary party next Friday. It's at noon?"

"Oh. Yes. Whoops." That would be smack dab in the middle of the Matthews and Millhouse meeting. "We'll have to miss this one, Brit. Gage and I will be with some consultants related to our marketing project. I'm sorry."

"But we need you there. You're the *owners*. Can't you reschedule this marketing thing?"

"We can't. No. But we'll be with you in spirit."

"It won't be the same without you." Brittany's cheeks flared with red blotches and she bit her lip. "I thought we were a family. Are we just cogs in a machine now?"

"How can you say that? Of course not."

She softened. "I don't know. After that speech Gage gave at the meeting… I just worry. He said we were so important, but it felt like he was saying goodbye or something."

"That wasn't it." Sugar's heart clutched. She could see how it might have sounded that way. And, if she couldn't convince Gage to stay, that speech might be close to his farewell. "Spice It Up is my life, Brittany. Everything we do is aimed at making it a better place for guests and employees. That's what the marketing project is about, too."

"Okay," she said, but her face still held doubt. "And I was wondering if Daisy's in trouble because of the mistake she made with the Coppolas?"

"Of course not. It was a mistake. We'll make up the reserves. We're a great team, Brittany. All of us working together."

Brittany seemed relieved by her words. Relieved and thoughtful, as if she was figuring something out. What was with her? Maybe she'd picked up on the tension between her and Gage. If Brittany felt it, then other employees would, too. The last thing they needed was a fearful staff.

Another worry to add to her already troubling list.

10

THREE NIGHTS LATER, on Sunday evening, Sugar pulled into the parking lot for the opening reception of Happily-Ever-After Week, cranky and tired—which was a shame since the reunion week was usually the high point of the year for her. For Gage, too.

She parked and checked herself in the rearview. Her face was pale and her hair as limp and lifeless as her mood. She applied lipstick and blush for color, brushed and fluffed her do. A little better.

What troubled her the most was the recent change in Gage. Ever since the Coppola problem, Gage had had something on his mind and it wasn't her. He seemed distant, preoccupied. She practically had to wave her hand in his face to get his attention. What was he thinking so hard about?

She missed him. His friendship, of course, but also, selfishly, she missed his desire for her. Which was stupid because that was her best hope for normalization.

Something irrevocable had occurred without her knowing and it made her feel ill. She couldn't bring herself to ask Gage what was wrong.

She had her suspicions. Pink message slips from Rionna Morgan littered Gage's desk. Something was going on between them. That was a good thing. An excellent thing.

If Gage hooked up with Rionna, maybe he'd be content to remain Sugar's partner.

Easy. Perfect.

Agony.

Gage pulling away had made her want to grasp at straws. Even, stupidly, wonder if maybe she'd stopped them too soon.

Hell, she should give Conner Jameson a call. Except the idea made her feel weary. The last thing she wanted was sex with a new man. She'd learned that much since Expo Night.

Meanwhile, staff seemed to be picking up on the tension. More than once, she'd caught Brittany jerking to attention when Sugar and Gage left a room, as if she'd been listening in, the way children obsess over every exchange between quarreling parents.

The one good thing that had happened was a sudden spike in bookings. A national organization of sex therapists was coming in November and, in December, a regional church group had booked fifty rooms for their marriage recommitment retreat. Couples bookings, too, were at an all-time holiday high.

That made this Friday perfect for the consultants to check out their census cycle. That meeting would be a turning point for the resort. They would go forward with the franchise or give up the idea altogether. Then Gage would decide to stay or go.

Friday was crucial. Everything had to be perfect. So much was at stake. Her future. Her life. She'd put everything into the resort. She'd thought Gage had, too, but his willingness to leave told her she'd been wrong. Her stomach churned with acid, her head throbbed with worry.

Settle down. Smile. It'll work out somehow.

For now, she had to get through this reception. *Get through?* What a tragic way to think of an event she usually adored. Reunion week proved what a gift Spice It Up was to the couples who stayed here. Gage felt the same way, she knew. She would enjoy this one, too, dammit, no matter what.

She forced a smile, tugged the hem of the jacket she wore over her purple silk dress, threw back her shoulders and eased into the banquet hall.

The room was bursting with energy, talk and laughter. Romantic music played overhead, the bar was busy and people were enjoying the sensuous appetizers laid out on the elaborate banquet islands.

Judging from the happy chatter, her ice breaker was working. Return guests wore blue-edged name tags with the words, "Ask me about…" beneath which the guests wrote something they'd loved at Spice It Up—fantasy role-plays or intimacy workshops or romantic dinners for two.

Red-edged tags on the newcomers said, "I'm curious about…" The idea was to connect the two groups in a way that gave the new couples hope and reminded the returning guests how far they'd come.

So far, so good. Sugar was looking forward to videotaping the three couples Erika had selected earlier in the day. The first was tomorrow morning. Erika had handed her the list and said something odd. *There are lessons for you here.*

Sugar had politely reminded Erika she wanted to promote Spice It Up, not hear morality tales.

Just listen to learn, Erika had said with a mysterious smile. Honest to God, sometimes the woman's inscrutable advice got on Sugar's nerves. She didn't need a Danish Yoda in her life.

Which normally was something she'd bitch to Gage about and they'd laugh. Except they were awkward around each other now—another nasty side effect of their misadventure.

She spotted him across the room and their eyes met. For one brief second, time and space blurred, making it seem that only she and Gage were in the room, seeing only each other, wanting only each other or life lost all meaning.

Her heart turned over and her knees gave way.

This can't happen. You said no. That made her feel hollow inside, as if she'd said no to her one chance at happiness.

She gave herself a shake, smiled, then nodded to her left, telling Gage she would be mingling.

He nodded back, still watching her.

She forced herself to move, to focus on what mattered— *Spice It Up,* which was the center of her world, her main achievement. The rest of it, the personal stuff, was too complicated, too much trouble, and guaranteed to go wrong. She would stick with what worked. Right now, it was all she had.

GAGE TORE HIS GAZE from Sugar. *What are you doing?* For a second there, he'd forgotten that everything was screwed up and over, that he was ready to move on.

He'd made a decision. He was taking the job with TravelQuest. He'd faxed over his résumé and talked to Rionna about the details of the job and been intrigued. He'd be challenged as he hadn't been in years.

When he took Sugar out of the equation, the charm of working at Spice It Up seemed to fade. He loved Spice It Up, of course, but it was too linked to Sugar for him to be able to stay.

He would tell Sugar about the job tonight after the reception, then talk to Rionna in the morning. He would promise Sugar a smooth transition. If she still wanted to do the franchise, she could work that out with Oliver. He hoped to investigate the consultants before their meeting Friday. Competent consultants made all the difference, he knew, so she could depend on them, too, in Gage's absence.

Gage needed to move on. Hell, he sounded like Sugar, who kept her eyes on the horizon while she tripped over the beauty—the roses—at her feet. Gage had been stuck in the rose bed too long, tangled in the brambles, sinking in the soil. Time to get out.

He watched Sugar talk to a group of people. She said something that made them all laugh. She was so good at making the guests feel at home and hopeful and special. That was one of her gifts. One of the gifts of Spice It Up that was impossible to capture in an operations manual. She still didn't get the magic of the place. And he wasn't strong enough to show her more.

He wished he were at her side as usual. The reception was a shared triumph. They loved seeing the couples return, liked to talk about how each pair had grown. Seeing the new couples, hesitant and tense, always made Gage smile, knowing the good changes they would experience during their stay.

With a jolt, he realized this was his last reunion reception, the next seven days his last Happily-Ever-After Week. He swallowed the knot in his throat. *Come on. Get a grip. Things change.* He was a practical guy. He knew to cut his losses when failure was certain. Since when had he gotten sentimental?

Since Sugar. She headed his way, smiling, and his lungs closed down around his heart as if to stop its beat. Would he ever get over her?

As she got close, he saw how depleted she was. Gorgeous as ever in a slinky dress, but her smile was weak and she looked dead tired and frazzled. It was the tension between them, the uncertainty. Tonight he'd make things clear. Better a clean break than dragged-out agony. Sugar was good at moving on. Him, not so much. He'd have to learn. He had no choice.

"It's going well, don't you think?" she said when she reached him, her voice hesitant.

"I think so." They both looked around the room. He couldn't stand how sad she seemed. "I'm sorry that what's happened—"

"I'm sorry we've been so—"

They both laughed at their simultaneous words.

"I know things are tense between us, Gage, but I want us to enjoy this. I love reunion week."

"Me, too."

"I know. It's the best, isn't it?"

"It is. The best."

They stared at each other.

"I'm sorry, Sugar." His throat squeezed tight but he forced out the words. "We need to talk. After the reception?"

"Okay." Her eyes widened, surprised at his tone. "Sure."

"Let me get a shot of you two." The photographer he'd hired aimed his camera in their direction.

"That's not necessary," Sugar said. "Are you getting a lot of orders? The display looks great." She nodded at the Then And Now portable display, which held shots of the reunion couples from their first visit, beside new photos, along with shots of the first-timers. Sugar had had the idea of hiring the photographer and Gage had made it happen.

"I can't keep up." The photographer grinned. "I want to take your picture. It's on me. As a thank you."

"Why not?" Gage said, putting his arm around her. "We haven't had one taken since we opened our doors." He kept the framed snapshot on his desk. This one would be his farewell souvenir.

Sugar wobbled in her heels and he steadied her. "I've got you," he said. Her body molded so perfectly against his. How could he live without her in his arms?

"Gorgeous," the photographer said. "Say 'sex heals.'" Lord, could he get any cornier?

"Sex heals," they said in unison, but the words came out so sadly it broke his heart.

"Print'll be on the wall in ten minutes," the photographer said cheerfully and headed off, thankfully oblivious to the emotion between them.

Sugar pulled away, then glanced up at Gage, almost shy. "Shall we check out the buffet? Make sure we're stocked?"

He followed her to the tables, which contained a range of romantic and aphrodisiac selections—proscuitto-wrapped asparagus spears, oysters with a hollandaise sauce and sugared figs. The most popular spot was a fondue island, where couples fed each other strawberries, bread and veggies dipped in pots of melted cheese and white or milk chocolate, giggling and kissing between bites. That made Gage smile.

"What are you thinking?" Sugar asked him gently.

"That I can tell the reunion couples from the new guests."

"It's the name tags. They're different colors."

"It's more than that," he said. "I can't see the tags on that couple by the wine bar, but I can tell they're return guests."

"How?"

"The way they keep a hand on each other and track each other's eyes." He watched the woman brush crumbs from her partner's cheek. "Those two are close."

"Interesting," Sugar said. When the pair turned their way, she said, "You're right. Blue tags. Let me try." She surveyed the crowd, then said, "I say those are newbies over by the oysters. See how she gives him a hard glance, then searches the room?"

"Yeah?" he said, glad he had her intrigued.

"She wonders if she settled for less. She's checking the other couples to see if they seem happier."

"You think?"

"I'd put money on it." The couple turned their way. Red tags.

"That's exactly what I would be doing, Gage," she said softly. "Like you said, I'm always checking out the guy on the next bar stool." She laughed, making light of herself, but he heard despair, too.

"Maybe you're misreading her," he said. "Maybe she's just afraid the bubble will burst. Maybe she doesn't want to get her hopes up for fear she'll be disappointed."

She studied the woman, then him, opened her mouth to speak, then stopped. She seemed confused and troubled and he had to touch her. He cupped her cheek.

She leaned into his hand, closed her eyes for a second and when she opened them they were full of anguish. "Don't you think I would if I could?" she said. "Be in love with you?"

"Have you even tried?" he asked.

She just looked at him, answering him with her silence. What could he say to that? His thudding heart slowed to a painful throb.

His phone rang then. He heard her sigh of relief. *Saved*

by the bell again. It was Oliver, who wanted him to look over the waterfall repair and decide whether the patch the workers had done was enough or if they should do a full renovation.

He told Sugar where he was going and headed off.

When he got back, the reception would be over and he would tell her he was leaving, end the tension once and for all.

Outside the reception door, he turned to look back at Sugar. A guest was talking to her and she was smiling, but he could tell it hurt and her eyes held sadness. He dreaded upsetting her more, but what else could he do?

"How's it going, Gage?"

Startled to hear Erika's voice so close, he spun on his heels. She'd materialized again. How the hell did she do that?

"Going well. Good turnout. Got a few last-minute reservations to fill the gap caused by the Coppola problem."

"That's not what I mean." Erika nodded across the room at Sugar.

"Oh. Not so good." He shook his head.

"You are not a man who easily concedes defeat," she said. "Perhaps you do not want the climb?"

He considered her words. Not true. He wanted Sugar with all his heart. "It takes two, Erika."

She didn't answer. Instead, she looked out at Sugar. "Sometimes we fight hardest what we most want."

He'd seen the longing in Sugar's face, the don't-dare-hope in her eyes before she shut away the possibility like a padlocked door.

Then Erika looked straight at him. "And sometimes we ask for yes, but welcome no."

"What is that supposed to mean?"

Erika only smiled, patted his arm and glided away.

Shaking his head, Gage set off for the casita. Erika thought he didn't really want to be with Sugar? Not true. Love was tough enough if both people wanted it. And Sugar didn't want it. What did Erika expect him to do? Grab her by the hair and drag her into his cave?

That would never happen.

HE'S LEAVING YOU. The thought pounded through Sugar as she walked among her guests, trying to be a good host, feeling numb and scared and so small. *We need to talk,* Gage had said, and it wouldn't be good, she could tell from his expression.

She shook hands with first-time guests from Chicago and wished them good luck. In a daze, she accepted a hug from a bubbly return couple. *Thank you so much... Staying here changed our lives....* And then another hug. And another. *You saved our marriage...our relationship...our love.*

This happened at all the reunions, but this time the words seemed to stick in her head and reverberate, playing again and again, overlapping like carillon bells.

A couple beelined her way. She recognized them from their first visit. They'd had a fight right in the lobby, she recalled, on check-in. This time they beamed.

"So glad to see you." Sugar shook both their hands.

"Check this out." The woman wiggled the fingers of one hand, where a diamond gleamed. "We're engaged and I'm not terrified."

"That's wonderful," she said.

"I know. Especially that I'm not terrified. I didn't think I could do forever. I mean, *forever.*" She widened her eyes as if that were an incomprehensible concept. Then she gave her fiancé a look of wonder. "But love changes you. It does." She turned back to Sugar. "I learned that here, so I just want to thank you."

Her fiancé put his arm around her and mouthed "Thank you" to Sugar.

"I'm so happy for you," Sugar said, letting the woman's words sink in.

"While I was here it just all came clear. You just do one day at a time until forever catches up with you." She shrugged happily and the couple moved on to the food table.

Sugar watched them go, smiling. Sugar didn't think she could do forever, either. Could love change her?

Have you even tried? Gage had asked her.

Maybe not. Not really. She'd been too afraid.

Now she turned slowly, taking in all the couples in the room, zoning in on the ones hugging, clinking glasses in a toast, kissing for the photographer, showing her that love was sturdy, love lasted. Love could change you.

I want that. For the first time, she let herself admit it.

You just do one day at a time until forever catches up with you. Maybe she could do that. For the first time, she allowed the possibility that she, Sugar Thompson, could fall in love and stay there.

She had to talk to Gage. Quick, before she lost her nerve. He was at their casita checking on the waterfall. What could be more perfect?

She rushed out of the ballroom. The registration table, littered with unclaimed name tags, made her pause. Some couples hadn't made it yet. Or weren't coming at all. Perhaps because their relationships had failed after all.

She wouldn't think about failure. Not now. She barreled out the door of the main building onto the resort grounds, then along the vine-covered breezeway, her heels clicking on the bricks as she ran, the sea breeze lifting her hair, puffing out her jacket. Her heart pounded as she flew up the hill over-looking the Jungle Bungalow and paused at the top.

The casita glowed with light—Gage was still there—a peaceful haven in all that wild greenery. She ran downhill, blocking out her doubts, her fears, her second guesses.

She was almost there when the casita went black, the door opened and Gage stepped out.

She just ran to him, calling his name.

He looked startled. "Sugar?"

She threw her arms around him and kissed him.

He broke off. "What happened?"

"I want to try," she said. "I do."

"You do? You want to try?" She watched him reverse whatever it was he'd wanted to talk about. His face filled with relief, his mouth widened into a grin, and his eyes went molten.

"Come on, then," he said and took her by both hands into the bungalow, letting go just long enough to work the key card.

Inside, there was no golden light, no jungle sounds, no waterfall, no worker rock and roll, and no jasmine, but standing there in the dark with Gage, breathing in sawdust and plaster and silence, it felt like wild heaven to her.

Gage cupped her face and kissed her.

Shivers ran down her body in waves, her own private waterfall of tingles all the way to her toes.

"No deals this time," he said, shoving her jacket off her shoulders to the floor.

"No deals," she said, unzipping her dress, letting it fall, and stepping out of it. She kicked off her shoes so that she stood in bra and panties and lacy thigh-highs, shaky and scared and happy.

Gage swept her into his arms—thank God, since her legs had stopped working—and carried her to the bed, throwing back the covers and laying her on the black satin sheets, leaning over to click on one golden lamp.

He sat beside her, watching her as he tossed off his shirt. His muscles gleamed, round and smooth in the low light, reminding her of the Rodin sculpture in Erika's office.

He unclasped her bra and her nipples tightened under his hot gaze. Her sex felt swollen and so wet, ready for him, eager for his touch, his thrust, his release.

She went for his belt, yanking open the buckle.

"My way, this time," he said, stopping her hand.

"Your way?" she breathed.

"Nice and slow." He ran his hands down her bare arms, across her stomach, then cupped her breasts before lowering his mouth to kiss each one with agonizing care, running his tongue over the nipples to delicious effect, warming her more than the cinnamon gel ever could.

"Slow is torture," she moaned.

"Slow is sweet." He rolled her stockings down, then her panties with leisurely care. The fabric scraped her skin with exquisite friction. The more naked she got, the hotter and hungrier was his gaze.

Stripped bare under his eyes, her body felt like one huge nerve that quivered and sparked everywhere he looked.

"Now you," she begged, a desperate edge to her voice.

He took off his pants and boxers, naked at last, his erection prominent against his tan skin, rendered golden in the dim lamplight.

She reached for his cock, but he shifted out of reach.

"Not yet. I want to enjoy every second of this." He kissed her mouth, soft and slow and promising, then ran his hands down her stomach, millimeter by millimeter.

Impatience rose in her. He was going to make love to her the way he did revenue projections or chose a wine or decided a stock to buy. Taking too much time and way too much care.

"Slow is brutal," she breathed.

"Slow is hot." He brushed his lips against her forehead, over each eyebrow, then each lid, the movement tender and remarkably arousing.

"You're killing me."

"I'll revive you." He kissed her mouth so thoroughly, so deeply that she just dissolved into the sheets, whimpering against his lips.

"Maybe I can stand a little more."

He looked at her in a way that made her feel *more* than naked, completely exposed, bared to her soul.

He kissed between her breasts and she arched up, wanting more of his mouth. He licked around her nipple, then pushed his tongue against the small nubs, giving her little thrills—quick tickles and throbs of pleasure that built an urge deep within her.

Maybe he had a point about slowing down. She had time to breathe in his cologne, his skin, his hair, to feel every slide of skin, every quiver of muscle, every tiny lick or nip or brush or tease.

He ran his palms along her abdomen, fingers wide, making her his. He raised her bottom so he could hold it, fingers meeting and sliding down the crease of her ass, taking in the shape of her, sculpting her like clay.

She wanted his body, too, to touch the length of him, to get him inside her. She reached for him again.

"Eh-eh-eh," he warned, crossing her hands at the wrist, pulling them over her head, taking power over her. "Do I need that sash or will you behave?"

In counterattack, she grabbed him with her legs, locking her ankles and sliding her sex against him.

"Ah, hell." He groaned and buried his face in her neck. "You win." He released her hands. He knew she needed that little victory and she loved him for giving it to her.

"Tell me what you want," he said, repeating her words from the last time they were together. His biceps rippled and twitched. He was straining to hold back, she could tell. He kissed down her neck.

"That. I want that," she breathed.

He kissed across her collarbone, outlining the bone with his tongue, memorizing her under the skin.

"That, too," she said. She flung out her arms, letting go at last. "I want whatever you want to do to me."

"Look at me," he said, but he meant *let me in*.

She did. She let him see her fear and her hope for as long as she could bear it.

She realized abruptly that she couldn't keep him out. Without a handcuff, a manacle or a sash in sight, he had her in his power. It was the way he looked at her and touched her, as if he adored her, had adored her forever.

And it was delicious. Like a warm bath that made her stop and notice every inch of her skin, every nerve ending, every molecule of air in her lungs.

Since his blurted confession of love, she realized she'd gradually opened that door in her soul she kept jammed shut. It had always seemed safer to prop a chair under the knob. But not now. Not with Gage.

When she couldn't stand it anymore and broke contact,

Gage smiled. "I know that wasn't easy for you." He kissed between her breasts. "Let me show you it was worth it." He shifted lower to her stomach, where he ran his tongue around her navel, the pressure so delicious she had to gasp. She lifted her hips, wanting more.

Her orgasm built, tightening, getting ready. She felt the usual anxiety, the urge to hold on, manage it, not to get carried away.

Gage's fingers were making lazy circles on her thighs, getting closer and closer to her clit. She would still need to touch herself to get there, she knew. Surely that hadn't changed.

Except then Gage stroked her just the way she would have done, his fingers moving like her own thought. *There on that side, yes. Now up above...press down a little, now the other side.* She started to tell him how perfect it was, but then he slid a finger into her and she made a choked sound.

"I love how you feel," he said, sliding his body down, lifting her legs up over his shoulders. Then he shifted again to place his warm lips on her, his tongue giving the perfect pressure to the perfect spot.

Her hips pivoted, out of her control. She felt the shiver that told her an orgasm was right...*there.*

"Yes," he murmured, sensing the change.

But that reminded her he was there. *Too* there. Waiting for her, coaxing her over the edge, wanting it, wanting to feel her come.

And just like that, her climax flitted away, the way a deer sensed movement and zipped off with a disappointing flick of white tail.

Gage stilled. He'd felt the shift.

"I want your cock," she said to cover the loss. "I want you inside me."

He hesitated, but only for a moment before lowering her legs and angling himself so he could slide in deep. His shaft brushed her clit, a position she liked, but her body had gone numb.

Go for it, she told herself. *It's good. For Pete's sake, let go.*

"Okay?" He watched her face, not letting her escape.

"It's great. Keep it up." Her voice cracked.

He pulled out slowly, then entered slowly, too. "We have all the time we need." But his arms trembled and she could see how hard he was fighting for control. He stilled, still looking into her eyes.

"Please. Just go," she said, frustrated beyond belief.

He hesitated, then seemed to give in and move deliberately, going after his orgasm, as she'd asked.

Thank goodness.

"Go faster," she said, not able to hold his gaze any longer. She wanted him to climax, needed him to, to escape this intensity. This was pleasure, too, right?

But there was more there for her, if she'd only let go. Why did she hold on so tight? What was she afraid of?

She wrapped her legs around Gage's waist, digging her heels into his backside, pushing him deeper until she saw the fire catch in his eyes, knew he was helpless against it. "I want you to come," she said. "I need you to."

He thrust into her hard. Then hard again and breathed her name as he exploded, crushing her against him, shuddering and shuddering as the spasms rippled through him.

"You're incredible," he breathed in her ear. He slid his hand down to stroke her with his finger. He was still inside and somehow managed to keep moving in and out at the same time.

"That was wonderful," she said, telling him it was enough.

He kept going, though, and she knew he'd keep at it as long as it took.

She stopped his hand with her own, their two hands cupping her sex, while she said what she had to say. "I won't get there now."

He searched her face. She saw he wanted to continue, but he deferred to her wishes and kissed her. "Next time, then."

Next time. She stilled at the thought, feeling a flicker of alarm. *It's okay. This is the plan.* She'd said she wanted to try, right?

"You wore me out," he said, cuddling her against him.

"I intended to." She listened to the soothing thud of his heart, felt the slow rise and fall of his rib cage under her ear. He was calm and relaxed. She was not.

The missing orgasm had left her tight and she was nervous about what they were doing, so when Gage's breathing told her he'd drifted off, she eased out of bed and headed to the shower to take care of herself.

11

In a few seconds, Sugar had the rain showerhead going and sat on the tile seat, one leg up, using the detachable showerhead to good effect, her head against the tile wall, her eyes closed, thinking of Gage, of how intense it had been with him, how close he'd brought her, how much she wished she'd been able to come with him. She waved the pulsing water back and forth between her legs, enjoying it, getting into it, swelling and aching, aiming for the pleasant spasms to come.

A sound made her open her eyes.

Gage stood inside the shower, naked and aroused, watching her, his dark eyes intense.

Embarrassed, she jerked the water away from her body and lowered her leg.

"Don't stop," he said, moving closer, the water beading on his skin, deepening the color of his hair, shaping it into thick strands. He lowered himself to his knees before her, then lifted her leg back onto the bench.

"Show me what feels good." His voice was soft, his tone humble and he took her hand, which still held the showerhead, and guided it so the water drummed warmly against her thigh—close enough to make her clit pulse with anticipation.

"Watching you do that turns me on," he said, releasing her hand.

She considered how that would be, felt a flutter of excitement, and decided to try it. Since when was she shy about sex? Since Gage, of course. He changed everything.

She shifted the stream of water so it struck her clit. Gage's presence made the jolt of hot pleasure more intense. He pressed his fingers into her thighs. She could tell he wanted to touch her, was holding back, letting her do what she preferred.

As she moved the water's pulse, his face seemed to reflect her own reactions. He tried to hold her gaze, but that was too much to bear all at once. She closed her eyes and leaned her head against the hard tile wall.

She felt Gage move and opened her eyes to find him scooting onto the bench. "Rest against me." He settled her in front of him, her legs inside his, his aroused cock snug against her back. "I want to hold you," he breathed in her ear.

She leaned back and let him wrap his arms around her, making her feel safe and secure, the way he made her feel every day, she realized. She put the water to work again and the combination of being held by Gage while the water caressed her clit was almost more than she could bear. She gasped from the rush of it and pressed herself more firmly into Gage's warm chest and against his cock, which showed her how aroused she'd made him.

She used her index finger to add to the sensation. Then Gage's finger took over. The water was warm and insistent, pulsing and pulsing, his finger perfect, nudging her closer and closer to release until…

Wham. Her climax hit so hard and strong she cried out,

the sound echoing in the shower. Gage held her tight while she rode the rush on and on and on.

Being with him like this, knowing he was focused on what she was doing to herself, was strange and glorious all at once. She dropped her leg to the shower floor, her sex still throbbing, relief rushing through her body like medicine.

She turned so she could kiss his warm, wet lips. His erection pushed into her stomach, exciting her all over again.

"So beautiful," he murmured, grasping a breast, kissing her deeply.

She rocked her pelvis against him.

He shifted her so she sat on the bench, then kneeled before her. Taking the showerhead from her limp hand, he smiled up at her. "Can I give it a try?" He ran it briefly between her thighs, then checked her reaction. "Too soon?"

She was startled by an instant throb of new need. "No. It's *wooonnnderful.*" If only he could be two places at once—in front of her and behind her back—but for now this would do.

Fabulously. She leaned back and spread her legs, wanton and wanting, while he stroked her with the water.

"I want to taste you," Gage murmured, shifting so the water pulsed at the top of her clit, while his tongue pressed the bottom.

Electricity zinged so sharply she feared she'd squirm off the bench or burst into flames. She grabbed Gage's head, trying to keep herself from flying away.

Gage was right there for her. She looked down at his mouth laboring on her and it was a beautiful sight, so sexy, so carnal, so right.

He ran his tongue in a slow stroke, with little pushes like the pulsing jets of water. Pure genius. She moved her hips, adding tension to the mix. Could she come with his mouth on her?

The urge tightened and locked. She was on the brink, she was doing it for the first time ever….

Then she panicked. *Oh, no.* The feeling drained away like she'd pulled a plug. She squeezed her eyes tight. *Pretend it's just you. Pretend it's just water.*

Gage lifted his face to her. "Look at me, baby," he said softly. "Look at me."

She looked at him, expecting disappointment, concern, hell, pity, in his eyes. Instead she saw a wicked glint.

"Whatever you do, Sugar, don't come."

She stared at him. "What are you…?"

"I mean it. Promise me you won't come." His voice was hoarse with heat.

"Okay, I…won't." She could hardly get out the word.

Then his mouth was there and his thumbs separated the lips of her entrance more fully so there was sideways tension to match the lengthwise pull of his lapping tongue. Water streamed down onto his broad back as he shifted so he could push a finger into her, giving her an exquisite thrill. She rocked into the movement.

He stopped. "You promised," he warned.

She stilled. "O-k-kay."

He started again, slowly, a cat licking cream, his finger working in and out, steady and slow, as though he could go forever, would go forever. Whatever it took for her *not* to come.

She rested her head against the tile, let her fingers dig into his hair, aware of the building pressure. Reflexively she pressed her thighs together for more friction.

"Uh-uh-uh," he warned.

This time she shoved his head onto her spot, not caring whether it was lips or tongue or teeth, she just needed him to keep up the pressure, the tug, the building urge.

Don't come. Don't come. Don't come. She chanted in her mind.

Right in the middle of all that denial, her orgasm hit, catching her completely by surprise, like someone jumping out from behind the door.

She cried out, the sound sharp in the steamy shower, and the waves of pleasure went on and on and on. This was bigger and better than any orgasm she'd given herself. She was so startled that tears sprang to her eyes. Thank goodness she was in the shower and Gage would not be able to tell the tears from the water. She'd broken down over a simple orgasm.

There was nothing simple about that orgasm. It was jam-packed with complexity, having to do with her feelings for Gage, his feelings for her and all the possibilities between them.

"Gage," she said. "Oh, Gage." And she dropped her cheek to his head, her flesh melting away from her bones.

Still kneeling on the tile, he wrapped his arms around her.

"Your knees must ache," she said and pulled him up to the bench. "We should put a sponge pad in every bathroom for this kind of thing."

In answer, he just kissed her, his mouth superheated from the shower, and kept it up for long, lovely seconds. "I thought I told you not to do that," he chided gently.

"I couldn't help it."

"You never do what I tell you to do."

"And that's what you love about me."

"Ah, Sugar. There's so much more I love about you." He

smiled and his eyes were warmer than the water pouring down on them. "I guess we'll just have to keep it up until you get it right," he said with a weary sigh, his eyes twinkling with fire and affection. He lifted her into his arms and she put her arms around his neck, loving his strength, the way she felt safe to rest in his arms.

He carried her to the vanity, yanked down a towel for her to sit on, then dried her with a second one with slow, careful strokes. "Do you know how beautiful you are?"

"You make me feel that way."

"Men follow you like dogs, remember?"

"If I went out like this, maybe," she said, so dazed and happy she didn't know what to do with herself.

Gage dried himself quickly, then carried her to the bed, where she stretched out on the cool satin sheets. Gage lay beside her, heat blazing in his eyes and she couldn't wait to give him some of the pleasure he'd given her.

She rose on her knees and guided him inside her, happy when his eyes rolled back in his head in reaction. She rocked up and down on him, enjoying every groan and thrust she earned.

After a few moments, though, he pressed his thumb to her nub and thrust up into her and the sensation was so powerful she gasped and her inner muscles knotted in sudden spasm.

"I hope you're not doing what I think you're doing," he warned, struggling for breath.

"I'm *noooot*... Absolutely *noooot*." But she fell forward against his chest, quivering into an orgasm that he soon joined, pulsing into her body in sweet spasms.

Just as they finished, Gage reached behind her and tugged gently on her opening, which nudged her into another startling release.

"You're being a very bad girl," he breathed, while she quivered through the ecstasy of it.

"You're punishing me, *riiight?*" she managed to say, amazed at herself and him.

"With everything I've got," he said, turning her so they were spooning. He separated the cheeks of her bottom and slid into her, bringing his hands around to stroke her with the fingers of both hands, so that she was soon gasping and twitching out of control. She couldn't even pretend not to come. He joined her again, groaning her name.

How had this happened?

He'd invoked the command to not come like a magic spell, but she knew it was more than that. She'd just let Gage in, let her feelings go and she'd climaxed…again and again.

She was limp with exhaustion, so physically sated she didn't think she could move.

Was this love? Maybe it was just the relief of finally taking something they'd denied themselves. Maybe it was just great sex—great because they knew each other so well. All she could think of to say was, "Thank you."

Gage chuckled softly. "No, no. Thank *you.*"

"But you don't understand. What happened was…new for me. How did you know…what I needed?" She felt funny talking about it.

"I just realized things work better when you drive."

"What does that mean?"

"Don't you remember when we were looking at properties for the resort? You had to be behind the wheel. You were exhausted and frustrated, but you wouldn't let me take over."

"That was because you're a better navigator. I can't read a map to save my soul." She remembered in the end she'd burst into tears and had to take an exit. Gage sensibly asked directions at a service station, then calmly drove them to their destination. He was so patient, so dependable, so…

"You're safe with me, Sugar. You know that, don't you?" He looked deep into her eyes, willing her to see what he offered.

"I know that." Gage would never hurt her if he could help it. And she would never hurt him, either. But sometimes, no matter what anyone intended, people got hurt. That's why you had to manage yourself, not get carried away, keep an exit strategy in mind. What was her exit strategy now?

Maybe she didn't need one. Right now she was just too tired, satisfied, too awestruck to figure it out.

For now, she would just let it be.

GAGE HELD SUGAR tightly against him, hardly able to contain his joy. Whooping "yes," he knew, would ruin the mood. He intended to make no sudden moves that might scare away his skittish kitten of a lover.

He couldn't believe his good fortune. He'd been headed back to tell Sugar he was leaving and she'd thrown herself into his arms. *I want to try.* What a miracle. It took two to make love work and she'd joined him.

And now she was so relaxed in his arms. She'd given in to her feelings, given in to him. Everything would be better now. Happiness would settle around her and she'd stop fighting so hard. Now they would run the resort together, all strife and struggle gone, in perfect harmony. Well, not perfect, but they'd stop having stupid arguments over everything. With the tension of unmet desires out of the way, it would be smooth sailing from here on out.

To think he'd almost given up. *Perhaps you do not want the climb?* Maybe Erika had a point there.

He had loose ends to tie up, though. Thank God he hadn't told Rionna yes yet. He'd call in the morning and tell her she'd need that headhunter after all. He realized he was grinning into the dark like an idiot.

Should he tell Sugar what had almost happened? That he'd almost gone to work for TravelQuest? Maybe when things were truly settled and she rested more easily in his love.

He buried his nose in her tangled hair and breathed in. He would hold her all night long.

Well, he'd hold her as long as she'd let him.

SUGAR WOKE UP, aware that someone had her tied down and was choking her. Well, not quite. Gage's hand dangled over her face and he'd wrapped his legs around hers.

She fought panic. This was new, so of course it would be scary at first. She forced herself to relax against Gage's warm back, copied his slow, easy breaths. Pretty soon her heart stopped pounding and she felt more normal.

She squinted at the clock: 3:00 a.m. Already she'd broken her pattern, since she never fell asleep with a lover. She went home or sent him there. Not this time.

But maybe that was because they were lying in satin sheets in a jungle fantasy. They'd slipped into a romantic time warp and were far away from their real lives, which, she realized, included a 9:00 a.m. videotaping in Erika's office.

She needed some solid sleep for that. She had to get out of here, get home. She didn't want to wake Gage, so she heaved to the left and away quickly. He smacked his lips, groaned, then settled back down. Whew.

She realized she didn't want to talk too much about the

tentative new situation they were in. It seemed too shaky, too tender. Like a bubble too easy to pop.

She sat up, feet on the floor, and noticed she ached all over. It was all the sex. Her clitoris had gotten such a workout, she should be able to bench-press something big with it.

She felt achy, but peaceful, too. Having an orgasm fully aware of her partner's presence was new for her and worthy of celebration, of overdoing it to the point of exhaustion, for sure.

She looked down at Gage's dear face buried in the pillow, his hair tousled. He looked so childlike and vulnerable and goofy that she grinned, probably looking pretty goofy herself.

Every time he'd made love to her, he'd ordered her not to come. Being the stubborn person she was, she'd disobeyed again and again. Her grin spread even wider and a breathy laugh escaped.

Gage's eyes opened. He smiled and reached for her.

"I've got to get to bed," she said, resisting his hold.

"You are in bed."

"I mean *my* bed, Gage. We have a big day tomorrow and it's almost here."

"So, don't waste another minute. Got the pillow right here." He patted his chest and held out his arms.

"I have to go," she said, forcing herself to stand. She was so light-headed that she wobbled.

Gage braced her, helped her to sit on the edge of the bed. "You can't even walk, Sugar. Come back to bed," he said with a sleepy huskiness that was nearly irresistible. He ran a warm palm, soft from sleep, along her arm, up and down, soothing her, seducing her.

The idea of crawling back under those satin sheets and

disappearing for endless hours sounded delicious. She felt detached from reality, like a boat that had snapped its mooring and slid out to sea. Deep, deep sea.

"We won't sleep and you know it."

Gage didn't answer her, just linked fingers and tugged, coaxing her down and down. She could smell their mingled scents and she wanted to get swallowed up in the warmth of how they were together.

"You're forgetting all we have to do," she said, forcing herself to think. "The consultants come in five days. If you think you can keep me naked and make me forget, it won't work."

"Don't pick a fight with me, Sugar," he said lazily. "We don't have anything to argue about anymore."

She was too dazed to disagree at the moment. Hope had sprung up like an ambitious bit of Johnson grass on a freshly clipped putting green. Hope that this thing with Gage was right, would grow, would last.

She bent to kiss him. "I have to go. That was so nice."

"Nice? It was heaven." He cupped her cheek, holding her gaze in the dim light, pinpoints of light in his dark eyes that seemed to come from deep within. "And it will be even better tomorrow, if you let it."

"Let me decide that, okay?" she said, frowning. She didn't like to be pushed. The twinge of annoyance gave her the strength to stand and dress, her muscles quivering, her head fuzzy.

She zipped up her dress, her back to Gage, but she felt his eyes on her, calling her to him. She whirled on him. "Quit that. Go to sleep, for heaven's sake."

He only smiled, his teeth flashing white in the dim room.

It was as though they were castaways on a private island,

with only the beauty of the place and each other for company. It was like a dream, really, and she was afraid to wake up.

There had to be an adjustment period, right? She'd never felt this way before. Maybe she'd just needed the right man, someone who knew her so well. She'd hold off her doubts as long as she could and just be with Gage until the dream became a reality she could live in.

BECAUSE HE'D SLEPT in the Jungle Bungalow, Gage was early for the videotaping in Erika's office. Exhausted, but happy, he dropped onto one of her chairs and leaned his head against the soft surface, closing his eyes for a few seconds of remembering Sugar.

He hoped no one noticed he was wearing the same clothes as the day before. His sturdy classics looked so much alike, probably no one but Sugar would be able to tell. Sugar had a point about Clinton's second term and his fashion habits. Maybe he should change it up a little. Show her he wasn't a complete fashion throwback. He knew that was a problem for her—that she liked variety and he was so predictable. He was determined to meet her needs, prove to her they could be together despite their differences.

He couldn't believe he had Sugar in his bed, in his arms, in his life. His dream had come true and he couldn't stop pinching himself.

"Hello."

His eyes flew open. Erika loomed over him, appearing again like magic. "Erika. Hi." He got to his feet.

She seemed to look him over carefully. "So, you made it?"

"I beg your pardon?" Was it that obvious? Was it the same clothes, his expression, the just-laid aura about him, the—

"For the videotaping?" She smiled kindly at him.

"Oh, yeah. I'm here. Sure." He blew out a breath.

"And the other?" Her eyes twinkled. "Your partner issue? That is better, I see. Your face is soft, your eyes are tired but happy."

"Yeah. That's working out. Turns out we both want the climb." He was so euphoric he wanted to hug Erika and dance her around the room.

"Then you will appreciate the couples who will be taped. Learn from their stories."

"You think we need lessons?"

"You will see what there is to see," she said, going to greet the video crew, who'd just arrived, followed by the couple.

If Roy and Varla Tortelli had something to teach him, it wasn't about fashion, Gage was sure. Roy was dressed like a used-car salesman in clashing pants and shirt. Varla looked like a visiting princess, with diamonds gleaming from every body part you could attach jewelry to. They seemed happy, though, so maybe that was the lesson.

Roy placed a sample case beside his chair. Gage didn't have time to ask about it because Sugar arrived and his heart banged his ribs.

She seemed to float into view, her face pink, her eyes shiny, as if with a fever. She drank him in, as if he were a stunning piece of art, the way she'd admired the Rodin sculpture, and he would do anything to keep her looking at him like that.

Roy and Varla stood to greet Sugar and she thanked them for being willing to help them with their marketing project.

"It's a pure joy," Varla said, shaking her hand. "Your resort changed our lives. And made us rich."

"Love can be fulfilling, I know," Sugar said breathlessly, glancing at Gage, who nodded, still unable to believe his good fortune.

"Oh, I don't mean that kind of rich," Varla said with a laugh. "I mean stinking rich." She held out her jewelry-bedecked fingers. "Roy discovered sex toys when we were here and now he invents them." She sat beside her husband and patted his hand.

Roy grinned like a kid who'd just scored a hot baseball card. He touched the case beside his chair. "Got some samples right here. When we're done, I'll show you one or two you might want to carry in your shop. We'll give you a good price."

"Sex toys, huh?" Gage said. Hmm. Sugar liked variety. Sex toys offered that. He itched to dig into that case.

"So, shall we get started?" Sugar looked at the videographer, who nodded at his camera guy, then at her.

"Why don't you just tell us your story?" Sugar said to Varla. "How you came to us and what happened for you here."

"Sure. See, Roy is a mechanical engineer and he was a project manager at a big computer company. He made good money and all, but he worked sixty-hour weeks, so that he was so tired at night that, well, he fell asleep before I could even shimmy into something sexy. I was…lonely."

She glanced up at Roy, who kissed her forehead. "So sorry, darlin'."

She patted his hand, then turned to Gage and Sugar. "I saw your brochure at my beauty salon and it just set me on fire. I knew this was our answer. Of course, Roy needed convincing. How could he take vacation? What about the new project? His manager wouldn't like it, etcetera. I told him our marriage hung in the balance."

"I'd never seen her so ferocious," Roy inserted. "So I worked it out with my boss and we went."

"So we get to the front desk and the girl asks us what theme we want—Roman holiday, fairy-tale castle, harem den or whatever…"

"And I can see this whole scene will be crazy pressure and my ulcer flares up."

"So, Roy goes off to get Maalox and leaves me all by myself," Varla said. "I'm turning pink as cotton candy listening to the sexy things at the resort. The minutes tick by and no Roy. How long does it take to buy antacid? I get the room key and all the welcome materials and march right into that gift shop to give him a piece of my mind."

"I was busy," Roy says, chuckling at the memory.

"Very," Varla said. "He's standing at the counter holding this rubbery thing shaped like a you-know-what only with rabbit ears and he looks at me like he's just seen glory."

"I had," Roy said.

"He'd laid out all these devices—a hard plastic rocket thing, a clear one that could be iced or heated, some beads and rings—things I'd never seen before, except on weird e-mail spam. So I asked Roy what he was doing and he said—"

"Getting interested." Roy grinned.

"Just like that, he had the old twinkle in his eyes. So, while he bought all that equipment, I pretended to look at gift cards, blushing and cringing the entire time."

"And we went to our room—"

"Roman Holiday," Varla inserted. "That's the one I chose."

"—and took off from there."

"I changed into my nightie and when I came out of the bathroom Roy was stretched out…naked and…you know…ready…and he was holding one of the dealies and he said to me, he said—"

"I said, 'Let's take this baby for a test drive.'"

"So we did." Varla's face was bright with remembered pleasure. "We tried that one and Roy asked me to describe how it felt and what worked best—faster or slower and what if it had a warming effect—and then we tried the rest of them until I didn't know what hit me."

"Me, either," Roy said, his cheeks red, but he looked so pleased with himself Gage had to smile. "I was figuring out how to improve on the engineering."

"There was a problem, though," Varla said. "The next morning, I woke up and started crying."

"I asked her what was wrong, wasn't it good for her?"

"I was afraid it was all about the toys," Varla said, with a laugh. "I was afraid he only wanted to play with the electronics, not me."

"But that wasn't it. It was about making her feel good and waking myself up at the same time."

"The real problem was that Roy's mind was numb because of his work. There was no creativity. Playing with the engineering in bed with me made him feel alive again."

"So we talked about it," Roy continued, "all that day and all that night—when we weren't otherwise busy—" he nudged Varla affectionately "—and we decided that I needed to get back into design work. We'd have to tighten our belts, I told her, but I had to quit the company."

"I knew it would be worth it if it made Roy happy and kept us close." She sighed. "We didn't plan on Roy inventing sex toys full-time, but it took off so fast that…well, the rest is history."

"The toys woke me up," Roy said. "Kept it interesting,

reminded me what mattered." He hugged Varla against him.

"Spice It Up gave me back my Roy," Varla said. "Staying here saved our marriage and made us rich in every way."

Gage smiled and looked at Sugar, who smiled back.

"That's a wonderful story," she said to the couple. "Thank you so much. I'd like to ask you a few extra questions about things you enjoyed at the resort, if that's okay?"

"Fire away," Varla said.

"While she does that, how about if I take a look at your samples?" Gage said to Roy.

Roy nodded and Gage took him and his sample case into Erika's private office. The first item he found was a skin-surfaced latex glove.

"Ah, the Love Glove," Roy said. "Our biggest seller. Try it on. Vibration tips for each finger, activated by the thumb."

Gage donned the glove and pressed his thumb against his index finger, which vibrated. Hmm. Definite possibilities. For Le Sex Shoppe, of course, but he wanted to surprise Sugar, too.

"Consider that one a gift," Roy said. "You'll find it a treasure, let me tell you."

"I'll bet. I'd like to have Leticia, our gift shop manager, look over your other items, if that's all right."

"I'd be honored."

They discussed some details, then closed up the sample case. Gage kept the Love Glove in his pocket, since he had immediate plans for its use.

12

As they walked Roy and Varla out of Erika's office, Sugar was relieved that she'd managed to focus on their story and not be completely distracted by Gage beside her.

It had been a struggle. They'd only been apart a few hours and she found she *missed* him—his crooked smile, his knowing ways, his warmth, his arms. Just sitting near him had been heaven. She could smell his skin. Every shift of his body made her think about making love with him. She felt drugged, entranced, lost in memory and awareness.

They said goodbye to Roy and Varla, then Gage took her arm and she practically passed out from the rush of it.

"I need a moment with you alone," Gage said in her ear.

Her heart lurched in her chest. Then her phone lurched in her purse.

Gage grabbed it and read the display. "Marketing can wait," he said, dropping it into her bag. "I want to show you something in the tower."

"In the tower?" she said. They had so much work to do, but looking into Gage's wicked eyes she didn't care a bit.

Gage's cell phone sounded. "They can wait, too," he said, not even checking who'd called. He grabbed Roy's sample case and walked her to the elevator.

They stepped inside and Gage turned away, messing

with something in his pocket—his phone?—and when he turned back he wore a mischievous smile. As soon as the door closed, he pulled her into his arms, cupping her bottom through her dress.

Then his hand began to vibrate.

"What is that?" she gasped.

"Roy calls it the Love Glove. Feel good?" He slid it up her back so that her whole body trembled.

"*Verrry* good," she said, as her entire body liquefied. "This is what you wanted to show me?"

"Mmm-hmm. And we're in the elevator. And we're so hot we can't keep our hands off each other."

She turned to him, eyes wide. "Are you…?"

He nodded, pulling her against him, his hand back on her bottom, vibrating deliciously. "How does it go again? We're trying to get to our room, but we can't wait?"

"No, we can't," she said, barely able to speak. "And the elevator takes—"

"Forever," he finished, reaching under her dress now, putting a vibrating finger between the cheeks of her bottom so that she could hardly bear the trembling rush. She felt completely helpless, absolutely in his hands.

"I didn't push the delay button," he whispered in her ear, running his tongue along the edge. "The door could open anytime and we could get caught."

"We could," she echoed. And if he didn't have a good grip on her, she might drop to the floor.

"You like that, don't you? That someone could catch us?"

"Yes," she breathed. "I like that."

The elevator stopped and the door began to open and she instantly changed her mind.

"Should have pushed the delay." Gage straightened her

dress, backed them into the mirrored wall, keeping his hand beneath her skirt buzzing away between the legs.

Two maids, Rosa and Lydia, entered with a cart stacked high with towels. She managed to return their greeting, relieved when they faced the door and spoke in Spanish to each other.

Sugar breathed in the rosemary-mint of the freshly laundered towels and bit her cheek to keep from crying out, pinned as she was to Gage's shivering fingers. She was afraid she'd come right there, standing up, fully clothed, with two chatty witnesses.

Finally the elevator opened and the maids left. Gage slammed his hand on the ten-minute button, shoved up her skirt and stroked her full-on with the Love Glove.

In seconds, she climaxed, muffling her cry against Gage's shirt, completely swept away. "That was so good," she said, gasping for air. Being surprised by the act, by the vibrating toy and almost getting caught had been an utter thrill.

Mirrors reflected them back to each other, as if there were more couples around them, watching them perform.

"We need a room. Now," she said, even though they had phone calls waiting and work to do. "Let's use the model suite." It was the room marketing used for conference planners.

"Yeah." Gage stripped off the glove, grabbed the sample case, and took her arm. They used the master key to get inside and went for the bed, whipping down the covers, knocking pillows every which way, then stripped each other with the same crazy haste. Gage tore her nylons and scraped her thighs getting her panties off and she broke a nail on Gage's pants button.

Finally, finally they tumbled naked onto the bed, Gage

on top. Above him, Sugar noticed their reflection in the ceiling mirror. "Look." She pointed.

He rolled onto his back to see. "Ah. Nice."

"It's your twin fantasy. And one of mine—being watched. It's like we're watching ourselves."

"Two fantasies in one," he said. "Check this out." He motioned at the side of the bed, where the closet doors were mirrors, too. He sat up and so did she, looking at their reflected images in the huge mirror. "We look good together," Gage said, wrapping his arm across her stomach, cupping a breast. He kissed her neck, then looked into the mirror. "I can't believe I have you."

"It's like a dream," she said, afraid to wake up. She felt like she was still holding her breath, suspended again in that time warp. It felt strange and wonderful.

Gage bent down for his pants and pulled out the vibrating glove. She shook her head. She just wanted him.

Misunderstanding, he flipped the latch on the sample case. "Something new?"

"I just want you," she said, stopping his hand.

"We should keep it interesting," he said, a flicker of something—concern?—in his face.

He was afraid she'd get bored. "We're interesting enough on our own, Gage." She hardly remembered the woman who'd claimed to always get restless. She felt so totally here with Gage now.

"I'm glad you think so," Gage said, shifting so she was sitting on his lap facing the mirror, their feet on the floor. He cupped her breasts, teasing each tip with a finger. She leaned into him, her head under his chin, and reached back to trace his lips with a finger. He sucked it in and she gasped at the warm suction, the suggestive pull.

His hands slid down her stomach, to her sex, which he brushed lightly with first one index finger, then the other.

She watched him touch her, her sex swollen and wet, eager for him.

"I love how you feel, how wet you get for me."

She arched against his touch, moving against his fingers, which rubbed her, priming her, sending jolts of urgent need along her nerves, readying her for release.

She'd never seen anything more sexy in her life, her body rocking against his fingers, his dark eyes so hungry for her. She moved faster and he matched her. She wanted more, so she spread her legs, opened to him.

Sensing her need to be filled, he pushed a finger into her. She gasped and twisted against his movement.

"That's it, baby. Come for me. I love to watch you come." His eyes drew her in, wouldn't let her go, not ever, and she loved that.

Her release came like a snapped wire. She gave a sharp cry and her entire body went limp.

He held her up, supporting her, kissing her neck, her favorite spot. "Mmm, that was nice."

He'd told her to come and she had. They didn't need the game of denial. They didn't need elevators or mirrors or a fantasy. They only needed this—this miracle of being in love.

She turned her body and rose to her knees so they were face-to-face, a position she'd never before wanted to try because it seemed too personal.

With Gage, it felt right. She eased him into her body, lowering herself until her bottom reached his thighs. He groaned with pleasure, a lazy smile on his face, and she wrapped her arms around him, loving the way their bodies met, the way he filled her completely.

"I need your eyes," he said, leaning back to look into her face.

She looked straight at him, giving him her eyes and the rest of her, too. All of her.

As if he knew what she was thinking, Gage thrust up, deeper into her body, his thighs trembling beneath her. She felt the force of him inside her, his arms holding her, his eyes adoring her. She had all of him, too.

Emotion swelled inside her, filled her heart the way Gage filled her body, climbed her throat and had to be shared. "I love you," she whispered.

He stilled, took in her words, his eyes shining with pure joy. "I love you," he said. "But you know that."

"And I'm so glad." They remained that way for a few glorious seconds, seeing everything in each other's eyes. Then desire built again and they moved, rocked together, spurred on by the feelings they'd shared.

In a few seconds, she felt Gage tense, ready to release and that brought on her own orgasm, easy as breathing. They came together, rocking and rocking in the endless float of pleasure, coming down finally, finding themselves in each other's arms, holding each other tightly.

She'd never climaxed at the same time as her lover before. Certainly not without helping herself and never while looking into his eyes. She couldn't believe how easy it had been, how natural, how right. Because they were in love.

There was something, though, some worry at the edge of her mind. Something about the dream of this, the distance she felt from her usual life, from herself. She fought the idea, focused instead on how their breathing matched perfectly. Their heartbeats, too. Even their thoughts. They weren't so different, after all.

Then her phone rang. Gage's, too, and she remembered distantly that they'd both gotten calls earlier—way back in another lifetime—that they'd ignored.

Gage pulled out of her body and went for her phone first, then his.

Saved? The usual thought rose in her mind, but it was too late this time. The phone calls hadn't saved them. They hadn't wanted to be saved. She accepted her phone from Gage, smiling like a goofball.

She shook her head, struggling to get back to who she was and where she was—at work in the middle of a busy day, with very little accomplished and the hours flying by.

They both said hello at the same time, sounding equally dazed.

"It's Maribeth, Sugar." Her marketing manager sounded impatient. "Didn't you get my message?"

"Sorry. No. I was, um, busy." She glanced at Gage, who looked extremely tense.

"That won't work…. I'll have to call you back," he said. "No. My plans have changed." Who was he talking to so secretively? He didn't want her to overhear?

"What is it?" she said to Maribeth, struggling to focus on her own call. Since when had she obsessed about Gage's conversations?

"I need your feedback on the ads," Maribeth said. "We have to book today, if we want the discount. Also, you need to talk to Daisy. She's cutting corners on bookings. If I hadn't checked, she would have double-booked two groups the second week in December. You really need to sort her out."

"I'll talk to her, don't worry." Sugar got off the bed, fighting to clear her head. She should have handled this conflict already. She'd been too preoccupied with the franchise and with Gage, who'd hung up his phone and was pulling on his pants, frowning, head down.

"Can you get down here?" Maribeth said. "Where are you anyway?"

"Oh. Uh." She forced her attention back to Maribeth. "We're up in the tower rooms. Checking on the, uh, demo suite. We'll be right there."

Gage's phone rang again and he answered it, still dressing.

"Gage is with you?" Maribeth asked.

"We had that videotaping and we just headed up here." *And we've been naked ever since.*

"We're on our way, Brittany," Gage said to his caller.

They both clicked off.

"Brittany's panicking over a call from the linen service," Gage explained. "She claims they're worried about us paying our bill. What's with her? Every little problem and she acts like the world's coming to an end."

"It was your pep talk, I think. She's been so nervous lately. Maribeth and Clarice, too. Everyone's on edge. It's probably the tension between us."

Gage smiled. "Thank God that's over now." He reached for her, that slow, sexy look on his face. This was simple to him. They'd fallen in love, now everything was easy. She knew that wasn't true, knew, also, that she wasn't quite herself.

"We've got to get to work," she said, avoiding his arms. She noticed the mess they'd made of the room, pillows tossed everywhere. "Help me clean up."

He gathered pillows into a pile.

"We can't be doing this kind of thing in the middle of the day," she said, roughly yanking the bedspread into place.

"Why not?" He shrugged.

"Because we have responsibilities. We've got staff frantic, looking all over for us. Maribeth and Daisy are at each other's throats."

"It wasn't that big a deal. We'll straighten that out."

"It could have been," she said.

"Whatever happens, we'll handle it," he said.

"You can't possibly know that." Sometimes his placid nature got on her nerves. Some things *were* a big deal, dammit.

He stopped, pillow in hand. "What are you doing, Sugar? Don't scare yourself."

"I'm not. We just can't drop the ball now because of what's going on between us."

"We're not dropping any ball." He went to her and pulled her into his arms. "Sugar, stop."

She resisted, refusing to melt into him again.

"We're on the same team," Gage said, running his hands up and down her arms. "Everything will be easier now. We're together. We don't need to argue over every little thing."

"We don't argue. We debate. We discuss. We work things out."

He chuckled. "That was before. We're different now."

"There's nothing wrong with how we were. We were great partners before."

"We'll be even better now."

She remembered the partnership fantasy Gage had shared in their meeting with Erika. He saw them hand in hand skipping past rainbows, cartoon bunnies in their wake, bluebirds circling their heads. That was so not her view.

She got a queasy feeling in her stomach. "We have to keep

what we're doing in perspective, Gage. We can't get over-whelmed by it. Look at all we have to do for the consultants."

"What's the rush? Postpone the meeting." He shrugged.

"Postpone it? We're lucky they could fit us in."

"If they can make money, they'll squeeze us in, Sugar. Don't worry about that. We can slow it down if we need to. Or cancel, for that matter."

"I still want the franchise, Gage."

"And I still think it's a bad idea." His voice had an edge and that made her mad.

"We had a deal, Gage. Do you think you've won? Because I'm in love with you we'll forget about the franchise?"

"Not exactly. I think you were restless, looking for a change, when what was really going on was that we wanted to be together. We're together, so—"

"You think my looking out for the future is just restless-ness? I was bored so I decided to throw everything in turmoil? You think I'm that shallow?"

"Not shallow. Just confused. We both were. I was ready to leave, remember? But now I'm happy to be here with you." Something flickered in his face, some doubt. The resort had never been as vital to Gage as it was to her. She'd chalked it up to his laid-back personality, but maybe it was more than that.

And his attitude pissed her off. This conversation was not a debate or discussion or their usual banter. This was an argument, pure and simple, and she did not like it a bit.

Gage's face softened suddenly. "We're not at war, Sugar. Falling in love with me isn't losing. I'll hear your consul-tants out, okay?" he said. "Let's not fight."

She softened. "I'm sorry. I guess I don't know how to act."

"Neither of us does. Maybe we need some time to

ourselves. Away from the resort. So we can get our priorities straight."

Her insides churned as though she was back in the washing machine from Expo Night. "Our priorities are straight, Gage. Spice It Up is the most important thing. That doesn't stop because we happen to be sleeping together."

"We *happen* to be sleeping together? This feels that temporary?"

"I didn't mean it that way, I just… It's new." She looked at him, not wanting to hurt him, but unhappy that the ground seemed to be shifting under her feet. "It doesn't seem quite real."

"Yeah. I get that." He tried to smile.

"Now we need to get downstairs before the staff really freaks out." She straightened his collar, trying to smile. "You should leave first, so no one suspects us."

"They'll find out soon enough we're together, right?"

She froze. "Let's give it a little time. We have to get used to it first, don't we?"

"I suppose."

But she could tell she'd hurt his feelings. She hadn't meant to, but she didn't like how many assumptions Gage was making. "We'll tell them when we're both ready."

"Okay." He sighed and his eyes shifted, reminding her of that strange phone call he'd taken. He'd wanted to hide it from her. Why? And why was she all of a sudden afraid to ask?

You're in love. It's new. And not easy. Everything seemed different, including things she'd liked just the way they were.

13

WHEN HE COULD escape to his office, Gage called Rionna back. She'd phoned at a terrible moment earlier, interrupting him and Sugar in bed.

When Rionna answered, he apologized for being so abrupt and told her he'd decided to stay at Spice It Up.

"I'm very disappointed, Gage," she said. "This would be a great spot for you." Then she hesitated. "Did something happen?"

He and Sugar had decided to be together, but he wasn't going to share that with Rionna. Not before the resort staff even knew. "We worked out some issues."

"That's good, I guess. If it's what you want. You struck me as dissatisfied, open to the opportunity."

"Dissatisfied? No. We're a good team." He was startled that Rionna had that impression. "I'm happy here."

"And you're loyal. I understand."

She thought only loyalty held him here? Maybe he'd sounded more eager than he'd meant to. "I wish you the best of luck," he said. "I know it would be a great job." Hell, he sounded downright wistful.

"Thanks, Gage. If you change your mind, let me know. By the way, are you making big changes over there? One of our PR guys says you're revamping your marketing. Booking problems?"

"No. Not at all." The hospitality industry churned gossip like nobody's business. "It was time for an update, that's all. Speaking of rumors, our concierge is convinced you sent us a spy."

"That's a good one." She laughed. "Like we'd want to offer sex classes to harried business execs."

"That's what I figured."

"You can't believe everything you hear," she said.

"No, you can't."

Or everything you felt, either, he realized as the day wore on. He and Sugar tiptoed around each other, tentative and nervous and careful. Sugar seemed to be expecting an argument every time he opened his mouth.

At the end of the day, Sugar closed his office door with her body and smiled, clearly trying to get past the tension. "So, I'm done for the day. You?"

He nodded.

"So what do we do now?" she said, looking uncertain.

"This," he said and cupped her face to kiss her. She softened against him in apparent relief.

"Sounds good."

"Let's go to bed." He put his arms around her, breathing in her hair, trying to make her feel like it would all work out now that they had each other. Why was this still so hard?

She tensed in his arms. "Mine or yours?"

"Mine is closer." The sooner they got naked, the faster they'd forget this odd friction between them.

She leaned back to look at him. "My bed is bigger and softer." She was trying to tease, but he could tell she was uneasy.

"The housekeeper just changed my sheets. And how do you know my bed isn't soft?"

"Because you're a firm mattress kind of guy."

"Touché. Better traction." It was the usual banter, but it felt flat as day-old champagne.

"We have the taping early in the morning. I don't want to have to rush home to get ready."

"So don't. I have a great shower."

"I'll need to change clothes."

"We'll set an alarm. I'll even drive you over and you can sleep on the way."

She blinked at him, frowned, then opened her mouth to object again.

"Why are we arguing?" he said, forcing a smile. "Let's go to your place. Whatever makes you happy."

"You're right. This is dumb," she said, breathing out an exasperated breath. "Your house is closer. I don't know why it matters."

But it did. Every word seemed highly charged. The afternoon's quarrel lingered between them like cooking smells. The tension about the franchise…the tentativeness of their feelings…how committed each was to the resort… what, exactly, being in love meant.

He led the way to his house in his car, even though he'd offered to drive Sugar home and to the resort. She wanted to hang on to some control, he could tell. He didn't know how to fix this, except to love her with all his might.

It didn't get easier at his house. Sugar perched stiffly at his kitchen counter while he poured wine neither of them drank. They kissed, got aroused, but their bodies were tight, their movements awkward. They clunked teeth and bumped noses.

"Let's hit those crisp sheets," he said, leading her by the hand. She stood uncertainly in the doorway, like a cat about to flee, then removed her earrings and set them on the bureau.

He wanted to make her feel comfortable, so he pulled out one of the bottom drawers. "This one's empty if you want to bring some things over." He went to the closet and opened it. "And there's lots of room here." His clothes took up barely a third of the space. "Maybe you can take me shopping. Help me pick out something post-Clinton?"

She laughed tightly. "Sure."

"Or I can bring some things to your place," he said. "If you'd prefer. Or both. Both is better."

"Let's not rush this, Gage." Her voice was sharp.

"I'm not asking you to elope, Sugar," he said, a little angry. "I'm trying to make it convenient for us to spend time together."

She sucked in a breath. "Sure. I know. It's just so…new." She waved her hands in the air.

"I know." He put his arms around her and kissed her softly. "Remember me?"

She sighed, melting against him a little. "Yes. I do." But her kiss was tentative and she didn't soften all the way. Where was the intense rush, the frantic kissing, the crushing embrace, the moans, the gasps? Gone, like they'd never happened.

They undressed, strangely shy, and climbed into bed together. "What time do you want to get up?" he asked her, rolling toward his alarm clock. He set it at the time she requested, then pulled her into his arms.

"I'm pretty tired," she said gently.

"Me, too," he said, knowing she could feel the lie of his erection against her stomach.

"You're not that tired." She chuckled, her old self for a moment. "We could try." She kissed him, reached for him.

Maybe sex was the answer. Sex had showed Sugar

how she felt about him. But there was too much hesitation in her face.

"Let's get some sleep tonight," he said. "We've got plenty of time."

She nodded against his chest and he focused on how good it was to have her in his arms.

Be careful what you wish for.

He had Sugar in his life, in his bed at last—all he'd wanted in the world—and he had no idea what to do next. He'd assumed that once Sugar admitted her feelings, let love grow, everything would smooth out.

Sugar seemed to treat falling in love like a defeat, like she had lost their bet or deal or whatever it was. She'd backed away, scared or sorry, and that feeling that a shoe was about to drop came again into his heart. A big, heavy shoe.

A boot. With spikes.

When the alarm went off in the morning, Gage found Sugar gone. She'd made coffee and left a note, but he could almost feel her relief at beating him up and out.

He was surprised that he was relieved, too.

Getting up early meant he was early for the testimonial taping, so he helped the videographers set up for Sam and Sylvie Dale in the same place they'd taped the first couple. It took a while and involved lots of wires and reflective umbrellas and they were all set when Sugar finally arrived.

"What are you doing?" she demanded, hands on her hips. "This is wrong. We have to move the set."

"We're fine, Sugar," he said. "We don't want to slow the crew." He gave her a look. *They're on the clock.*

"We need to create the illusion of multiple locations," she insisted, ignoring him.

"Can I speak to you?" He motioned her to Erika's office and shut the door behind her, holding in his frustration. "This is a promotional piece, not an entry for Sundance. We don't want to pay any more than we have to. They're set up."

"You should have waited for me."

"You were late," he snapped.

"You started early."

"You're being obstinate."

"*I'm* being obstinate? You don't even care about the video. You just don't want your authority to be questioned."

"The longer we argue, the more this costs us."

"Exactly." Sugar was breathing hard, furious with him.

"Why are we fighting?" he whispered.

"I don't know," she said, her voice full of despair. "We never fight."

"We do now," he said. And he knew why. Love had changed Sugar, changed their partnership.

Erika popped her head in. "They're waiting for you."

"We'll be right there," he said.

Erika looked from one to the other. "I have an hour this afternoon if you two need a progress check?"

"No, thanks." They both spoke at once—it was the first thing they'd agreed on since making love in the tower suite.

"WE'D BETTER GET OUT there," Sugar said to Gage, miserable and scared about what was happening between them.

"Yeah," he said grimly and marched out the door.

They were fighting. Not debating. Not discussing. This would not result in a good decision. It would end in hurt feelings. It would tear them apart.

Being in love was turning out awful. Even when they tried to be nice, they ended up arguing. Their usual back-and-forth banter felt like hurtful jabs. They'd quarreled over whose house to go to, for God's sake.

And once there, Gage treated her as though she were made of glass and she acted tense and numb. Lying on Gage's hard mattress, telling him when to set the alarm had felt a lifetime away from the glory of making love face-to-face in the tower suite.

She'd treated Gage's kind offer of closet space like an attack, hurting his feelings while she was at it. She'd never been in love before, after all. She had no idea how to do it.

Or even if she could.

That was the crux of it.

For now, she had work to do. She followed Gage out to the new location she'd insisted on—wasting time and money, even though the first setup had been fine—to interview Sylvie and Sam Dale from St. Paul, Minnesota.

She greeted the couple, apologizing for the delay, and soon she and Gage were seated in the observer chairs.

Erika had told Sugar the couples had *lessons* for her. What had she learned from Roy and Varla Tortelli? Better sex through electronics? More like *keep it lively*. That's what Gage had attempted with Roy's Love Glove and her elevator fantasy. That was sweet of him. She smiled at him, sitting beside her, hoping to ease the tension.

He smiled back, trying, too.

Now it was time for Sylvie and Sam Dale's story and whatever lesson Erika thought they had for Sugar and Gage.

"We're a little nervous, I guess," Sylvie said. She was a petite woman in a trim suit and hat, her hair in a pageboy. "Our story is kind of funny, isn't it, Sam?" She had the melodic voice of someone who sang in a church choir and deep dimples.

"I sure wouldn't call it funny." Sam, big and barrel-chested in a plaid shirt, hugged his wife close.

What a sweet couple. They disagreed with love and affection. Maybe that was the lesson. Maybe their stay at Spice It Up taught them to be forgiving and—

"Well I would!" Sylvie snapped. "Do we need more than two hours in the Control Room, Mr. Dale?"

"No, Mrs. Dale," Sam said humbly.

Oh. Well. Sylvie and Sam were into domination and submission. Sugar was surprised. She glanced at Gage, who suppressed a grin.

"So, shall we start?" Sugar nodded at the camera guy to roll tape, then turned to the couple. "Tell us how your stay here helped your marriage."

"You start, sweetheart," Sam said. "You're the boss."

"Never forget it." She smiled, easing the put-on terseness.

"I never do." He sighed happily.

Hmm.

"You see, I never really liked…S-E-X," Sylvie said to Sugar. "It just seemed embarrassing and awkward and, well, what was the point?"

"You're making it sound bad, Sylvie."

"It was bad. The kissing was okay, but before long, you got on top, did your thing and, bam, it was all over."

"Now, sweetheart, **you're** giving these folks the wrong idea."

"The real problem was that I didn't know what I wanted. We married young, and Sammie got transferred right away. I was pregnant, so it didn't make sense for me to get a teaching credential and a job with a baby on the way. So I was just a housewife. And because Sam worked so hard for me and the baby, when he wanted sex, I went along, even when I wasn't in the mood."

"I didn't think you even liked sex."

"Well, I didn't. Not then. But then the neighbor asked me to a Bunko game with her friends and after a few apple martinis, they started up about orgasms and how to have them and my hair just curled, let me tell you."

Sam rolled his eyes.

"One of the ladies had been to Spice It Up and she gave me a brochure and loaned me a book she'd bought when she was here and I decided a trip was just what we needed."

"Without explaining one blessed thing to me," Sam said.

"You should have heard him when we got here. 'What have you done, Sylvie?' he said, all gruff, his face beet-red. 'This place is all about sex!' And I said, 'Maybe we can get some…you know…pointers.'"

"She tells me to have an open mind. Good Lord Almighty, I wanted to get the hell out of there right smart."

"He went on about how we were paying top dollar for workshops we wouldn't go to and did I even know what this hotel was all about?" Sylvie said, then leaned forward conspiratorially. "Of course I did, but I didn't have the nerve to explain it to him. He wanted our money back, but I wanted to learn something and I told him he was going to learn with me, dammit. And when I said that, he gave in."

She stopped and widened her eyes at the memory. "I got the funniest feeling. You know. *That* feeling. Over bossing him around. I yanked his arm and he looked surprised and…real sexy. And I liked that."

"She had the fire in her eyes," Sam said.

"It didn't take Erika, bless her heart, twenty minutes

to figure out what made me hum. She told me I had to have power over sex and she sent us to the Control Room, but I was intimidated by all the equipment and the hand-cuffs and such."

"Then Sylvie spotted this DVD in our room."

"It had a woman giving her partner a little spanking. And I just got so hot that I pointed at the screen and whis-pered, '"That. I want that."'"

"I argued at first, but Sylvie marched to the gift shop and bought handcuffs and ordered me to strip and lie down."

"I was so proud of myself. I said, 'Sam Dale, I will cook your food and keep your house and raise your children, but I will have sex my way.'"

"Then she handcuffed me to the bed and—"

"I took charge. I kissed him the way I wanted to be kissed—no tongues flopping around. And I rubbed around on him, stopping when I wanted to, moving when I preferred. It was amazing. And then I…well, I did the oral thing—"

"Let's not do details, Sylvie."

"I will if I want to," she snapped. Then she patted his hand. "They get the point. I got what I wanted the way I wanted and for as long as I wanted it. And it was—"

"Spectacular," Sam finished.

"It was the start of an adventure. Sam got better at sex."

"And Sylvie got better at ordering me around."

"Spice It Up gave me back my power. I thought because Sam was the breadwinner that I was beneath him."

"It's not a competition, Sylvie. I want to take care of you. I want to support our family."

"And I want to take care of you, too, Sammie."

"Oh, you do. You surely do."

"Mmm." Sylvie kissed him. "So, anyway, maybe I'm

low on the income scale, but I'm on top in the bedroom and that works just fine for us. We trade off some, too, now," she added, "since we figured out how love makes it all fair."

Interesting, Sugar thought. Sylvie's issue was power. Maybe that's what had happened to Sugar. She felt as though she'd lost control and that made every disagreement with Gage into a power struggle. Maybe all they needed was a Control Room session or a pair of handcuffs. That sounded far too simple. But it was worth discussing with Gage, who, right now was apologizing to the third couple for making them wait.

14

GAGE WATCHED Sugar find a seat beside him for the final taping. Larry and Patti Mitchell were getting their mikes clipped to their clothes.

"I'm sorry I caused the delay," Sugar whispered in his ear.

"We'll work it out." Like Sylvie Dale, Sugar had power issues. Erika had a point about the couples having lessons for them. He wondered if Sugar realized it and what, exactly, they should do about it. He'd wear manacles and a dog collar if it would help Sugar work this out in her mind.

"So, we're ready?" Sugar nodded at the video crew. "Thank you both for agreeing to be taped," she said to the couple.

"So glad we could help," Larry said. He was a good-looking guy who knew it, but didn't make a big deal about it.

"Anything to help other couples not make the mistake we almost did." His wife, Patti, had a no-bullshit look that reminded Gage of Sugar, though she wasn't nearly as pretty.

"We were lucky we figured it out in time." Larry looked down at his wife with pure love, as if his life depended on her happiness.

"We were. So lucky." Patti smiled up at Larry, loving him flaws and all. That's what Gage wanted with Sugar, but it seemed so far away at the moment.

Sugar invited them to tell their story and Patti spoke first. "It all started with the babysitter. Larry had the hots for her." She shot him a look.

"That wasn't it."

"Sure it was. She watched our son after preschool while I worked part-time. She was pretty, with a darling giggle and long, blond hair. And she was on the JV cheer squad, which, of course, was Larry's Achilles' heel, since he was a football star back in the day."

Larry smiled. "High school was good to me."

"Whatever." Patti rolled her eyes. No bullshit, like Gage had thought. "So, Larry got home before me on those days and he and Bonnie sometimes were still chattering away when I got there. One day her car wouldn't start and when Larry offered to take her home, the look on his face stopped my heart."

"It was you I pictured in a cheerleader uniform."

"Meanwhile," Patti continued, "Larry was just dialing in our sex, his mind a million miles away. Finally I couldn't take it anymore. Whatever was wrong, I knew we had to fix it, so I asked the scary question."

"She asked me if I was sleeping with the babysitter, can you believe that?" Larry asked.

"Why not? She was sixteen and perky, no cellulite or puckered nipples or Cesarean scar. Any man would want her."

"It was just a fantasy," Larry said morosely. "I was seeing you, Patti. Your face. Your body."

"At first I cried. Then I yelled. Then I stopped talking altogether."

"I could tell we were in trouble," Larry said, "so I hit

the self-help aisles in the bookstore, read about fantasies and one of the books mentioned Spice It Up."

"He showed me the Web site and I said, 'Let's go.' Why not? I'm a practical person and if this worked, then great. So we decided to do Larry's fantasy. We reserved a grotto. I put on a blond wig and a cheerleader outfit and Larry wore a football uniform and we pretended we were on the field after a big game."

"Except Patti laughed."

"I felt stupid standing there getting felt up, while I told him how great his touchdowns were. I'm not an actress."

"Ruined the whole fantasy, believe me," Larry said.

"So we tried again. Cop and hooker, except when he asked me what I charged—"

"She made a joke."

"I said, 'Visa or MasterCard?' I couldn't help it."

"So I wilted."

"Then we did doctor and patient, but I got ticklish and Larry pouted."

"I was trying to save our marriage."

"With idiot games." She shook her head. "The problem was that Larry was bored and I wasn't. I told him I was done playing and he should find another playmate."

"I didn't know what to do, so I asked Erika for an emergency session."

"I spent the day thinking about being single and that night I marched right into the bar to try it out. I ordered a double rum and Coke and drank it fast, but everyone was paired up, dancing and laughing, and I was so lonely and my heart was breaking. I refused to cry. I was mad, dammit. Life went on, even if Larry didn't want me anymore. I was young and decent-looking and—"

"You're gorgeous, Patti. You take my breath away."

Patti patted his thigh. "Anyway, I was about to leave in despair when this hot guy sat beside me and asked me why I looked so sad. Turned out his wife was bored with him, too."

"What a coincidence." Larry grinned.

Patti slugged him. "So we talked and we had so much in common that I thought, *I could sleep with this guy.*"

"Meanwhile, I was watching from across the bar," Larry said. "Erika told me I had to make the fantasy real for Patti and the guy was an Intimacy Associate. The plan was for me to order him to leave my wife alone."

"Larry assumed I wouldn't let the guy kiss me." Now Patti grinned.

"Not only that, but she kissed him back," Larry said. "And I just came unglued. For the first time, I realized I could lose my Patti. My rock. My life."

"He was a good kisser, too." Patti sighed with pleasure, though her eyes sparkled with mischief.

"Don't even joke," Larry said.

"So Larry comes over and practically decks the guy."

"The IA kept telling me to lighten up, signaling that I was overacting, but I couldn't stop myself."

"It was kind of sweet," Patti said. "When I found out what was really going on."

"Once I realized how easily I could lose Patti, I changed completely. Screw the fantasies. I had to hang on to her."

"It wasn't all Larry. I was taking him for granted. I saw that I had to keep things interesting, too. So, sometimes I bring up the pool man or how cute my boss's ass is in khakis and we're off to the races."

"Works like a charm," Larry said.

These two had figured out what mattered, Gage saw. Worked through their problems. Surely he and Sugar could, too.

After the interview, they wrapped up with the video crew, arranging to see the rough cut of the video, then Gage and Sugar were alone in his office.

"So, feel like trying on that cheerleader outfit?" he said, thinking he'd ease into the discussion with humor.

"Wasn't that the saddest story?" Sugar said. "They had to scare themselves into staying together."

"That's not it at all. They figured out that what matters is each other, not fantasies or babysitters or fancy resorts. That's a happy ending."

"Their relationship is based on fear, Gage. And I understand that completely." She paused and gave him such an anguished look his heart cramped in his chest. "When you said you might leave the resort, that was how I felt. And I panicked."

"What are you saying, Sugar?" He dreaded her answer.

"I'm saying that maybe we're together because we're afraid to move on."

Frustration made him want to punch the wall. "What are you doing?" he asked tightly. "Why are you picking us apart, treating everything as a sign that we can't be together?"

"We can't ignore the truth."

"You're looking for an excuse. These couples have shown us how to work things out, not that it's hopeless."

"I'm doing my best, Gage," she said levelly. "And so are you. What if our best isn't enough?"

"We have to want the climb," he said, repeating Erika's advice, wishing like hell it didn't fit so well.

He was tired and confused and a little angry. He'd just

turned down a great job to stay with Sugar, dammit, but he knew full well that, even if he felt safe to tell her, she'd use it to prove how they couldn't be together.

15

SUGAR WAS BUSY for the next two days putting the finishing touches on the presentation for the consultants. She was glad her mind was occupied. Every time she thought of Gage she fell into despair.

What if their best wasn't enough? The question hung in the air like a sour note held too long. Gage had been angry, as if he resented her already. For not trying? For making him stay? She couldn't bring herself to ask.

Tuesday night, they slept together at her house, but they were tentative with each other and didn't make love. Wednesday night, they slept apart because they needed to catch up on sleep.

Thursday, the night before the consultant visit, Gage had his regular poker night, so they didn't need to discuss sleeping arrangements. She was relieved.

Which was a terrible, terrible sign.

Restless at home, she missed her friends. Their thirty-fifth birthday prickly-pear margarita night seemed years ago. Esmeralda had e-mailed her about her new job managing the Dream A Little Dream Foundation and Autumn must be closing in on finals. She probably needed a pep talk for that, so Sugar hit the speed dial number.

"Hey, Sugar."

The whiskey sound of Autumn's voice warmed Sugar to her toes. With a jolt, she realized *she* was the one who needed the pep talk. "So how's school?" she asked her friend.

"Just great. I think I aced my finals and I'm still pinching myself."

"I'm not surprised. You're pretty smart for a stripper."

"Hey, hey, watch yourself." But Autumn's voice was light with joy.

"So, that's the *head* part of Esmie's prediction for you. What about *heart and hearth.*"

"Lord, Esmie." They laughed, sharing an affectionate skepticism about their friend's psychic messages. "Who knows? For hearth, I'm moving to Copper Corners for a month."

Autumn explained that she'd agreed to take a temporary job in a small town working for the mayor, who was the brother of a friend of hers. A fellow stripper would be there, too, and wanted her company. Autumn always took care of her friends.

"And as for heart…forget it. I don't have time for heart."

"I know exactly what you mean." Sugar had let hers take charge and she felt lost and confused.

"What happened?"

She filled Autumn in on the situation with Gage.

"You know what I'm going to tell you," Autumn said.

"Stick with what I know best?" Autumn and Sugar shared a focus on work over emotions. "That's the franchise. The meeting is tomorrow. Maybe that will turn Gage around."

"Or not. The point is you're strong, you know what you want and you can go for it, with or without a man."

"True," Sugar said, feeling better hearing the words.

She just wished she could have both—what she wanted *and* a man.

"You okay?" Autumn asked.

"Talking to you helps." Romantic commitment might be a problem for Sugar, but she was hooked to her friends for life.

"You figure Gage is what you've been ignoring? From Esmie's reading?"

"Who knows? Cut it out or I'm going to think you believe that stuff."

"Esmie's got something going, you gotta admit that."

"I guess." And sometimes Sugar wished she'd just keep it to herself.

She was deeply asleep late that night when the phone rang. "Hello…?" She could hardly get out the word.

"Don't scare yourself."

"Esmie? Is that you?" She sat up in bed, pushing her hair out of her eyes.

"I had a dream," Esmeralda said. "A man was chasing you with a bouquet of roses and you ran straight off the cliff."

"It's the middle of the night, Esmie. Couldn't this wait for morning?"

"Sorry, hon. The spirit never sleeps. I have to speak the dream before it fades. Do you get the message?"

"Stay away from cliffs? Sure." She remembered the roses Gage had bought her on Expo night. *So you'll stop and smell them.* And Esmie had said something about opening her eyes and smelling roses.

"Sugar," Esmie's tone was stern. "Don't run from your happiness."

"I'll try not to," Sugar said, lying back on the pillow. "So what's new with you?" She did not want to talk about Gage with Esmeralda. She wasn't ready for her advice.

Esmie was excited about the new job she would soon start for a foundation to fund people's dreams, but nervous about handling the business aspects of the work. She still expected her ex-husband to return the way the psychics had predicted. Sugar reminded her friend that she needed to trust herself and her own intuition when it came to work or love affairs. Sugar knew that it would take more than that to convince her stubborn friend who, for all her confidence in helping others in their lives, was clueless when it came to her own.

The next morning, despite her interrupted sleep, Sugar awoke full of hope for today's meeting. Maybe it was Autumn's pep talk or Esmeralda's dream, but she had a feeling that things would work out fine.

She got to the resort early and told Brittany to let her know when Foster Matthews and Mark Millhouse arrived.

Brittany confirmed the time twice and seemed strangely nervous. Maybe it was the anniversary lunch she was planning, though those should be second nature to her by now.

Sugar was stapling the last copy of the franchise materials for the meeting when Clarice stuck her head in the business office door. "We need you. Fast. And Brit says those consultants are waiting."

"How long have they been here?"

"I don't know. She's talking to them now."

Sugar grabbed Gage from his office on the way out and opened the door to the counter area. She was shocked to see the lobby was full of unhappy guests, some in silk robes, towels on their heads, as if they'd rushed down from a shower or bath.

The phones were ringing off the hook and Brittany and

Luigi had lines of people in front of them. She recognized Foster Matthews standing with another man—Mark Millhouse, no doubt—at the counter to the left of Brittany's post.

"What's the problem?" she asked Brittany, who covered the phone she was talking into.

"The power is off in the tower rooms," she said.

"Where is Nestor?" Gage asked.

"Can't find him. Oliver, either. Or any maintenance guys."

"I'll handle this," Gage said to Sugar, opening up his phone.

Sugar smiled at the consultants. "Gentlemen, I'm so sorry about this. I can't imagine what's going on."

"And the cancellations!" Brittany said to her. "That's a disaster."

"What cancellations?" She was painfully aware that the consultants were listening.

"Fifty guests gone. Just like that. No explanation. Also, I got a call from a travel agent who thinks we're—" she leaned in, as if to be private "—going out of business."

"Are you kidding?" What the hell was going on? Before she found out more, she had to get the consultants away from any more bad news. "Let me get you situated in my office." She led them down the hall. As she passed Maribeth, the woman motioned her over.

Sugar hesitated.

"We can wait," Foster said.

She grimaced internally, but moved to where Maribeth stood.

"We just lost another batch of reservations," Maribeth said. "Canceled, just like that."

"You're kidding," she whispered, glancing at the consultants, who could easily hear what she'd said.

"Is it more cancellations?" Brittany called over. *Great.*

"I don't know what's happening." Maribeth looked worried.

"See what you can find out. I'll be back. I'm sure it'll be straightened out," she said to the two men, acting more confident than she felt.

She left them in her office with the packets and promised to return with Gage soon.

Back in the lobby, Gage told her Oliver and the crew had been on a wild-goose chase at the casitas—plumbing problems and an ant infestation, both bogus—and they'd be back any minute.

She and Gage calmed the guests and Sugar agonized over the waiting consultants. When Oliver returned, he found a bank of suspiciously blown breakers and quickly fixed the problem.

That didn't solve the mystery of seventy-five lost bookings, but she and Gage had to get back to Matthews and Millhouse.

"What the hell caused the breakers to blow like that?" she asked Gage as they rushed to her office. "The consultants overheard about the lost reservations, too."

Gage shrugged. "Things happen."

Sometimes he made her furious. She was shaky and nervous and dripping with perspiration, but to him it was no big deal. At the door to her office, she stopped to paste a calm smile on her face, then breezed in and introduced Gage.

"I'm so sorry about the confusion," she said. "It's never, ever like this."

"Things happen," Gage repeated.

"You're having reservation problems?" Foster asked. The question was polite, but she felt the concern behind the words.

"They'll get sorted out," Sugar said. "Like I said, this never happens."

"But we do have dips in our census," Gage interrupted, making her turn to him, mouth open. "November, December and part of January. You'll see that in our materials."

"But that might vary for the franchises. And focused promotions could overcome it." She signaled Gage with her eyes. *Cut it out.*

"Your materials look great," Mark Millhouse said. "We appreciate the depth of analysis."

"We brought you some preliminary ideas, as well." Foster pushed folders toward her and Gage.

Sugar opened hers. Gage clasped his hands over his, as if he didn't care what was in it. "So what does this 'diagnosis' consist of exactly?" he asked.

There was a pause, while the consultants absorbed Gage's tone. "We look through your materials, ask you questions, tour your property. Nothing too complicated."

"What percentage of your potential clients pass this 'exam'?" he asked, putting finger quotes around *exam*.

"Most do, but that's because we screen our clients," Foster said, smiling. "Ms. Thompson and I spoke, as you know."

"Yes, I know." Gage gave Foster a steely look. Sugar wanted to throttle him. He was acting like a dad who disapproved of his daughter's boyfriend.

"I'm not sure our profile matches your previous hospitality clients," Gage said. "We're unique, as I'm sure Sugar told you."

"Customized service is a hallmark of our business. Which is why Ms. Thompson contacted us in the first place." He shot her a puzzled look. *What's with the suspicion?*

"You'll have to forgive Gage. He likes to play devil's advocate." She tried to smile.

"It's important to have all the facts," Gage said. "Wouldn't you agree, gentlemen?" Had he always been such an arrogant jerk?

"Certainly," Foster said, "but—"

"For example, I've read that half of all franchises fold because they're undercapitalized. Spice It Up was very capital-intensive at start-up. If franchisees crash, that would hurt us, correct?"

"Yes…" Foster glanced meaningfully at his partner, then looked back at Gage. "If finances are an issue, we don't recommend a franchise. By the same token, we wouldn't recommend a franchise fee or a royalty level that wouldn't adequately compensate you."

"We realize that, don't we, Gage?" Sugar said firmly.

"I'm just trying to understand the dynamics. I'd like to see the demographics to show the viability of an expansion in the markets Sugar has in mind."

"We have that information, but it's proprietary. When we sign our agreement, we'll share it."

"So, you're saying, 'Trust us'?"

The consultants were silent. The clock ticked, tension mounted.

Sugar wanted to kick Gage under the table. "I have an idea," she said finally. "How about if we take you on a tour so you can see what the resort is all about? Sound good?"

The consultants exchanged glances and Foster spoke. "Maybe we're getting ahead of ourselves here."

"What do you mean?"

"You two should decide if this is the direction you want to go. We're not interested in forcing the issue."

"You're not. We want to pursue this," Sugar said.

"We'll leave our materials." He nodded at the folder that Gage hadn't even opened. "We'd be happy to work with you when you're ready."

"Sometimes businesses take a few years to stabilize enough for franchising," Mark added. "It's just a matter of time."

"You don't think we're stable? Of course we're stable." She thought about the lost reservations and the chaos in the lobby. "What you saw out there was an anomaly."

"We'll talk it over and get back to them, Sugar," Gage said in a tone she hated. As if he were in charge. She'd never felt this way with him before. They were equal partners, dammit. She felt like Sylvie before she seized her sexual power.

She managed to gather her dignity enough to graciously walk the consultants out, promising to get back with them. Gage hadn't bothered to come along, heading for his office. Without the folder.

"That was quick," Brittany said. "Didn't it go well?" She seemed oddly hopeful.

"It went fine," Sugar said, gritting her teeth. She marched back to her office, grabbed Gage's folder and took it into his office, shutting the door behind her. She tossed the folder on his desk so hard it sent papers sailing to the floor. "What the hell were you doing in there?"

"Asking legitimate questions," he said mildly. "Questions you should have asked."

"You sabotaged that meeting. You couldn't convince me to give up, so you chased away the consultants."

"You were jumping into this blind, Sugar."

"You were being an asshole."

"You and I always discuss things. Or at least we used to."

"That was before you turned into an arrogant prick."

"And you became a shrill bitch." His voice had a snap she'd never before heard. "Sorry," he said. "But you heard them. We need to stabilize. We've got problems."

"Because of the bookings and a power outage?" A terrible fear zinged through her. "Did you do that? Arrange for the breakers to be turned off? To make us look bad?"

"That's ridiculous, Sugar."

She was so upset she couldn't think straight. "You seemed damn happy about it. And you had to mention the slump, didn't you? You had to— Hey?"

Her gaze snagged on a paper that had fallen to the floor. It was a fax cover sheet addressed to *Rionna Morgan* with the subject, *Résumé, Gage Maguire.*

"You faxed your résumé to Rionna?" She jerked her gaze to his face.

He frowned, looking sheepish. "That was before. I was going to mention it to you."

"You applied for a job at TravelQuest?" Cold washed over her as if she'd been plunged into a mountain lake.

"When I called about the franchises, she offered me VP of new properties. The guy retired. I turned her down. After you and I got together."

"You didn't say a word to me."

"It didn't seem relevant. I told her no." He shrugged.

"You lined up a new job." Emotions rose in a wave. Jealousy, betrayal, fear.

"At the time, I thought I had no choice. It would be a challenge. It's a different business model."

"And you want that? A challenge?" She understood. That's what the franchise represented for her. Gage needed a challenge, too. Of course.

"It's over. I love you. I'm staying."

Sugar believed in change, in moving on, but the idea of Gage leaving scared her. It had from the beginning. Just like Patti and Larry, she'd been clinging to Gage out of fear.

"Whatever you're telling yourself, stop now," Gage said. He bent to pick up the fax sheet and the résumé, tore them in two and tossed them into the trash. "I said no."

Gage wanted a job with Rionna, of all people. She hated the rush of jealous possessiveness that ran through her.

"I don't want you to stay out of obligation or fear or habit." Her voice shook with emotion. She wrapped her arms around herself and held on tight.

"This was why I didn't tell you. Because I knew you'd use it against me." Gage looked angry, hurt and confused all at once. And it was her fault. She'd been right to fight falling in love. She was terrible at it.

"Maybe you can hide from the truth, Gage, but I can't."

There was a knock at the door.

Sugar took a deep breath, fought to settle herself before she opened the door to Maribeth.

"Sorry to bother you, but something's very wrong," she said. "Those reservations we lost? The twenty-five new ones? They were phony. The call-back numbers weren't real."

"What are you saying?" Sugar said.

"Someone deliberately gave us false reservations."

"Who would do that? And why?"

Maribeth paused. "I didn't want to say anything, but Daisy wants my job. Maybe she was trying to make herself look good."

"Daisy wouldn't do that," Sugar said. "Just like you wouldn't fake reservations to make her look bad."

"That's true, I guess." Maribeth hung her head.

"No one who works here would deliberately harm us," Gage said, shooting Sugar a look. She'd accused him of doing exactly that.

"But someone who saw us as a gold mine might. Someone who would set up false reservations, start rumors, send a spy."

Like Rionna Morgan.

"What you're suggesting is crazy, Sugar, and you know it," Gage said levelly.

"Do what you can to recover the losses, Maribeth," she said. "We'll figure it out later."

When Maribeth was gone, she and Gage looked at each other.

"You think I know something about this, don't you?" Gage demanded. "How could you think that? TravelQuest has no interest in a sex resort. I even asked Rionna about that stupid spy rumor and she laughed."

He was right. It made no sense. But she was still angry. "Hell, you didn't need fake reservations or flipped breakers to ruin my plan. You treated the consultants like criminals."

"I was just asking—"

"Questions. Right. Angry ones. I don't get it. In fact, I don't get you. I don't even know you anymore, Gage."

"Yes, you do. And that's what scares you." His voice had a dead sound she'd never heard before.

"You're wrong. You're acting strange. One minute you're swearing undying love and the next you're applying for a job with a woman who wants to sleep with you."

"Cut it out, Sugar. Stop creating a fight over nothing."

"Over nothing? You want out. I know you do. You don't want to work here anymore. Why else would you fight the franchise idea so hard?"

"You're turning that into some kind of test? Love you, love your franchise? That's ridiculous."

"You've changed, Gage."

"So have you."

"Fair enough. We've both changed."

"You act like I'm your enemy, not the man you love."

"You're my partner, too, Gage. It's a separate issue, or I think it should be. Except it's not working anymore. All we do is fight."

"I love it here, Sugar. I love you. I want us to be together and be happy, but you don't seem to want that."

"Yes, I do," she said faintly.

"What are you so damned afraid of? I do everything I can to show you I love you, that I'll be here for you, but you accuse me of sabotaging our bookings! What is enough for you? What would it take?" He was breathing hard, angry, and she had no idea what to tell him.

Luckily, Gage's desk phone rang, saving her from coming up with an answer. He pushed the speaker button. "Yes, Brittany?"

"You and Sugar have to get out here." Her voice was high and scared and she seemed to be crying. "It's all messed up. I'm sorry."

Gage looked at Sugar, his expression matching her own, she was sure. They were together in alarm, at least, and they rushed to the lobby, where they found Maribeth and Daisy in a standoff, surrounded by a group of pale-faced employees.

Daisy raised her face to Sugar and Gage, tears streaming down her cheeks. "I quit," she said. "You hear that, everyone?" She indicated the group. "All I did was try my best. Maribeth blames me and I know you will blame me, too. I made one mistake—I misbooked the Coppolas. That was all. I did take those new reservations. I swear. I don't know what happened to them. And I didn't fake anything. I can't live with everyone thinking I did."

"Let's slow down now," Sugar said, fighting her own emotions so she could calm Daisy. "We have a problem we need to solve, that's all. No one's leaving." Except maybe Gage, but she'd deal with that later.

"I told her not to quit," Brittany said, her voice squeaking. "I told her everything would be all right. And it will be, right? Everything will be back to normal, right, Sugar? The marketing thing is over, and, look, I found these reservation forms. They fell behind the trash can and didn't get keyed in." Brittany's face was pale with blotches of bright red. She looked utterly terrified and the papers shook in her hands.

Sugar took them. They bore dates from the previous week. Looked to be about fifty of them. "What happened here, Brittany?"

"I just found them, like I said. We can make up the lost guests, can't we? I mean, they were future bookings, not real losses, right?"

"Brittany…?" She looked at the papers, then back at the receptionist.

"It was a mistake, okay?" Brittany wailed. "I only wanted to keep things the same. When Daisy goofed with the Coppolas, I saw how you guys got together to fix it. You said we always work together, so I thought maybe this was a way to remind you."

"What are you talking about?" Gage said.

Brittany lifted miserable eyes to Gage. "I overheard you talking after the staff meeting—about the franchise and needing Oliver for the franchise team. There's a vent above the kitchen sink and I heard every word. I know about franchises. I used to work at a Bunny Burger. I knew Oliver would be all over the country and I'd never see him anymore."

"So you hid reservations?"

She nodded. "And faked some that I canceled. I mean, we never had them in the first place, so it didn't seem such a big deal. How could we lose money we didn't really have?"

"But I don't get it." Sugar shook her head.

"I just wanted you to forget the franchise."

"Because of Oliver?"

"And because Spice It Up is perfect the way it is. Everyone knows that. I did it for everyone." She waved out at the listening staff. "I heard you set up that meeting with Matthews and Whosis, Sugar, and I figured if they saw we were a mess, that would be the end of it. So I sent Oliver and the crew away and flipped the breakers."

"Unbelievable," Sugar said.

"I know it was dumb. But I had to do something. And now you two are fighting and Daisy's quitting and nothing's going to be the same anyway." She burst into tears.

Sugar and Gage looked at each other. Sugar wanted to sob, too. Her head ached with all that had happened—the consultant visit, Gage's job hunt, Brittany's scheme. She had to get hold of herself, remember who she was and get back to what mattered.

"We let things go out of control," she said, looking at Gage first, then Brittany. "We have to settle down and do what we know will help."

"That's right," Gage said softly.

From the moment she and Gage had launched their plan to change each other's minds, all hell had broken loose. Now she had to fix it. For Spice It Up. For herself and for Gage.

Maribeth, Daisy and Brittany got busy confirming the

"lost" reservations and Sugar drafted a reassuring letter to staff, with Gage's input. At the Monday staff meeting, she and Gage would answer any remaining questions. In the meantime, she and Gage had things to settle.

GAGE ROUNDED the hall by Erika's office and ran straight into Sugar. For a second, he was swept away by the feel and smell of her, but she pulled back. "We need to talk," she said, her face pale and sad.

"I suppose we do." Gage dreaded the conversation—he'd been grateful for the delay of the last few hours—but they had to clear the air.

Erika's door opened abruptly between them. "Ah, my two favorite partners. You are here for a session?"

"We need to talk to each other," he said. "Alone."

"Please use my office." She let them pass her. "I'll be off for tea, but you have my cell number." She gave them a look of sad commiseration, as though they were about to attend the funeral of someone dear. Of course, that was how Gage felt. Sugar had to be equally sad, but she was hiding it. As usual.

They shut the door and paused, staring at the plush chairs where they had interlocked knees, stared into each other's eyes and described what they valued in each other.

The chairs were now side-by-side, angled toward Erika's straight-backed chair. Without a word, Sugar chose Erika's chair. Gage pulled one of the plush chairs away from its mate and faced Sugar dead-on.

They were still surrounded by Erika's intimate artwork, including the Rodin sculpture, but Gage felt immune to the atmosphere. His gut was tight and he felt isolated and hopeless.

Part of him hoped for some kind of magical solution, but Sugar's drawn face and empty eyes told him it wouldn't come from her and he was out of ideas.

"I think we'll be okay out front," Sugar said. "Everyone's working hard to pick up the slack."

"We'll gain ground by the end of the quarter," he said. He'd crunched the numbers. "No permanent harm done."

"Good." She sighed. "If we'd told everyone about the franchise at the staff meeting, we might have prevented Brittany's panic."

"We did the best we could," he said. "With everything."

She jerked her eyes to his. "We did, didn't we?"

He nodded. His chest ached with the pain of it. He could feel her slipping away.

"Brittany thinks we should withhold one of her paychecks as punishment," Sugar said.

He shook his head. "She learned her lesson."

"I agree."

"Good." He tried to smile. "We haven't agreed on much lately."

"When people are in love, they're supposed to bring out the best in each other. We seem to bring out the worst. You're arrogant and bossy. I'm shrill and bitchy."

"A disagreement doesn't have to be a power struggle."

"I know, but I can't seem to help it. I feel like Sylvie, except a leather vest and a riding crop won't turn this around." She smiled, but her lip quivered. Even as she slipped away from him, he loved her so much.

"Maybe we just need time," he said.

"Time won't help. Hell, we've had twelve years. The truth is that I don't know how to be in love. I can't handle it."

"Sure you can."

"I think we wanted to be in love so much we made something happen that wasn't meant to be."

Perhaps you do not want the climb? He'd dragged himself up there to the top, dammit, but Sugar had let the rope burn through her fingers. Now he was worn-out. "So now what?"

"We can't take back what happened."

"Is that what you want? To take it back?" Gage saw in her face she did. "I'm not sorry. We had to try."

"Maybe so." Her eyes had lost their usual gleam. "I'll buy you out, Gage, assuming you're serious about giving me good terms?" Her lip trembled as she tried to smile.

"Is that what you want? For me to leave?"

"How can you stay? I intend to pursue the franchise idea and I really don't want to fight with you over it."

"If that's what you want."

"It is. Falling in love ruined our partnership. Every dispute feels like a breakup."

"You're right." He had an eerie sense of relief. The decision felt right, the way the sad ending of a tragedy felt inevitable. Like his parents' divorce. He'd longed for them to get back together, but somehow knew they wouldn't. At some level, all along, he'd accepted it.

"So, you'll take that job with TravelQuest?" she asked.

"I'll have to see."

"You'd be good at it. You'd be good at anything." Her voice cracked.

"I want the best for you, Sugar," he said.

"Me, too. For you." Her eyes shone with tears.

"Many couples don't have that wish," he said, imitating Erika.

Her laugh sounded choked.

He reached for her hands and linked fingers, looking into

her eyes for the last time. He remembered making love to her, face-to-face, eyes open, and how happy she'd seemed.

He'd been happy, too. Happy, but holding his breath.

"At least we tried," he said.

"At least that."

He released her fingers, but felt their warmth for hours.

16

ALONE in her booth at the travel convention, Sugar clicked off her PowerPoint display, leaned back in her chair and grinned. She wanted to shriek with triumph, but there was an entire convention of people outside who might think she was nuts.

The consultants had connected her with four motel owners who might be interested in a Spice It Up franchise and their eyes had lit up during her presentation. In fact, she'd booked visits for two of them in the coming weeks.

She closed down the laptop and projector, packed up and headed back to Spice It Up to put some notes together.

Everything had gone like clockwork—the testimonial video had brought laughter and applause and she'd answered every question. Nothing stood between her and a franchise now.

She wanted to share her success with Gage, but that was utterly inappropriate. It had been two weeks since they'd "dissolved their partnership"—a miserably legalistic name for such a painful heartache—three weeks since they'd called it quits on their relationship.

Gage was due to start with TravelQuest soon, she thought, though he was still in town. He'd been in to the office several times to work out details with her and to orient Oliver.

She missed him so much—missed having him down the hall to argue with or joke with or just plain spend time with. Luckily, she'd been too busy to mope about what had happened. There had been no time to figure out why it hurt so much, why she couldn't let go of the memories.

Now she'd have more excitement to distract her. She had to prepare for the visits, put the final touches on the franchise agreement, get the franchise lawyer to look everything over. The consultants would fill in the gaps, so it wouldn't even be difficult to manage without a partner.

If only she could work 24/7. Nights were the worst, when she broke down like a fool, sobbing like she'd lost everything, when she had all she wanted.

Esmeralda had left her two messages—one "sensing her pain," the other threatening to fly out there and shake her by the shoulders if she didn't call back soon. Sugar would do so now that she had the good news about the franchise.

She had called Autumn, who urged her to trust herself and to suck it up. *Love stuff is a pain.*

Yeah. A pain. That wasn't the half of it.

Back at the resort, she headed for her office, but when she noticed Erika's door open, she found herself going in.

Erika didn't look up from her computer and Sugar had to call her name.

"Sugar!" She pulled her glasses from her nose. "You surprised me." Usually Erika surprised her.

"Is this a bad time?" Sugar asked.

"For you, I always have time." She gestured at one of the soft chairs that felt like a hug when you sat in it.

Sugar sat. She hadn't talked to Erika about what had happened, had actually avoided the woman, just as she'd avoided Esmeralda, fearful of what either might say.

"I was just talking to our spy," Erika said. "The book she is writing sounds fascinating."

Louise Waters, the woman Clarice had identified as a possible spy, turned out to be a writer doing research for a romance novel she intended to write. She'd called not long after the consultant visit to ask to interview Sugar and various staff members. And here Sugar had suspected Rionna of trying to sabotage the resort.

She'd allowed herself to get carried away with everything.

"I wanted to thank you for your help, Erika. Even though it didn't work out with Gage."

"Changing your life is not easy. There are fits and starts." She shrugged.

"And now it's over," she said firmly.

Erika just looked at her.

"We took your advice, but we couldn't make it work. It was all to the good. At least we tried."

"And your eyes are wet with tears."

She said it so simply, so directly, that Sugar blinked twin drops into her lap. She swiped at her cheeks. "What is wrong with me? It was for the best."

"So sleeping together did not help?"

"You knew?"

"I have eyes. I can see." She smiled.

"Well, it ruined everything. It changed us. We couldn't be partners anymore."

"So you, who enjoy the thrill of the new, don't want this in your partner? A change?"

"No. I guess I didn't." She hesitated. She hadn't thought of it that way.

"But you do want changes in your resort?"

"I want the franchise, yes. It will be a relief to be busy."

Except her whole body ached with the pressure of what she faced. Letting soup burning on the stove because she was too enthralled to eat sounded fun when it included a partner. Alone, not so much.

"You look exhausted. And sad."

"I guess I feel that way. I miss Gage." Her heart felt hollowed out by the loss.

"Perhaps you miss the familiar, after all? Your old partner? Your old resort?"

"Spice It Up will still be here. I'll be away a lot, it's true." The idea gave her a pang of regret, similar to how she felt about losing Gage. "You think I'm making a mistake?"

"What do you think?"

"I'm not sure…." She spoke slowly, uncomfortable with her uncertainty.

"That is new, correct? For you to be not sure?"

She laughed. "Yeah. Gage says I have more opinions than anyone he's ever known. Right now, I'm not so sure."

She looked around the room, at the Rodin statue, at the watercolor of a couple kissing. She loved this room. It made her feel warm and safe. The way she felt about Spice It Up. Which she'd only noticed when Gage grabbed her hand and made her slow her down and look.

"Perhaps you must become sure."

"Perhaps." She thanked Erika, said a vague goodbye and set off in a daze to look at her resort.

In the lobby, she saw Maribeth and Daisy with their heads together. After the crisis, the pair had reached a new level of cooperation. Brittany was showing a couple the amenities, her voice bright with enthusiasm. Luigi was busy snapping his gum and taking reservations. Clarice was bubbling about a sailboat cruise to another couple. Jolie led a nervous pair toward the elevators and their rooms, where they would have a fabulous time, Sugar knew.

In the past, she'd let her gaze skim over the resort and its events and people. Now she took it in, absorbed it. Gage had taught her that. He'd pulled her close and turned her to see what they'd built together.

Why had she been so eager to move on? She'd been afraid to let things reach her, afraid to let her feelings take hold. Why?

Because she might lose what she loved. And that would hurt so much she'd fall apart, the way her mother and her sister had done. She'd assumed the worst.

But she was sturdy. Just like the couples she saw in the gazebo, when she stepped outdoors. They focused on Mary E. as she showed them how to give and receive intimacy. How brave they were to fight for their love.

Wasn't she brave, too?

She walked on, pausing to look through the window at a cooking class, where couples tasted each other's dishes, smiling and nodding, whether it was burned, raw or too salty. The idea was to make food a gift. She waved at the instructor, then moved on.

At the top of the first hill, she stopped, her heart in her throat. She remembered holding hands with Gage on this spot.

Look at what we built. She'd taken all this for granted. Now the sea air smelled crisper, the sun felt warmer, the grass and trees greener, the sky more blue. Because she was in love?

This could never last.

Why not?

There was joy in staying. There was reward. There was value in slowing down, as Gage had shown her.

What had Erika said? *You must risk what you know....*
See each other with new eyes.

Sugar was different, after all. She'd told herself she was
afraid to be trapped, but she loved it here. She'd committed to this business, why couldn't she commit to Gage?

Have you even tried? Not long enough and not hard
enough. Gage was right. She'd seen every problem as proof
they couldn't be together. She'd been so afraid to hold
still, she'd trampled right over her happiness—run away
from Gage and his bouquet right off the cliff, just as in Esmeralda's dream. What had Esmie said? *Open your eyes*
and smell the roses.

She kept walking. She had one more place to visit. And
a decision to make. If it wasn't too late.

"RIONNA? This is Gage."

"Oh. Hello!" Rionna sounded startled that he'd called.
Again. He'd checked in with her every few days.

"I wanted to let you know I'll be at that management
meeting you mentioned," he said.

"You will? Really?"

"I should hit the ground running, don't you think?"
Moving on was better than stewing over old dreams. Sugar
was right about that. Gage glanced toward his bedroom
doorway, where he'd set the bags he intended to use for the
trip. All that remained was buying his ticket.

"That's a good idea, of course." Rionna hesitated. "The
thing is that we're not quite ready for you. We have some
things to finalize still. I just…well, I assumed you'd have
loose ends to tie up."

"We handled them. Sugar and I are on good terms."

They were being quite rational about everything, though every time he saw her his heart seemed to break even more.

"That's good to hear. I imagine Sugar wasn't surprised you were leaving."

"Why would you think that?"

"You seemed poised to go. How could she miss it?"

That stopped him cold. Rionna had said something similar when they first talked about the job. *You struck me as dissatisfied.* "Maybe you're right," he said, needing to figure this out. He finished the call, promising to check with her in a week.

He glanced again at his suitcases. The moment Sugar told him to go, he'd mentally packed his bags. He'd felt *relief* when they broke up, like the shoe he'd been waiting to drop had finally landed.

He walked around his place, restless. Had he ever truly believed he and Sugar could be together? Had *he* ever really tried?

What the hell was his problem? Didn't he think he deserved to be happy? He sure as hell hadn't acted like it.

How could he expect falling in love with Sugar to be easy? Nothing about the woman was easy. Why would love be?

And at the very moment Sugar needed his patience, his compassion, his steadiness, he'd bought a one-way ticket out of town. As long as Sugar remained elusive, he hadn't risked anything.

He'd waited twelve years, but he'd never believed he'd get what he wanted. He'd given Sugar a month, but what if it took six months or a year or more? For the woman he loved, the woman he would love for the rest of his life? That was nothing. A blink, a twitch of time.

He had to talk to her. Had to make it clear. Just like that

moment of recognition on that vibrating water bed from weeks ago, he saw now how it had to be.

WHEN SUGAR reached the Jungle Bungalow, the maid was just finishing up. She stepped inside and flipped on the jungle sounds, her heart banging her ribs, her throat tight with pain. She breathed in the jasmine, listened to the water feature bubbling gently—all repaired—looked at the bed where she and Gage had made love weeks ago.

The gift basket was waiting for the next couple with fresh chocolates and a new bottle of cinnamon gel.

Oh, Gage. How she missed him. How she loved him. How she loved this room they'd shared together, worked in, made love in.

All these weeks, she'd tried to push past, move beyond, turn the corner, but she hadn't managed it. Now she didn't want to. Not when she'd finally seen the value in staying, in sticking with, in holding on.

She sank onto the bed, flopped onto her back. Was it too late? How could she ask Gage to come back? He'd gone ahead and she was stuck. Lost and in love.

She heard a key card in the door. Damn. New guests checking in, no doubt. She stood, brushed away her tears and prepared to smile and say something encouraging.

But it wasn't new guests. It was Gage.

"What are you doing here?" she asked, her heart in her throat.

"This," he said. Just like on their birthday night, he grabbed her face and kissed her. She felt the same startling rush, then the wallop of all the kisses that had come after that, and the millions to come in the future.

Finally he broke it off. "I'm not giving up, Sugar. No matter how long it takes. I've unpacked for good."

"You've what?" She shook her head, dizzy and confused.

"Never mind. The point is we need more time. We have to work at this. Hell, that's the whole message of Spice It Up. Love takes work, but it's worth it."

"I think you're right," she said tentatively. "I was afraid I couldn't do it—be in love—that I didn't know how. That I couldn't stay with it. But I can. I can stay with the resort and with you."

"So you've seen yourself with new eyes? Erika will be delighted."

She could only laugh and then he kissed her, soft and slow, the way she loved. When he broke off the kiss, he pressed his forehead to hers. "I'll tell Rionna I'm out."

"If you need the challenge, Gage, keep the job. I don't want you to feel trapped."

"I was escaping. Because I didn't think I'd get what I really wanted. If you're set on this franchise, I'll help you as much as I can, even though I still disagree."

"Let's hold off for now. We have to learn how to be partners again, now that we're in love." She could pursue the franchise leads later.

"I thought we would stop the debates," Gage said.

"How can we? That's how we work best."

"Some things don't change."

"Afraid not." She looked into Gage's eyes, no longer fearful of what would be there, no longer scared to show him her heart. There was risk in falling in love, but there was also reward. So much reward. "I was scared."

"You're safe with me, Sugar. And you can drive anytime."

Tears sprang to her eyes. He knew her, in some ways, better than she knew herself.

"Wouldn't Erika love to see us now, staring into each other's faces, seeing everything in the eyes, the mouth, the hitch of breath—was that what she said?"

He smiled. "I'll keep things interesting. I promise."

"We have each other and our imagination. What more do we need?" She loved how Gage's gaze never wavered from her face. He would be there for her always—when she was scared or worried, when they struggled with the resort or the franchise or whatever they chose to do next. And she would be there for him.

"We'll make it work." Gage stroked her hair away from her face, looking into her eyes, coaxing her to have faith in them both. "Just like we made the resort work."

Open your eyes...see what you've ignored...smell the roses. Esmeralda's advice had been correct, her crazy dream right on. Gage had brought the roses to her life. He'd opened her eyes to what she loved. Erika had been right, too. Thank goodness Sugar hadn't been too stubborn to ignore their wisdom.

"Let's do a fantasy, huh?" she said.

"I'll tie you to the bed, hell, put on a prom dress and pink tights if that's what you need. Just say the word."

"Not that kind of fantasy. Not this minute, anyway. I mean a fantasy about our future. I see us enjoying Spice It Up and each other. I see us doing ordinary day-to-day things, like reading the Sunday paper and eating eggs cooked a certain way, and taking vacations...say an Alaskan cruise." Her voice faltered. *An Alaskan cruise?*

Gage laughed. "You on a cruise?"

"It's my fantasy." She pretended to slug him.

"Trapped on a boat with nothing to do but play bingo and eat? That's so not you."

"You're right." She felt a rush of relief.

"So we compromise. Maybe a three-dayer down the Mexican Riviera, a long stay in Acapulco with hikes to the ruins. We'll rent a sailboat, hit the club scene every night...like that."

"I love how you get me."

"Here's mine." He stroked her arms, held her closer, tucked her head under his chin. "I see us making love in every casita in this resort—how else to really know it? I see us laughing over new plans—this franchise thing if we decide it's right— letting the soup burn on the stove because we're so busy—"

"Making love?"

"Or working or laughing or just being together." He put his hands against her face and brought her close to kiss her.

He broke off, grinning. "Who knows, maybe by the time our Happily-Ever-After reunion comes again, we'll be ready to go permanent. Maybe have a wedding during the reunion?"

"Better to keep each other guessing."

"That's the plan," Gage said and kissed her, and it was fun and easy and deep and strong and Sugar knew they would keep each other guessing for a very long time. Maybe forever...one day at a time.

* * * * *

Look for the next book in the
DOING IT...BETTER! *Series*
AT HER BECK AND CALL
by Dawn Atkins
Coming in February 2007
from Harlequin Blaze

*Experience entertaining women's fiction for
every woman who has wondered
"what's next?" in their lives.
Turn the page for a sneak preview of a
new book from Harlequin NEXT,*
WHY IS MURDER ON THE MENU, ANYWAY?
by Stevi Mittman

On sale December 26, wherever books are sold.

Ambience is everything. Imagine eating a foie gras at a luncheonette counter or a side of coleslaw at Le Cirque. It's not a matter of food but one of atmosphere. Remember that when planning your dining room design.
—Tips from *Teddi.com*

"Now that's the kind of man you should be looking for," my mother, the self-appointed keeper of my shelf-life stamp, says. She points with her fork at a man in the corner of the Steak-Out Restaurant, a dive I've just been hired to redecorate. Making this restaurant look four-star will be hard, but not half as hard as getting through lunch without strangling the woman across the table from me. "*He* would make a good husband."

"Oh, you can tell that from across the room?" I ask, wondering how it is she can forget that when we had trouble getting rid of my last husband, she shot him. "Besides being ten minutes away from death if he actually eats all that steak, he's twenty years too old for me and—

shallow woman that I am—twenty pounds too heavy. Besides, I am *so* not looking for another husband here. I'm looking to design a new image for this place, looking for some sense of ambience, some feeling, something I can build a proposal on for them."

My mother studies the man in the corner, tilting her head, the better to gauge his age, I suppose. I think she's grimacing, but with all the Botox and Restylane injected into that face, it's hard to tell. She takes another bite of her steak salad, chews slowly so that I don't miss the fact that the steak is a poor cut and tougher than it should be. "You're concentrating on the wrong kind of proposal," she says finally. "Just look at this place, Teddi. It's a dive. There are hardly any other diners. What does *that* tell you about the food?"

"That they cater to a dinner crowd and it's lunchtime," I tell her.

I don't know what I was thinking bringing her here with me. I suppose I thought it would be better than eating alone. There really are days when my common sense goes on vacation. Clearly, this is one of them. I mean, really, did I not resolve less than three weeks ago that I would not let my mother get to me anymore?

What good are New Year's resolutions, anyway?

Mario approaches the man's table and my mother studies him while they converse. Eventually Mario leaves the table with a huff, after which the diner glances up and meets my mother's gaze. I think she's smiling at him. That or she's got indigestion. They size each other up.

I concentrate on making sketches in my notebook and try to ignore the fact that my mother is flirting. At nearly seventy, she's developed an unhealthy interest in members of the opposite sex to whom she isn't married.

According to my father, who has broken the TMI rule and given me Too Much Information, she has no interest in sex with him. Better, I suppose, to be clued in on what they aren't doing in the bedroom than have to hear what they might be doing.

"He's not so old," my mother says, noticing that I have barely touched the Chinese chicken salad she warned me not to get. "He's got about as many years on you as you have on your little cop friend."

She does this to make me crazy. I know it, but it works all the same. "Drew Scoones is not my little 'friend.' He's a detective with whom I—"

"Screwed around," my mother says. I must look shocked, because my mother laughs at me and asks if I think she doesn't know the "lingo."

What I thought she didn't know was that Drew and I actually tangled in the sheets. And, since it's possible she's just fishing, I sidestep the issue and tell her that Drew is just a couple of years younger than me and that I don't need reminding. I dig into my salad with renewed vigor, determined to show my mother that Chinese chicken salad in a steak place was not the stupid choice it's proving to be.

After a few more minutes of my picking at the wilted leaves on my plate, the man my mother has me nearly engaged to pays his bill and heads past us toward the back of the restaurant. I watch my mother take in his shoes, his suit and the diamond pinkie ring that seems to be cutting off the circulation in his little finger.

"Such nice hands," she says after the man is out of sight. "Manicured." She and I both stare at my hands. I have two popped acrylics that are being held on at weird angles by bandages. My cuticles are ragged and there's marker decorating my right hand from measuring carelessly when I did a drawing for a customer.

Twenty minutes later she's disappointed that he managed to leave the restaurant without our noticing. He will join the list of the ones I let get away. I will hear about him twenty years from now when—according to my mother—my children will be grown and I will still be single, living pathetically alone with several dogs and cats.

After my ex, that sounds good to me.

The waitress tells us that our meal has been taken care of by the management and, after thanking Mario, the owner, complimenting him on the wonderful meal and assuring him that once I have redecorated his place people will be flocking here in droves (I actually use those words and ignore my mother when she rolls her eyes), my mother and I head for the restroom.

My father—unfortunately not with us today—has the patience of a saint. He got it over the years of living with my mother. She, perhaps as a result, figures he has the patience for both of them, and feels justified having none. For her, no rules apply, and a little thing like a picture of a man on the door to a public restroom is certainly no barrier to using the john. In all fairness, it does seem silly to stand and wait for the ladies' room if no one is using the men's room.

Still, it's the idea that rules don't apply to her, signs don't apply to her, conventions don't apply to her. She knocks on the door to the men's room. When no one answers she gestures to me to go in ahead. I tell her that I can certainly wait for the ladies' room to be free and she shrugs and goes in herself.

Not a minute later there is a bloodcurdling scream from behind the men's room door.

"Mom!" I yell. "Are you all right?"

Mario comes running over, the waitress on his heels. Two customers head our way while my mother continues to scream.

I try the door, but it is locked. I yell for her to open it and she fumbles with the knob. When she finally manages to unlock and open it, she is white behind her two streaks of blush, but she is on her feet and appears shaken but not stirred.

"What happened?" I ask her. So do Mario and the waitress and the few customers who have migrated to the back of the place.

She points toward the bathroom and I go in, thinking it serves her right for using the men's room. But I see nothing amiss.

She gestures toward the stall, and, like any self-respecting and suspicious woman, I poke the door open with one finger, expecting the worst.

What I find is worse than the worst.

The husband my mother picked out for me is sitting on the toilet. His pants are puddled around his ankles, his hands are hanging at his sides. Pinned to his chest is some sort of Health Department certificate.

Oh, and there is a large, round, bloodless bullet hole between his eyes.

Four Nassau County police officers are securing the area, waiting for the detectives and crime scene personnel to show up. They are trying, though not very hard, to comfort my mother, who in another era would be considered to be suffering from the vapors. Less tactful in the twenty-first century, I'd say she was losing it. That is, if I didn't know her better, know she was milking it for everything it was worth.

My mother loves attention. As it begins to flag, she swoons and claims to feel faint. Despite four No Smoking signs, my mother insists it's all right for her to light up because, after all, she's in shock. Not to mention that signs, as we know, don't apply to her.

When asked not to smoke, she collapses mournfully in a chair and lets her head loll to the side, all without mussing her hair.

Eventually, the detectives show up to find the four patrolmen all circled around her, debating whether to administer CPR, smelling salts or simply call the paramedics. I, however, know just what will snap her to attention.

"Detective Scoones," I say loudly. My mother parts the sea of cops.

"We have to stop meeting like this," he says lightly to me, but I can feel him checking me over with his eyes, making sure I'm all right while pretending not to care.

"What have you got in those pants?" my mother asks him, coming to her feet and staring at his crotch accusingly. "*Baydar?* Everywhere we Bayers are, you turn up. You don't expect me to buy that this is a coincidence, I hope."

Drew tells my mother that it's nice to see her, too, and asks if it's his fault that her daughter seems to attract disasters.

Charming to be made to feel like the bearer of a plague. He asks how I am.

"Just peachy," I tell him. "I seem to be making a habit of finding dead bodies, my mother is driving me crazy and the catering hall I booked two freakin' years ago for Dana's bat mitzvah has just been shut down by the Board of Health!"

"Glad to see your luck's finally changing," he says, giving me a quick squeeze around the shoulders before turning his attention to the patrolmen, asking what they've got, whether they've taken any statements, moved anything, all the sort of stuff you see on TV, without any of the drama. That is, if you don't count my mother's threats to faint every few minutes when she senses no one's paying attention to her.

Mario tells his waitstaff to bring everyone espresso, which I decline because I'm wired enough. Drew pulls him aside and a minute later I'm handed a cup of coffee that smells divinely of Kahlúa.

The man knows me well. Too well.

His partner, whom I've met once or twice, says he'll interview the kitchen staff. Drew asks Mario if he minds if he takes statements from the patrons first and gets to him and the waitstaff afterward.

"No, no," Mario tells him. "Do the patrons first." Drew raises his eyebrow at me like he wants to know if I get the double entendre. I try to look bored.

"What is it with you and murder victims?" he asks me when we sit down at a table in the corner.

I search them out so that I can see you again, I almost say, but I'm afraid it will sound desperate instead of sarcastic.

My mother, lighting up and daring him with a look to tell her not to, reminds him that *she* was the one to find the body.

Drew asks what happened *this time.* My mother tells him how the man in the john was "taken" with me, couldn't take his eyes off me and blatantly flirted with both of us. To his credit, Drew doesn't laugh, but his smirk is undeniable to the trained eye. And I've had my eye trained on him for nearly a year now.

"While he was noticing you," he asks me, "did *you* notice anything about him? Was he waiting for anyone? Watching for anything?"

I tell him that he didn't appear to be waiting or watching. That he made no phone calls, was fairly intent on eating and did, indeed, flirt with my mother. This last bit Drew takes with a grain of salt, which was the way it was intended.

"And he had a short conversation with Mario," I tell him. "I think he might have been unhappy with the food, though he didn't send it back."

Drew asks what makes me think he was dissatisfied, and I tell him that the discussion seemed acrimonious and that Mario looked distressed when he left the table. Drew makes a note and says he'll look into it and asks about anyone else in the restaurant. Did I see anyone who didn't seem to belong, anyone who was watching the victim, anyone looking suspicious?

"Besides my mother?" I ask him, and Mom huffs and blows her cigarette smoke in my direction.

I tell him that there were several deliveries, the kitchen staff going in and out the back door to grab a smoke. He stops me and asks what I was doing checking out the back door of the restaurant.

Proudly—because, while he was off forgetting me, dropping by only once in a while to say hi to Jesse, my son, or drop something by for one of my daughters that he thought they might like, I was getting on with my life—I tell him that I'm decorating the place.

He looks genuinely impressed. "Commercial customers? That's great," he says. Okay, that's what he *ought* to say. What he actually says is "Whatever pays the bills."

"Howard Rosen, the famous restaurant critic, got her the job," my mother says. "You met him—the good-looking, distinguished gentleman with the *real* job, something to be proud of. I guess you've never read his reviews in *Newsday*."

Drew, without missing a beat, tells her that Howard's reviews are on the top of his list, as soon as he learns how to read.

"I only meant—" my mother starts, but both of us assure her that we know just what she meant.

"So," Drew says. "Deliveries?"

I tell him that Mario would know better than I, but that I saw vegetables come in, maybe fish and linens.

"This is the second restaurant job Howard's got her," my mother tells Drew.

"At least she's getting *something* out of the relationship," he says.

"If he were here," my mother says, ignoring the insinuation, "he'd be comforting her instead of interrogating her. He'd be making sure we're both all right after such an ordeal."

"I'm sure he would," Drew agrees, then looks me in the eyes as if he's measuring my tolerance for shock. Quietly he adds, "But then maybe he doesn't know just what strong stuff your daughter's made of."

It's the closest thing to a tender moment I can expect from Drew Scoones. My mother breaks the spell. "She gets that from me," she says.

Both Drew and I take a minute, probably to pray that's all I inherited from her.

"I'm just trying to save you some time and effort," my mother tells him. "My money's on Howard."

Drew withers her with a look and mutters something that sounds suspiciously like "fool's gold." Then he excuses himself to go back to work.

I catch his sleeve and ask if it's all right for us to leave. He says sure, he knows where we live. I say goodbye to Mario. I assure him that I will have some sketches for him in a few days, all the while hoping that this murder doesn't cancel his redecorating plans. I need the money desperately, the alternative being borrowing from my parents and being strangled by the strings.

My mother is strangely quiet all the way to her house. She doesn't tell me what a loser Drew Scoones is—despite his good looks—and how I was obviously drooling over him. She doesn't ask me where Howard is taking me tonight or warn me not to tell my father about what happened because he will worry about us both and no doubt insist we see our respective psychiatrists.

She fidgets nervously, opening and closing her purse over and over again.

"You okay?" I ask her. After all, she's just found a dead man on the toilet and tough as she is that's got to be upsetting.

When she doesn't answer me I pull over to the side of the road.

"Mom?" She refuses to meet my eyes. "You want me to take you to see Dr. Cohen?"

She looks out the window as if she's just realized we're on Broadway in Woodmere. "Aren't we near Marvin's Jewelers?" she asks, pulling something out of her purse.

"What have you got, Mother?" I ask, prying open her fingers to find the murdered man's ring.

"It was on the sink," she says in answer to my dropped

jaw. "I was going to get his name and address and have you return it to him so that he could ask you out. I thought it was a sign that the two of you were meant to be together."

"He's dead, Mom. You understand that, right?" I ask. You never can tell when my mother is fine and when she's in la-la land.

"Well, I didn't know that," she shouts at me. "Not at the time."

I ask why she didn't give it to Drew, realize that she wouldn't give Drew the time in a clock shop and add, "...or one of the other policemen?"

"For heaven's sake," she tells me. "The man is dead, Teddi, and I took his ring. How would that look?"

Before I can tell her it looks just the way it is, she pulls out a cigarette and threatens to light it.

"I mean, really," she says, shaking her head like it's my brains that are loose. "What does he need with it now?"

nocturne™

**WAS HE HER SAVIOR
OR HER NIGHTMARE?**

HAUNTED
LISA CHILDS

Years ago, Ariel and her sisters were separated for
their own protection. Now the man who vowed
revenge on her family has resumed the hunt, and
Ariel must warn her sisters before it's too late.
The closer she comes to finding them, the more
secretive her fiancé becomes. Can she trust the man
she plans to spend eternity with? Or has he been
waiting for the perfect moment to destroy her?

On sale December 2006.

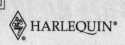

HARLEQUIN®

Happily Ever After Is Just the Beginning...

Harlequin Books brings you stories of love
that stand the test of time. Find books by
some of your favorite series authors and
by exciting new authors who'll soon
become favorites, too. Each story spans years
and will take you on an emotional journey
that starts with falling in love.

If you're a romantic at heart, you'll
definitely want to read this new series!

Every great love has a story to tell.™

Two new titles every month
LAUNCHING FEBRUARY 2007

Available wherever series books are sold.

In February, expect **MORE**
from

HARLEQUIN® *Romance*®

as it increases to six titles per month.

What's to come...

Rancher and Protector

Part of the
Western Weddings
miniseries

BY JUDY CHRISTENBERRY

The Boss's Pregnancy Proposal

BY RAYE MORGAN

Don't miss February's
incredible line up of authors!

www.eHarlequin.com   HRINCREASE

HARLEQUIN®

Blaze™

COMING NEXT MONTH

#297 BEYOND BREATHLESS Kathleen O'Reilly
The Red Choo Diaries, Bk. 1
When Manhattan trains quit and a sexy stranger offers to split the cost of a car, Jamie McNamara takes the deal. Now stuck in gridlock in a Hummer limo, she has hot-looking, hard-bodied Andrew Brooks across from her and nothing but time on her hands....

#298 LETTING LOOSE! Mara Fox
The Wrong Bed
He's buff. He's beautiful. He's taking off his clothes. And he's exactly what lawyer Tina Henderson needs. She's sure a wild night with a stripper will make her forget all about smooth attorney Tyler Walden. Only, there's more to "The Bandit" than meets the eye....

#299 UNTOUCHED Samantha Hunter
Extreme Blaze
Once Risa Remington had the uncanny ability to read minds, and a lot more....
Now she's lost her superpowers and the CIA's trust. The one thing she craves is human sexual contact. But is maverick agent Daniel MacAlister the right one to take her to bed?

#300 JACK & JILTED Cathy Yardley
Chloe Winton is one unmarried bride. Still, she asks, "Why let a perfectly good honeymoon go to waste?" So she doesn't. The private yacht that her former fiancé booked is ready and waiting. And so is its heart-stopping captain, Jack McCullough. Starry moonlit nights on the ocean make for quick bedfellows and he and Chloe are no exception, even with rocky waters ahead!

#301 RELEASE Jo Leigh
In Too Deep...
Seth Turner is a soldier without a battle. He's secreted in a safe house with gorgeous Dr. Harper Douglas, who's helping to heal his body. Talk about bedside manners... But can he fight the heated sexual attraction escalating between them?

#302 HER BOOK OF PLEASURE Marie Donovan
Rick Sokol discovers a pillow book of ancient erotic art, leading him to appraiser Megan O'Malley. The illustrated pages aren't the only thing Megan checks out, and soon she and Rick are creating a number of new positions of their own. But will their newfound intimacy survive when danger intrudes?